codename:

JUMPING
SPIDER

codename:
JUMPING
SPIDER

CHRISTINE J. W. CHU

PARTRIDGE
A Penguin Random House Company

To order additional copies of this book, contact
Toll Free 800 101 2657 (Singapore)
Toll Free 1 800 81 7340 (Malaysia)
orders.singapore@partridgepublishing.com

www.partridgepublishing.com/singapore

For my loving parents, Steven and Julia, who gave me the courage to follow my passion and to pursue my dreams

I believe that every man has, potentially, a strong will, and that all he has to do is to train his mind to make use of it.

—William Walker Atkinson

Acknowledgements

To the NaNoWriMo Team for encouraging writing and creativity;
to the Wattpad team for providing a place to share.

To Partridge Singapore for offering the necessary publication
tools and expertise; this book was made possible by you.

To my friends who read, criticised, and approved of the story.

To my teachers, especially Madam Mohana, who encouraged me to write.

And lastly, to my dear sister, Justine, for her awesome cover design
ideas and constructive remarks; this story was inspired by you.

Acknowledgements

One

Sharon Dylan was stirred from her sleep by a noise. There was something eerie about the noise. Dazed, she tried to open her eyes, but darkness flooded her vision. It was pitch black – everywhere. That was when she realised she was blindfolded.

She squirmed slightly, only to flinch in pain as the ropes around her wrists rubbed against her delicate skin. She was tied to a chair, and the ropes were tied so tightly that she could barely feel her hands, let alone move them. Alarm bells started to go off in her head, and she let out a low whimper, trying hard to remember how she had ended up like this.

The last thing she recalled was leaving a party with a cute guy. *What was his name again?* She hadn't even bothered to ask for a name. *Could I be any more stupid? What was I thinking, anyway, leaving a party with a stranger without the slightest sense of self-preservation?* She bit her lips, unable to recall anything else. How on earth did this happen to her?

A low chuckle echoed through the room as the eerie noise continued, coming nearer to her. Suddenly, she recognised the noise. It was the sound of someone sharpening a knife. *A knife.*

She swallowed hard.

A quiet voice spoke, sounding nearer to her than she had expected. "Hello."

Her back stiffened at the unfamiliar voice. It was a guy's voice – that was for sure. But whose was it? She couldn't be sure if this was the cute guy who brought her away from the party. Somehow, this voice sounded different – colder, crueller. Feeling unsettled, she started to wriggle in her seat, only to make her wince from the pain at her wrists again. A fearful gasp escaped her mouth as a heavy feeling tugged at her chest. This wasn't going to end well.

The voice spoke again, sounding gentle. "Hush, my dear. Stop squirming around, or you will hurt yourself even more. I have no intention of inflicting pain on you."

The gentle, quiet tone of her captor's voice sent a chill down her spine. She took in a shaky breath in an attempt to calm herself. She swallowed again and opened her mouth to speak.

She tilted her head in the direction where the voice came from and asked, "Who are you?" Her voice was trembling a little.

"Wrong question, darling."

She could hear the smile in his tone. Tears pricked her eyes. *Was this some kind of joke to him?* Maybe it was, given the fact that she was still in her party dress. Whatever he was planning for her, he wanted her to be awake to go through with it. Her gut told her that this wasn't going to be a rape but something much, much worse. She drew in another shaky breath, suppressing the urge to cry. She tried again.

"Why are you doing this?" Her hands shook violently. Her heart was banging against her ribcage, beating so fast and hard that she felt out of breath.

"Try again." His gentle voice sounded closer to her.

She bit on her lips hard, whimpering. What was he trying to do to her? *Wait. That was it, wasn't it?*

She bit back a sob as she asked, "What's going to happen to me?" Her voice was low, impassive, and barely audible.

But he heard her. "Finally, a question that makes sense. I was starting to think that you don't care for yourself at all." He laughed softly. "Well, to answer your question, all that I can say is that you won't have to suffer pain."

The words were clearly supposed to sound comforting to her, but they had the exact opposite effect. She pressed her lips into a thin line as she held back a cry. This sick man was going to kill her. She was sure of that. What else could he be referring to regarding that? She felt him placing his hand on her shoulder, and she flinched from his touch.

"Why are you doing this?" she asked, repeating her earlier question in order to stall. Her mind was racing to come up with an escape plan.

"Because."

She frowned, dissatisfied with his answer. Then the thick, metallic taste of blood filled her mouth, making her realise that she was biting her lip too hard. Why couldn't he at least let her know why he wanted her dead? Then she remembered the string of murders that had been taking place around town over the past few years. Young women around her age disappeared and were found dead in deserted areas.

Harsh realisation crashed through her head. *I'm his next victim,* she thought with sudden despair. He'd already done this before. She didn't stand the slightest chance in this. Not anymore.

"Make it fast," she whispered, losing hope. "Just kill me already."

He chuckled lightly at her words. He seemed to be enjoying this very much. "What's the rush? I have just promised you that I will not torture you. Are you suicidal?" He sounded merely amused. His hand left her shoulder. Then the sound of a knife sharpening echoed in her ears again.

She cringed at the unnerving sound. "You are already torturing me with all this talk," she cried out in frustration. "I want this to end. Just do it now. Please …" Her pleas trailed off when she heard him sigh loudly. Fear clouded her thoughts once again. *Did I upset him? Is he changing his mind about not torturing me?*

After a long period of silence, her captor finally spoke again. "Darling, that's not the right way to speak to your abductor." Although he was scolding her, his tone was still light and relaxed. "You do not make requests. You accept what I give you. Do you understand?"

At this point, she was defeated – completely. She could not even choose her own death. Perhaps she should just do what he said and just accept her fate. After all, she was going to die. It would not have made any difference to her.

"I don't understand why people get so depressed at times like this," he continued, seeming to be speaking both to himself and to her. "I mean, they do realise that death is coming to them anyway. Everyone experiences death at some point ..."

She tuned him out as he droned on. What he was saying meant nothing to her anymore. It did not matter now. Nothing mattered anymore.

"The truth is, death isn't something to be feared. I think it's the journey to death that people should be afraid of. Some people have to suffer so much before they finally reach the death part. Some just feel a long period of emptiness before they go. Personally, I think the latter sounds much more bearable, don't you?" He sighed loudly again. "You are not much fun, you know." The sound of knife sharpening stopped. "Well then, let's get this over with."

Her hands were almost numb, being tied by ropes, but she could still feel something graze against her wrist. *There,* she thought ruefully, *he had finally done it.* He was not lying when he said that she would not have to suffer physical pain. He had chosen the perfect place to cut her. She could hear her blood dripping to the floor, but she felt no pain.

Drip ... drip ... drip ...

She smiled humourlessly. This was surely a good way to go.

~

He was leaning against the door. From a distance, he watched her silently. He wore a grim smile as he watched the life drain out of her. His gentle touch, his comforting words; it was all carefully cut out for this. The girl would die thoroughly, both physically and mentally – he made sure of that.

Her breathing became shallower, and a glossy sheen of cold sweat covered her forehead. He smirked coldly. This was only the beginning. Her heart would weaken along with her will. He shook his head at the limp figure in the wooden chair. If only she had not given up that easily, she would not be going through all this.

But she was only human, after all.

And a human's will was always fragile. No matter how strong humans thought they were, all it took for him to break them into pieces was a blindfold, a knife sharpener, and a bottle of water. How pathetic. It was almost too easy for him.

Drip ... drip ... drip ... drip ...

He could see that she was getting weaker. He wanted her to feel the hopelessness, to feel the life being sucked out of her. That was what he felt, and he would make sure that *she* would suffer twice as much as he did.

Drip ... drip ... drip ... drip ...

He stared at this innocent little girl, her heartbeat fading slowly. A small part of him felt remorseful for using her as a painkiller today. He swore to himself that he would stop this kind of notorious act, but he would only stop when he made sure that *she* had paid her price. He let out a quiet sigh. Too bad *she* was always out of reach. If only *she* didn't make it so hard for him to get to *her*, he could have finished this once and for all.

Now he was walking towards the girl. He checked her pulse. As predicted, her heart had stopped beating. Feeling smug, he took his own sweet time putting away his tools and left the room, leaving no evidence of his presence behind. The dead girl was just another piece of the puzzle now.

This was his design.

Two

"You will go down within ten minutes. Take my word for it," Catherine said smoothly, giving the guy in front of her a lazy smirk.

The guard sneered at her. "You think?" he scoffed. "I'm the one with a gun here. All you have with you is a big bowl of nothing, if you count that as your weapon." He let out a derisive laugh.

She merely raised her eyebrows at him, studying him with narrowed eyes. "For some reason, I'd like to see you handle a gun," she stated in a challenging tone. "Maybe then you'll be able to look intimidating."

A corner of his eye twitched slightly at her words, and she knew that she'd hit a nerve.

She leaned back against her chair, crossing a leg over the other. "Look around you. I heard that this place is built with the highest-level security system, yet I managed to slip into the core of the building unnoticed – alone. Do you really think that I would have come unprepared?"

"Too bad you can't get out now," he jeered. "The whole building is on lockdown, and there is nothing you can do about it. You're stuck here with me."

Her ears pricked at the information, and she let out a low chuckle. "And who did you think put the building on lockdown? Hacking into your security system wasn't that hard, you know." That was a lie, of course. She wasn't *that* tech-savvy. She was going to have to deal with that problem later. For now, she would have to take him down first before security backup arrive.

For the first time, a hint of uncertainty passed the guard's face. The guard pointed his pistol at her, narrowing his eyes. "Do you think that I would believe that? Locking down the building is the dumbest act for a solo thief like you."

"A solo thief?" She pretended to frown, only to smooth out her forehead a moment later. "Right, I am in this alone." She nodded to herself. Then she gave him a taunting smile. "Or am I?"

A confused look appeared on the guard's face. Her eyes went to the exit door, and she gave a small nod in that direction. The guard caught her sudden movement, and immediately he spun around, bracing himself for an ambush. She quickly stood up, taking this opportunity to wrap her arm around his neck, pulling him into a headlock. Using the other hand, she smashed his head on the chair behind her. Immediately, the guard went limp in her grip.

She checked her watch. It had taken her less than five minutes. She laughed quietly, shaking her head. She had underestimated herself.

She briefly scanned her surroundings before sweeping out of the room, leaving the unconscious guard behind. Next stop: the database.

"You wished to see me, sir?" Catherine asked politely, knocking on the door before entering the major general's office.

The man behind the desk raised his head and smiled when he saw her. He was in his mid-forties, but the twinkle in his piercing blue eyes made it hard to tell his real age. He was properly groomed, with short blond hair, giving him a professional look. He stood up to greet her, addressing her with apparent delight.

"Special Agent Nelson. Good to see you in such good spirits."

Catherine simply smiled, waiting for the general to get to the point. Her best guess: there was a new case for her. However, General Warner continued with his small talk.

"I have to say, you did an excellent job in your previous case. You managed to bring down an infiltrated government database within three days – single-handedly, I might add. You have certainly made history."

She lowered her gaze to the floor, sighing quietly. Then her gaze returned to the general and she said, "Sir, I appreciate the compliments very much. Now that the ice has been broken, perhaps we can talk about my next case." When he raised an eyebrow, she simply nodded her head at the file on the desk. "I'm pretty sure that this is for me."

He gave her a mildly impressed look. "And how did you guess that it was for you?"

She just shrugged, smiling wryly. Instead of answering the question, she responded with a question of her own. "I'm guessing that this is no ordinary case?"

He arched his brows at her question, trying to hide the look of surprise on his face. Then he sighed. "Sometimes I really wish that you were not that sharp, but you are Jumping Spider after all. Come, have a seat." He sat down and picked up the file on his desk, flipping it open.

She did as she was told, part of her wondering what was so special about the case to make the general stall. She waited patiently for him to speak, wearing her poker face as she watched him intently.

The general peered at her fleetingly before turning his attention back to the file. "Your next case is to investigate a series of murders, and this case requires you to pay a visit to Tirjuan."

Her body went rigid. "No," she immediately declined, her voice stiff and impassive.

He gave her a tired look. "Look, I know how difficult it will be to return to Tirjuan, but there is no other agent better suited to take on this case. I've been alerted that this investigation has been going on for years and the local

PD are still no closer to closing the case. The orders given to me are that Major Crimes Unit will be taking over the investigation, and they want this to be over with ASAP." Then he leaned back against his chair, giving her a pointed look. "I need Jumping Spider on this one."

She frowned, understanding herself well enough to know that she was not going to turn him down, not when he seemed so torn to have made this decision. But she still needed some convincing to take on this case. "Why does it have to be me?"

"I'll talk you through this case. You'll see why."

~

Catherine sat in the stuffy little motel room she had rented, staring into the mirror. A pair of dark brown eyes stared back at her, reflecting nothing but emptiness in them. Her long wavy hair fell over her shoulder. Her dark hair used to be a natural shade of fiery copper, but she didn't like it. It made her stand out too much in a crowd, she thought, and she didn't feel comfortable with it. It wasn't because she had low self-esteem or whatever made people feel self-conscious; it was just that she preferred to lie low and not speak to people when she didn't have to.

After she lost her parents, Catherine felt as if the outgoing part of her had died with them too. She realised that her bubbly cheery nature had been a mask she had been wearing to please her parents all this while. The truth was, she had always felt more comfortable keeping to herself whenever possible. It was just that her parents didn't understand her preference of being an introvert. So now she would only talk when it came to dealing with work as well as when she felt the need to speak her mind, which usually didn't end up very well.

In the end, to make life easier for herself, she dyed her hair black and became a brunette. People didn't notice her as much as they used to, and it did make her feel better – for a while. Catherine parted her lips and exhaled a long breath through her mouth, trying to shake off the heavy feeling that was settling itself in the pit of her stomach.

She would be spending a night here before continuing on her way to Tirjuan. Until now, she could hardly believe that she was actually going back to her hometown. Starting now, she would be undercover. That was usually the sort of thing that filled her with excitement and anticipation whenever she was working on a case. For her, it was fun playing a non-existent character, fooling everyone else with her superb acting skills.

But this time she was supposed to play Jenn – the young and innocent girl she used to be. *Used to be.* So how was she supposed to play a role that she had spent so much time trying to forget about? But anyway, she was back to being Jennifer Cole – an identity that she longed to erase from her memory – and she was anything but excited.

It was because of this identity that her parents were brutally murdered by assassins. Of course, she had personally hunted down those thugs and even put a few bullets in their heads. Five, to be exact – three for the leader of the group that was hired to kill her parents and the other two for his two minions. That was her first time shooting and killing someone. In her report and her debrief, she had stated that she did it out of self-defence, but she knew it was just a lie. She had cleverly staged it in such a way that she would be able to get her revenge without getting caught, though she knew that the major general and her mentor suspected as much when they heard the news that the assassins were dead.

As for the mastermind behind the whole evil scheme, she had sought him out and put him behind bars. She didn't shoot him, for dying would be far too much of an easy escape for him. She wanted him to suffer for what he did to her family and the many other lives he'd tortured in vain, so she decided that letting him rot away in jail was the best punishment for him.

She did everything she could to bring him down, hoping that it would somehow bring her comfort to know that she had avenged her parents' death, but revenge never seemed enough to relieve her from her pain. Even until this current day …

Swallowing hard, Jenn took a deep breath and pushed away the bitter memories, trying to focus on more pressing matters. She quickly diverted her concentration to the case at hand.

Six teenage girls were murdered in her hometown in the past three years. Three of them were murdered on 5 May, while the other three died on 1 August, in their respective years. Also, forensics estimated that the time of death for each victim was after midnight – somewhere between twelve thirty and two in the morning. So she could pretty much sum up that the serial killer had a time pattern.

According to the general, the local authorities couldn't seem to find out how the girls were murdered. The lab reports stated that none of the victims suffered any sexual assault or physical abuse other than skin abrasion on the wrists, which in other words were rope burns. No traces of toxic substance or drug could be found in their systems. None of the evidence found in the crime scenes indicated occurrence of violence while the murders took place. The cause of death stated in each of the reports was major heart rhythm disturbance which led to heart failure.

It seemed as if the victims were simply tied to the chair and then their hearts just magically stopped working, but of course, Jenn didn't believe that this was scientifically possible.

It must be that the agents in charge were not looking hard enough. That was the only conclusion she could come to. Now that she was given jurisdiction over this case, she made a mental note to personally revisit each crime scene later. Jenn was aware that finding evidence years after a murder would be hard, but she had to start somewhere.

That was why she hated cold cases, especially when people who didn't seem to know their jobs well had obviously handled the case. Crime scenes could have been tainted, and any possible trace of evidence would have been wiped off by now. She was off to a rough start.

Right now, the only solid information that she had about the serial killer was his time pattern and his choice of location in presenting his victims – secluded areas in town. It made her wonder what the local police and detectives were doing throughout these three years. She heaved a deep sigh as the dates of the murders swirled around in her head: 5 May … 1 August. What was so special about these dates? Wait! She remembered something suddenly.

Three years ago, on 5 May, the first murder took place. Four years ago, on the exact same day, she left home and was recruited into the NSSS. She remembered the date so clearly because it was actually the day her parents were brutally murdered too. That was why she was taken into protective custody, which led to her decision to join the NSSS to have her revenge. Jenn pulled herself back to the matter at hand before she could start dwelling on the past again.

So was it just pure coincidence? Or could it be a clue to her investigation? But wait: the other date – 1 August – meant nothing to her at all. Hmm, so perhaps it was just a coincidence. Now she was back to square one. Great.

Smiling wanly at her reflection, Jenn turned away from the mirror. She wore a slight grimace as she moved to her backpack and took out the case files that the general had given to her this morning. Well, she would have to start from scratch now.

Jenn read the victims' biographies, though they were already imprinted in the back of her head. She needed to find some sort of link between the victims. But unfortunately, there was none, except for the fact that all six of the victims had auburn hair. For her, that did not count as anything much for a promising lead, not that she was going to ignore it. If the killer really was aiming for random redheads, that would mean that she was most probably dealing with a psychopathic homicidal maniac. That would not be pleasant.

A part of her was sure that these murders were not committed for a thrill or anything that suggested psychopathic killer; rather they were committed by a killer who loved puzzles. Studying the photos of the death scenes, it was obvious that she was dealing with a very sophisticated and somewhat elegant serial killer. For starters, all the victims were found dead without any signs of physical trauma and drug toxicity. In the photos, each girl was blindfolded and tied to a chair in an empty room.

What intrigued her most was that this killer could kill someone without actually doing her any harm. Well, physically anyway, according to the autopsies. This killer didn't want their blood on his hands, she thought, so that could mean that he didn't really want to harm them. In a way, he was still fighting his conscience and giving them a chance to live – if her hunch was correct.

When she learned about this case from the general for the first time, she already had a hunch about how the killer actually did it. But she needed to prove her theory right first, so she was not going to jump the gun and make assumptions right away.

Sighing, she put the files away and lay down on her bed. That was all she had for now.

When Jenn woke up the next morning, the first thing she did was cut her hair. She had decided to return as a new Jennifer Cole. Her hair was already dyed black, so she did not need to change her hair colour. She simply cut off her hair until it was shoulder length. When she was done, she put away her scissors and stood back to admire her handiwork, nodding in approval. *Not bad*, she thought.

The next thing she did was put on something casual. She had only brought along some plain clothes so she did not have much choice. Tirjuan was just a quaint little town after all, so she figured that fancy clothes would be a waste of space. Rifling through her backpack to double-check her things, she decided to keep her magazines and gun in her backpack. She wasn't planning to start any action on the first day in town, so she would not need the gun today, plus it would blow her cover if she accidentally flashed it in front of the people in town. However, she kept her badge in her jacket, just in case.

As Jenn started to sling her backpack over her shoulder, she heard her cell phone ring. Placing a hand on her hip, she slipped her hand into her pocket and took out her cell phone before glancing at the caller ID. She almost let out a groan.

It was him again.

Fighting the urge to ignore his call, Jenn pursed her lips and ran her tongue over her upper front teeth as she put the cell phone to her ear. She answered the phone in a clipped tone. "Warner."

Ben replied, "Catherine, I heard that you're going back home." His strong, masculine voice sounded concerned. "What's going on?"

She exhaled the breath that she was holding. If the general decided to tell Ben about this, why couldn't he just tell his son the whole story? She rolled her eyes, feeling annoyed. "I'm working on a case." She spoke in a businesslike tone, void of emotions, despite the emotions that were brewing inside her. "Is there anything I can help you with?"

"Oh." She heard him sighing in relief over the phone. "Uh … No, I don't need anything. I just—"

Jenn had decided that it was time to cut him off. "Well, if you don't need anything, you might as well leave me to do my job. Bye." She heard him calling her name before she hung up on him. Making an exasperated sound, she grabbed her backpack off the bed.

Jenn shoved her cell phone back into her pocket, muttering unintelligent things to herself. She quickly checked out of her room and continued on her way to Tirjuan, feeling irritated and distracted by the phone call from Ben. What a way to start her day.

Three

WELCOME TO TIRJUAN!

Jenn stared at the bogusly cheerful faded words on the signboard. A wave of nostalgia washed through her as she studied her surroundings. Softly Jenn whispered to herself, "I'm back."

The sky was still dark when she arrived. The silence around her was peaceful and calming as she walked along an empty street with her shadow stretching in front of her. At this hour of the day, no one was up yet, so she was free to roam around town.

The town was dimly illuminated by street lights. A light, gentle breeze caressed her cheek as if to welcome her arrival. Absentmindedly, she had strolled to the centre of the town – Eiry's Garden. This park got its name from one the oldest residents in town, Eiry Haste. It was filled with various types of trees and flowers that Eiry had planted.

Glancing around the park, Jenn wondered if Eiry was still around. She would have been more than a hundred years old by now. The park seemed to be in good shape, so someone was still taking care of it.

Moving towards a wooden bench, Jenn heard someone humming a tune from somewhere near her. The melodious tune floated peacefully in the fresh crisp morning air, sounding ever so gay and lively in this timeless little garden. Jenn glanced around and saw an old woman standing near a rose bush.

Eiry.

Jenn watched her humming softly to her roses. It seemed like Eiry was still in decent condition for her age. Then suddenly the humming stopped. As if sensing someone watching her, Eiry turned her head and spotted Jenn.

They exchanged polite smiles and nods. Then Eiry slowly moved towards Jenn. Seeing this, Jenn stepped forward in attempt to help her, but Eiry stopped her. "I'm still capable of walking, you know," Eiry said in an age-defying voice. It was quite a surprise to hear such a solid voice coming from her smallish frail figure. She sat down on the wooden bench and patted on the seat next to her.

"Well, I can see that age has not withered you." Jenn laughed softly and sat down beside her.

"Time has been kind to me," Eiry agreed in a smiling voice. "So tell me, Jennifer, where have you been all these years?"

Jenn widened her eyes at the old lady, genuinely surprised. Eiry remembered her. "I have been studying abroad in Australia," she lied, sticking to her cover story.

Eiry arched a delicate eyebrow, nodding. "I see. How about your parents? Are they well?"

At the mention of her parents, her heart dropped. This was the reason she hadn't wished to return. People always asked too many questions. Plastering a smile on her face, she tried to maintain a normal façade. "They are enjoying life, travelling around the world. I've barely seen them in the past few years." Her answer was simple. After all, the less detail she gave, the higher the chance that her lie would hold up.

"Hmm …" Eiry stared at her, her expression filled with sympathy. She took Jenn's hand in hers and patted it affectionately. "You must be missing them very much, then. It's a good thing that you understand them and feel happy for them. Some young people these days are just too self-centred. Good for you, young lady." A smile flicked the corners of her wrinkled old mouth.

"I suppose so." Jenn returned the smile politely, feeling her chest tighten.

They continued chatting for a few minutes before Jenn excused herself. It seemed that Eiry was still as warm and loving as she was four years ago. She was a nice old woman. For all Jenn knew, she was probably the only one in the town who still smiled at every person she saw. Jenn remembered how much she had looked up to her before she left Tirjuan. Well, Eiry did make a good role model at the time, even now.

As Jenn continued to stroll along the street, she saw the sun appearing on the eastern horizon, rising perpendicular to it. It was getting warmer now, and the town was coming awake. It amazed her how fast time had flown by. Soon people started filling the streets as she walked by the houses and shops in town.

The place had not changed much. She inhaled the fresh morning air, cherishing this moment. After this, she would have to view this town and its people through the eyes of a special agent. She had to keep reminding herself that she came here to investigate about a serial killer, not to make herself cosy and comfortable with her past. It actually surprised her that she was being so sentimental right now. It was so unlike her to let nostalgia get to her, she thought as she walked on, taking in every single detail of the town.

She halted as a familiar-looking building came into view. Memories flooded her mind, hitting like a ton of bricks. Coming back here was harder than she'd thought it would be. Slowly she walked towards the church. She stopped at the doorway and saw a reverend praying in front of the altar. It was Reverend Ed. She would recognise him anywhere.

She stood there watching until he finished his prayer. When he turned around and saw her, he gave her a warm smile, but it lacked familiarity. Jenn guessed that unlike Eiry, Reverend Ed didn't recognise her.

"May I help you, young lady?" He spoke with a voice filled with tenderness.

She gave him a pleasant smile. "Reverend Ed, how are you?"

His eyes instantly filled with recognition. "Jennifer?" Disbelief coloured his voice. "Jennifer Cole?"

She nodded, entering the church. "Good to see you again, Reverend. You haven't changed much."

Reverend Ed laughed heartily. "I wish I could say the same about you," he said, taking in her new whole look. "How have you been over these years?"

"Great," she lied smoothly. "The people there are quite friendly. I had no trouble fitting in. School is fine too. I'll be graduating next year."

"Good for you." He smiled, nodding in approval. "Are you coming back after graduation?"

"Uh …" She pretended to frown, filling her eyes with the right amount of hesitation. "I actually signed a contract with a company over there. I'll be on probation as soon as I graduate."

His face fell slightly at her reply. Then he composed himself and gave her a pat on the shoulder. "It's okay. Don't feel bad about it. Be happy that you have a bright future ahead of you. Psychology is, after all, what you're cut out for."

Jenn gave him a tight-lipped smile. "Yes, I should be," she said in an unconvinced manner. She felt guilty for lying to him, but she had no other choice.

Then she let out a breath and put on a pretend smile as she changed the topic. "What about you, Reverend? How are you doing over the past few years? In fact, how is everyone?" She planned to use this as a start to do some digging for the case, just to see if the citizens knew much about the murders that were taking place in town.

The reverend clearly got her hint and decided to go along with the topic. "I'm doing fine. Everyone else is okay too, but we have all been missing you. The church hasn't been the same without you around. Nick and the others rarely come over now. At first, we were really shocked that you left so suddenly. But then when we got your letter, it explained everything. You needed to register yourself for school on such short notice, so we understand." He gave her a reassuring smile.

Her lips parted as she tried to ask for more details, but their conversation was interrupted by the sound of her cell phone ringing. "I'm sorry." She gave him an apologetic smile as she fished out her vibrating cell phone. Taking a glance at the caller ID, she could barely suppress her grimace. It was Ben – again.

The reverend saw her expression and apparently took that as his cue to leave. "I'll let you answer your phone." With that, he began to head to his office. "Do visit again soon. God bless you always," he said with a smile before disappearing from sight.

Jenn muttered a goodbye to him and stepped out of the church before answering the call. "This better be good, Warner." Annoyance seeped through her calm tone.

"Hey, chill," Ben said in a light manner, apparently detecting the irritation in her voice. Then his tone turned hesitant. "Did I interrupt something? You usually don't sound this annoyed. I'm … sorry if I did, though."

She released a quiet sigh as she tried to recompose herself. "Whatever. Why do you keep calling me? Don't you have a case to solve?" she asked, sounding colder than she'd intended to.

Ben was silent for a moment before he let out a sheepish chuckle under his breath. "I'm on stake-out duty. There's nothing going right now, so I figured I'd give you a call. Nice of you to ask," he added in a joking manner.

She rolled her eyes at his comment. "Well?"

"Hmm?"

She sighed again. "What do you need?"

"Oh, right," he mumbled to himself, hesitating for a moment before speaking again. "Okay, just give me a few seconds and hear me out. I really need to get this out. Then he quickly added, "Please?"

Jenn immediately knew what he was referring to, and she exhaled a sharp breath. Seriously, he was still bugging her about this? She groaned inwardly. And here she thought that he called to consult her on something about his case. "What part of 'We're done' do you not understand?" she muttered monotonously. "You wanted to cut things off between us. You did, and I've accepted it. Now it's over, and there's nothing to talk about anymore. So move on, will you?" She then hung up on him.

Clutching the cell phone tightly in her hand, Jenn grinded her teeth together in frustration. She did *not* need this right now. She truly could not understand his stubbornness. They had been broken up for almost half a year now, and he was the one who had cheated on her. He had even laughed at her for being so attached. And now he was acting as if none of that had ever happened. She scoffed at the thought. What kind of sick joke was this?

Taking a few deep breaths, Jenn pulled herself back to the present. No, she thought to herself, she was not going to lose control of herself right now. She was a special agent who should be focusing on her case at hand. She should be more professional. No more emotional distresses. Shoulders squared, she strode away from the church to begin her investigation.

First things first, she needed a place to stay. She hailed a taxi and asked the cabby to take her to the nearest hotel in town. She contemplated the idea of renting a suite, considering that she might be working with many case files later and would need a huge space to keep her files and map out a work board. And suddenly she wondered if she would even be able to find a decent suite in this small town.

It turned out that she was thinking too much. The hotel she found was quaint yet accommodating, and the suite she rented was very much to her liking. It consisted of two bedrooms and a shared bathroom, a small office, kitchen, and a living area furnished with two couches, a coffee table, and a television.

Walking into the master bedroom, she set her backpack on the bed and unpacked. Meanwhile, she started planning her next move. Should she visit the local police department first? Or should she do some digging around the town to form her own baseline about the murders?

Jenn had finished unpacking and moved on to putting up her work board while she debated what her next move was. She went into the office, and conveniently there was a huge note board on the wall. In the middle of the room was a small conference table surrounded by six chairs. Pleased, she brought in the case files and started pinning up the victims' photos and their profiles, linking each of them to her respective time and location of death.

Jenn studied their places of death, but there was no apparent link between each location where the murders took place. They were just abandoned warehouses and cabins in secluded areas of the town. So as she had observed last night, perhaps the killer would stick to his pattern and make his next kill someplace similar. According to the killer's time pattern, the next murder would take place exactly one month later. Thirty days should be enough for her to solve this mystery, right? Well, either way, she would have to make it work.

She heaved a deep sigh when she realised that she still needed to come up with a suspect list of her own since the list of suspects provided by the local police consisted of almost half of the citizens of Tirjuan. No wonder they didn't get anywhere with the investigation.

When she took a second look at the crime scenes marked on the town map, she noticed that each location was actually quite close to the other. They were mostly focused in the south part of the town, which was where she was staying right now. Well, that made it a whole lot easier.

The reason she was so sure that the killer was nearby was because from his style of murder, she could see that he was smart, and she knew that he knew it too. So most likely the killer would attempt a double bluff to make the police assume that he would do his magic somewhere far away from home. Hence the long list of suspects. Plus, he needed to keep a close eye on the investigations, so he had to stay close to the police department, which was in this area too. Good – she just narrowed down her pool of suspects.

In the end, Jenn decided that it was better for her to do her homework first before going to the local PD. It briefly occurred to her that some of the cops here might be crooked, given the fact that this had been an ongoing investigation for more than three years now. Perhaps the killer had someone in the department feeding him information about the case or the agents in charge were just that slow. Either way, she needed to teach them about real police work.

Four

Jenn spent her whole afternoon aimlessly wandering around in town, eavesdropping and listening to town gossip. Unfortunately, she did not get a lot out of that small-town gossip. All she managed to gather was how the victims' families kept pushing the police to work harder to solve the cases, but the police had neither made a response nor disclosed any information about the ongoing investigations.

However, much to her relief, no one had recognised her so far, not that she knew every one of the town folks.

As the evening shadows began to fall, she decided that she'd reached her quota of walking for today. She leisurely bought a cup of coffee from a coffee house nearby and strolled towards the park. The pleasant aroma of the coffee mixed with the faint smell of sweet floral fragrance as she neared her destination, bringing a relaxed smile to her lips. Eiry's Garden had always been her favourite spot in town to think.

As she settled down on a bench at the far end of the park, that's when she noticed them watching her from the corner of her eye. They were hanging around the huge fountain which stood magnificently in the middle of the park. The two younger guys from the group were a year younger than she was, namely Ray and Tom, and the girl, Isabella, was two years younger than they were. The three of them were trying to observe her as subtly as they could, but they were failing miserably. As for the man who was now openly gawking at her with shock written all over his face, he was five years older than she was. His name was Nick.

How could she be so sure about who they were? Well, it was obvious. She knew them. And she was pretty sure that they remembered her. Or at least Nick did, judging from his comical expression of surprise. Well, he had never been one to be able to communicate or express his emotions without coming across as awkward or shy. It seemed he had not changed much.

As if just realising that he was staring at her the entire time, Nick quickly recomposed his face into his usual serene mask, but he didn't stop staring. As for the other three, they were whispering to each other. They were talking about her, she thought. Honestly, she could read them like an open book, and she knew that they thought she looked oddly familiar.

Jenn angled her body slightly towards them so that she could read their lips better. At the same time, she took out a notebook from her pocket which she'd brought with her for situations like this. She scribbled a few lines on her notebook and peered up every once in a while, trying to be as natural as possible while she studied them from under her lashes.

Isabella was whispering to Tom, "Do you think that's who I think she is?"

Tom responded by nodding his head once. "But she looks really different," he observed. "Maybe it's not her."

"A long lost twin of hers?" Isabella guessed, arching a brow. This earned her funny looks from both Ray and Tom.

"I thought that only happens in movies," Tom said mutedly, looking rather amused now.

Then Ray interjected by saying, "Jenn or not, she seems new in town. Might as well give her a warm welcome." Excitement coloured his expression.

Before Isabella could ask for Nick's opinion, Ray – always the most outgoing one – was already walking towards Jenn. As Ray approached her with a friendly smile, Jenn observed the mild change in his looks. It seemed he had grown a few inches taller since the last time she saw him. She also noticed his muscular physique. *Well, someone has been working out.* Ray opened his mouth, and she braced herself for his first question.

He introduced himself. "Hi, my name is Ray Darce." Then he asked, "May I have the pleasure of knowing your name?"

Time to start playing her role. Standing up, she turned to him and mirrored his smile. "How about you guess my name?" she answered smoothly, without missing a beat.

His smile faltered as he hesitated. Jenn knew the reason behind his uncertainty. There she was before him and he remembered her, but her different appearance and way of speaking had put doubt into his mind.

"Uh ..." He eyed her with a hint of playfulness, plainly trying his best to hide his uncertainty. "Is it Jennifer?"

"Not bad, Darce. Not bad at all." She smirked. "It's good to know that I'm still remembered after my long absence in town." Up close, she noted the slight change in his facial structure. He had outgrown his chubby cheeks, and his jawline was definitely stronger and defined. Ray had certainly turned into quite a handsome young man, she thought, smiling inwardly.

It was quite amusing to watch the uncertainty on his face morph into an enormous grin, his baby blue eyes widening involuntarily. "Jenn? Jennifer Cole?" His hand flew up and held her upper arm tightly, as if trying to convince himself that she was really there.

Jenn was surprised at the sudden contact, and she felt something spark inside of her at that very moment, but she hid it well with a chuckle. "Yes, it's really me. Now, can you let go of my arm? You're cutting off my blood circulation," she said in a joking manner.

Realising his thoughtless move, he abruptly let go of her arm and smiled sheepishly, blushing a little. "Sorry. I'm just ..." He trailed off, clearly at a loss for words, still looking dazed. He shook his head, struggling to gather his thoughts together. "I'm just excited to see you again," he explained, laughing at himself.

Tom, Isabella, and Nick watched their interaction with curious eyes, and Ray, as though suddenly remembering his friends, eagerly spun around to tell them the good news. "Hey, guys! It's really Jenn." He waved for them to come over.

Hearing this, Tom and Isabella started rushing over to Jenn's side, showering her with hellos and welcome-back hugs. Nick tagged along too, his face carefully arranged into a mask of surprise. Jenn saw through it immediately. Of course, she knew he'd known right from the moment he saw her. He simply did not tell the others. She wondered why. Perhaps he was too stunned to speak.

Nick gave her an awkward hug, pulling back as soon as he wrapped his arms around her. Hmm, still not much of a hugger, was he? "It's been a while," he mumbled in his quiet tone, giving her a tiny smile.

Jenn observed that his smile was a bit stiff, but he was never one who smiled much. He was more of the serious type, never a slacker, never a joker. He couldn't even laugh at his own jest, for heaven's sake. Jenn laughed quietly, recalling his failed attempts to joke with people.

"Four years since I left," she said smoothly. Turning to the others, she asked, "How are you guys?"

"Life without you was like hell," Ray said with mock sadness.

Tom nodded in agreement before grinning at her cheekily. "And now that you're back, hope is finally restored!"

Isabella gave him a light punch on the shoulder. "Oh, don't be so melodramatic." The guys guffawed in response, causing her to roll her eyes at their silliness.

Jenn smiled pleasantly at the scene before her. Still a pair of clowns the guys were.

Then Isabella turned to Jenn and said, "We're doing great, but we did miss you a lot."

Jenn felt genuinely touched at her words. "I missed you guys too," she said solemnly.

"Are you back for good?" Tom asked.

She sighed, adding a hint of regret in her tone as she replied, "Just back for a quick visit."

"How long?" This time it was Nick who spoke. He seemed more at ease now.

"Hmm …" Jenn thought about it for a moment. Then she decided not to answer the question directly. After all, she herself wasn't sure about her duration of stay. "Well, with school stuff, my schedule can never be fixed. But if I'm lucky, I get to stay for a whole month." She grinned.

Nick responded with a rare smile of his own, nodding. Then he let the others bombard her with questions again.

Suddenly, she noticed the absence of Jules, Nick's girlfriend. She and Jules were best of friends, and Jules was always the centre of Nick's world. They were inseparable. So where could she be now?

"Where's Jules?" Jenn asked, looking at Nick.

A shadow of emotions flickered across his face, but then it was gone. Jenn could literally sense the cheerful atmosphere around them being sucked away instantly by her question as a thick heavy cloud of stressful silence hung in the air. Nick would not meet her gaze as he excused himself and left in a hurry.

Confused by his reaction and sudden departure, she turned back to the others, only to find them wearing similar edgy expressions on their faces, staring at the ground. Jenn could see the underlying sadness in their eyes, and a small voice in her head told her that they were hiding something big from her.

"Something bad happened, right?" she muttered, her voice low and flat.

Tom was the first to meet her eyes. He smiled half-heartedly. "Jules is gone. Let's just leave it at that."

Jenn raised her eyebrows but said nothing. Suddenly, she remembered the last conversation that she had with Jules before she was recruited into the secret service. She recalled Jules confessing that she did not have feelings for Nick anymore and saying that she was in love with another guy. When she asked Jenn for some advice, all Jenn told her was to follow her heart.

The memory replayed itself in her mind as Tom's answer swam around in her head. So maybe Jules really did listen to her advice. But then Jenn thought that it was quite harsh of Jules to take off and leave all her friends for just one guy. It was really unlike Jules to act so impulsively ...

Sighing, Jenn pulled herself back into the present and glanced around. The others were watching her closely, the sadness in their eyes gone.

"You really have changed a lot," Isabella said thoughtfully. "I mean, it's not just your hair or the way you act. How should I put this?" She paused for a moment to think. "It's like you're a whole new person."

"A good change, I hope." Jenn lightened her tone. She could see what Isabella was trying to do: change the topic.

Isabella pretended to think about it for a while before breaking into a grin. "Yes, I suppose." Then her face turned serious. "I think I'm going to go check on Nick. I'm worried about him." Muttering a goodbye, she left in the direction that Nick had gone.

Tom stared after her. He said quietly, "I think I'll go with her." Then he gave Jenn a quick hug. "It's nice seeing you again, Jenn." With that, he left too.

Jenn was left alone with Ray. Suddenly, a light bulb went off in her head. It was quite a rare chance to get someone alone to talk to in this small town. Scanning their surroundings, she confirmed that no one else was there with them. Grabbing this opportunity, she invited him to sit down with her on the bench.

Ray stared at her curiously, but he showed no intention of turning down her invitation. As he sat down beside her, Jenn took a long sip of her coffee. "I can see that I have a lot of catching up to do now." She turned and gave him a lopsided grin, breaking the ice between them. Sitting so close to him, she was once again blown away by how much his looks had changed. She turned her gaze away from his face, willing herself not be distracted from the task at hand.

She asked, "So what's new in town?"

Ray laughed, his blue eyes twinkling. "I'll answer your questions if you answer mine – fair enough? I have a few questions of my own too, you know."

Pursing her lips, she raised a brow at him, wondering what he was going to ask. Then she thought, *What harm can he do?* So she readily agreed. "It's a deal."

Clearly feeling satisfied, he repeated her question. "What's new in town, huh?" He paused for a moment. "Let's see. VCS has closed down."

Her eyes widened in surprise when she heard this. VCS, abbreviation for Voluntary Community Service, was an association founded by Nick himself. It was initiated to assist the town folks in maintaining the town's beauty and cleanliness, plus it was involved in fundraising activities in the church. Ray, Tom, Isabella, Jenn, and a few other young people ran the association alongside him. She was pretty sure that they were doing quite well before she left. "How did this happen?"

A small frown appeared on his forehead. "Well, things weren't going very well after you and Jules were gone. Nick was crushed. He dismissed us a few months after you left."

She nodded, saying nothing. Jenn noticed the way he avoided talking about Jules. From what she could see now, Jules's departure really did make quite an impact on them.

Ray suddenly clapped his hands together. "Now it's my turn." He was silent as questions ran through his mind. Finally, he decided on one. "Please don't take this wrongly, but why did you return all of a sudden? I mean, for four year, we heard nothing from you. There were no calls, no letters. Then today, out of nowhere, you popped out in front of us. What's the ulterior motive behind your visit?" He pretended to narrow his eyes sceptically at her.

Jenn ignored the playful glint in his eyes and faked a thoughtful look as she slowly said, "Would you believe me if I told you that I came back because I missed you guys?"

"I thought you would have said that you came back because of me," he said with false disappointment, pouting.

36

His response made her do a double take. Was he actually flirting with her? She decided to play along. "Well, it would not be fair of me if I said that ..." She gave him an amused look. "And your puppy dog face is terribly comical," she added, bubbling with laughter now.

Ray pretended to grimace before chuckling lightly, obviously enjoying this. "There is no one else here to hear it anyway," he said boldly, staring at her with a confident look.

Yep, he was definitely flirting now. Jenn never knew that Ray was interested in her. This was new. "You know, I'm starting to think that you're trying to avoid my questions." She managed to brush off his comment. This was not the time to flirt around with her old friend. "So what else happened while I was gone?"

The sudden change in topic plainly threw him off a little, but he recovered quite fast. "Tom and Isabella are official now," he announced smugly.

She let out a laugh when she saw the look on his face. "Let me guess. You were their matchmaker?"

"You owe me dinner," he said in a singsong voice, grinning.

Once again, he'd surprised her. Ray actually remembered their bet from four years ago. "A bet is a bet." Jenn couldn't resist smiling at his smug expression.

"How about we have that dinner now?" she suggested. "I'm starving."

Ray glanced at the sky and let out a low whistle. "I didn't even notice the time. Okay, then let's continue Twenty Questions over dinner." He got up excitedly. "There is this new restaurant in town. Its food tastes amazing, and it's cheap. You've got to try it."

She shook her head at his enthusiasm, suppressing a laugh. Some things just never changed.

Five

Sunlight seeped through the parted blue curtains. As she lay in her bed, Jenn thought about the dinner she had with Ray yesterday. Ray seemed extremely interested in her life overseas. Fortunately, she managed to evade most of his questions by distracting him with witty remarks and occasional flirting. As for her own questions, she did succeed in digging up something interesting about the case.

According to Ray, all the victims attended parties around town before they went missing. He would not tell her how he knew about this, but Jenn saw no sign of deception in him, so she decided to believe him. Perhaps someone had made him promise not to tell.

It was totally unexpected for her to have obtained this piece of information. Although Ray did not elaborate any more about the murders, Jenn was sure that he knew more than he let on. However, she did not push him any further; she did not want to raise suspicions, and he seemed very uncomfortable talking about it.

It did strike her as odd that Ray would hold key information about the case, but it was a small town after all. News and rumours usually spread like wildfire in a small place like this. What was really odd was Ray's demeanour while they talked about the case. She remembered observing the sudden change in his gaze as his eyes glazed over when she breached the topic. A vacant, almost hollow look had filled his baby blue eyes, as if he had been there watching when the murders took place.

Of course, he went back to normal when they moved on to a new topic. It made her wonder how much he did actually know about the murders of those poor souls. Perhaps he knew one of the victims personally. That would explain his interest in these murders.

Her reverie was broken by the sound of her cell phone ringing. Uttering a groan, she silently prayed that the caller would not be who she thought it was. She got out of bed and fished her cell phone out of her backpack. Relief filled her chest when she saw that it wasn't him. But the feeling faded away when she realised that it was General Warner instead.

She greeted him, wondering the reason behind this phone call at this time of the day.

"Good morning, Agent Nelson." He spoke smoothly. "Did I wake you up?"

"No," she replied. "I was just doing some analysing about the case. Why did you call?"

"I just wanted to check on you." She could picture General Warner shrugging as he said this. "So tell me, how are you doing?"

The general wasn't usually like this, she thought. Lately, he had been much softer than before. She had asked herself before what had caused this change in his behaviour, but she couldn't come up with any logical explanation. However, it could be because of the return of his …

She shook her head suddenly, dismissing her train of thought. Turning her attention back to the conversation, she said, "I'm doing fine. I'll be heading to the local PD today."

"I thought you would have done it yesterday." There was not a hint of surprise in his tone, just mild curiosity.

"I'm not really off to a good start here. The information gathered by the previous case agents of this investigation is merely enough to give a public statement," she said bluntly. "So I thought that I ought to make my own baseline of this investigation before speaking to the agents in charge."

"I think that you'll do a great job in whipping them into shape." The general chuckled. "All right, I'll leave you to your work." They exchanged goodbyes and ended the call. Then she started to get ready for the day.

Today Jenn was going to speak to the agents in charge of these homicide cases. And she was going to do it with style.

~

As Jenn strode into the police department, all eyes turned to her. She maintained a confident gait as she flashed her badge at them and asked to see Agent Turner and Agent Potts.

"That would be us." Two men in suits came forward to greet her. Her brown eyes flickered to the cheap power suits that they had on and then to the arrogant looks on their faces. Jenn mentally shook her head. No wonder they couldn't even get a single case closed in three years.

"I'm Agent Turner and this is Agent Potts, my partner," the tall blond guy said, gesturing to his lookalike, who was slightly shorter than he was. "You're Jumping Spider," he added with a know-it-all smirk.

She regarded them with a cool, calculating gaze and then spoke without missing a beat. "If you want to impress me, you will have to try harder than that. Now, is there anywhere we can talk in private?" If she was going to work with them, she would have to take them down a notch or two.

Agent Turner gave her a flirtatious smile. "Don't be like that."

Jenn ignored him and turned to his partner. "Perhaps you would know the way around here, Agent Potts."

To say that Agent Turner looked surprised was an understatement. As for Agent Potts, he appeared to be stunned into silence. So this guy wasn't used to being addressed when his high-and-mighty partner was around, Jenn concluded when she observed their reactions. After a few moments, he finally managed to react. "Th-this way, please," he stuttered, turning around to lead the way.

Agent Turner was silent as he fell into step beside his partner. Jenn followed them, observing them closely. The agents led her to what seemed like a meeting room. It was carefully furnished and had been tidied up just recently, she observed as she did a quick inspection of her surroundings, noting the unorganised stacks of case files on the table and the stains of marker on the hastily erased whiteboard. Closing the door, Agent Turner, who seemed to have recovered from his shock earlier, turned to her and said, "So how can we be of your assistance?" There was a hint of mockery in his voice.

Jenn simply gave him a sardonic smile and placed the files she had brought along with her on the table. She pushed the time-worn file towards the agents. Agent Turner took a fleeting look at the files while his partner faded into the background.

"Why do you want me to go through my own file? I do remember what's in it, okay?" He said impatiently.

Jenn pushed the other file, a newer one, to him. He picked it up and went through it. Then he slammed it on the table. "Where did this come from? You have someone in the department working for you?" he demanded, narrowing his eyes at her.

"Calm down, Agent," Jenn said, her voice unruffled. First conversation they had and he was already showing such poor trust in his own department. Impressive, she thought with a sigh, very impressive.

"Don't tell me what to do," Agent Turner snapped. He scowled at her, his ears turning red. "Am I supposed to be happy that someone else is trying to take my case away from me?"

"No one is trying to steal your case here, Agent." Jenn wanted to point out how impulsive and unprofessional he was acting, but she decided against it, thinking that now was actually the best time to test his limits.

He scoffed. "Oh, really? Then where did this file come from? The only people working on this case are me and Agent Potts. It's obvious that the second file came from someone who wants us humiliated and fired."

She wanted to laugh at his words. Did that egotistical fool realise that he was indirectly admitting that she did a far better job than he did with the case file? "Trust me, Agent, after seeing that elephantine ego you possess, I do wish to have you humiliated, but to get you fired? I wouldn't go that far." She looked at him with a mixture of amusement and contempt.

"What?" Agent Turner stared at her, his anger replaced with disbelief. Talk about mood swings. "You mean you did this?" he asked, jabbing his finger at the new file. "But … but that's not possible. Where did all that information come from?"

"Hard work, Agent. Hard. Work," she replied, emphasising every word. "If it makes you feel any better, it actually took me a whole day to gather all this information."

"What?" He gawked.

"I'm not a huge fan of weeds, you know," she continued, knowing that he most likely wouldn't understand her comment. He stared at her blankly, unable to comprehend her words.

She had to stop herself from sighing at his dumbfounded expression. "'Without hard work, nothing grows but weeds.' It's an ingenious quote of Gordon B. Hinckley," she explained swiftly. "When you want to get things done, you do them properly. That's the trick. If you had put some effort in to this case, I would not have had to go through all that trouble to dig up whatever information that you didn't even bother to look at. In fact, I might not even need to be here."

"No, I don't believe you." Agent Turner slowly shook his head. "You must be in this department to have access to all this information."

"I beg to differ. I just arrived here yesterday and look what I've found." She gestured towards her file. "And I got all that just by asking around in town. The people know things, you see," she muttered.

"And you believed what they said that easily?" he retorted, opening her file. "Let's take this as an example. How can you be sure that all victims attended parties the night before they were killed?"

She gave him a tight smile. "I have a reliable informant, not from your department, of course." Then she added, "And I did some homework too last night. This information isn't exactly classified, so it could have been easily accessed with a simple tool called the Internet. The photos of them at the parties can easily be found on online. Young people love to share their life experiences on social websites these days. I thought you would have known that." She ended her speech with a raised brow.

"I-I do know that," he mumbled, seeming ashamed of himself for not figuring that out himself. But then he brushed it off. "I see what you're trying to do here. You want to belittle me and my partner, don't you?"

"I have better things to do than that." She waved her hand dismissively, giving him a look of absurdity. "What I'm trying to do here is merely let you see how your enormous ego and ignorant attitude could have ruined your career." Her tone became serious. "Six girls are dead now. There might be a seventh if you still fail to see the seriousness of the situation. You're just making a clown out of yourself if you keep this up."

"I'm not playing a fool in my job, if that's what you're saying. People do respect me for my service in the justice department." His voice was shaky.

"I just emphasised the death of *six* young girls and all you can think of is respect? And you even have the nerve to bring up justice." Her tone was filled with disgust and mockery. "Are you really that shallow?"

A corner of his eye twitched at her blunt words. Agent Turner balled his hands into fists as he struggled to contain his anger. He opened his mouth to make a retort, but Jenn gave him no chance for argument.

"You want to talk about respect? Fine." She stared at him blankly. "I noticed that your partner was silently choking with laughter a few times just now, and I'm sure that he wasn't laughing at me." She gave Agent Turner a pointed look. "Even your own partner doesn't want to back you up. What does that say about respect?"

The blond guy turned his head to give his lookalike a death glare. Agent Potts lowered his head and said nothing.

"Oh, don't try to put the blame on him, Agent Turner. You spend too much time on your high horse, which brings me to my next point: justice. If you're so immersed in yourself, it's no mystery why the case has not been brought to a close. Considering the fact that you and your team have failed to solve this series of murders after more than *three* years, what justice have you done to the six innocent lives that have been lost?" She sighed to herself, looking at her watch. "Why am I even talking about this?"

"If you're in a rush, please show yourself out. No one's stopping you," Agent Turner said, blatantly furious.

At this point, she laughed. "I'm not quite done yet." Jenn pressed her palms on the table, showing superiority. "I'm officially taking over this case, and I've requested for both of your assistance." This announcement once again earned her looks of surprise from the two agents.

Before Agent Turner could open his mouth to object, she continued. "I've spoken to your superiors about this, and my request has been approved, so there's no point in going against an order." Jenn gave him a knowing look. "I will contact you when I've come up with a complete list of suspects." Then she gathered the files and headed for the door.

"Wait." Agent Turner spoke suddenly, causing her to turn around to face him. "You've already made it clear that you don't respect me," he stated bitterly, "yet you're asking for my – or in this case, *our* – assistance. Why?"

Jenn smiled. "Because after wasting so much time fooling around, it's only fair for both of you to start contributing to the justice department. Don't you want a second chance to make it up to the families of the victims?"

"I ..." Agent Turner stared at her in wonder. "Yes."

"Me too," Agent Potts piped in. "Thank you. We'll try our best." He beamed, speaking up for both of them for the very first time.

Jenn nodded in approval. "Good. I'm counting on that."

~

In the afternoon, Jenn decided to visit all the crime scenes. She started from the latest one. She went to the address stated in the files and saw that it was an abandoned cabin. She searched the area thoroughly, but nothing came up. She proceeded to the next location but still didn't find anything useful. She continued on to the fourth, third, and second crime scene. No luck.

Finally, she arrived at the empty warehouse where this whole mystery began. Jenn was very much ready to return to the hotel at this point. But to her surprise, she did find something which seemed like a promising lead, though it would have been hardly noticeable without strict scrutiny.

In the middle of the warehouse stood an old wooden chair where the first victim was held when she was murdered. The victim's hand must have been tied to the arms of the chair because on one of the arms, the victim had managed to carve out a name. Jenn ran her fingers over the name before scratching her fingernail below the words, testing her theory. Indeed, the old wood was soft enough to be carved with her nails.

With the right amount of force, the victim could have easily carved the name onto the chair back then. But how did she get away with leaving such an important clue without being noticed by the killer? Jenn continued to study both arms of the chair, only to find deep rope marks at the sides and bottoms of the arms. So that was probably how the victim did it: She pretended to struggle forcefully whilst scratching her fingernail on the wood to leave this name behind.

Her eyes flashed back to the name and she took a photo of the evidence with her phone. The alphabets were scarcely visible but readable to her watchful eyes.

Ray.

Six

Jenn stared at her reflection in the mirror, uttering a grunt when she saw the dark circles under her eyes. Then she huffed and turned away from the mirror, running her hand through her tousled black hair. As another wave of exhaustion filled her foggy mind, she put a hand to her mouth and muffled a yawn. She dragged herself out of her room and into the kitchen to get a glass of water.

She had been tossing and turning all night, but she just couldn't fall asleep. She couldn't get her mind off the case since she saw his name on the chair. That one single name was the key evidence to solving this whole mystery. Yet she found it so hard to believe her own eyes.

She had even found a few witnesses who saw the third victim, Leigh Burnham, leaving a party with a guy the night before she died. When she asked for a name, all of them gave Jenn his name.

Ray Darce.

She narrowed her eyes as the name entered her mind. She recalled the way he acted that night in the restaurant when they talked about the murders and she figured it out. So that was how he got the information. He was the devil himself. How smart of him to act dumb all this while.

However, something felt wrong about this whole thing. How was it possible for Ray to stay under the radar for so long? And what could be his motive for causing such kind of uproar around the town? There must be a missing piece, she thought firmly. But what was it?

It occurred to her suddenly that the killer used a most unique way of ending the victims' lives. Her earlier suspicion was further confirmed when she visited the crime scenes yesterday. She thought about the enclosed room in a quiet area, the chair, the victims' body with no signs of physical trauma and drug toxicity. There was only one way of killing them – using their minds against them.

However, she found it hard to understand how Ray could have managed to perform this level of hypnosis. There was no record of his taking lessons on hypnosis, nor did he leave the town for long periods to learn it. Even if he did manage to master it through the internet, it usually took many years of practice and professional guidance to be able to put people in such a deep trance. Unless, of course, he was naturally gifted in hypnosis.

Another question popped up in her mind. If Ray really was the guilty party, how was she going to bring him in? She had consulted the situation with Agent Turner and Agent Potts. According to them, a carved name on a chair was not solid evidence to be used in court to take him down. It could easily be brushed off as planted evidence. She was going to need to find stronger evidence in order to pin him for the crime in front of the judge. She was going to need a confession.

And she would get it from him.

~

Getting out of the taxi, Jenn tipped the driver, asking him to wait for her. Then she turned around and took a good look at the house in front of her, remembering how often she had been there for friendly visits and parties up until four years ago. And now she was here for an interrogation. *The wonderful twists of life*, she thought cynically.

Breathing a deep sigh, she went forward and pressed on the doorbell. A few moments passed before someone answered the door. It was Ray. Great.

"Jenn?" His eyebrows lifted in surprise. A curious smile crept onto his face. "What brings you here today? Think about me much?"

He had no idea. "Yes, I do, and I need your help with something," Jenn said, plastering a smile on her face. "Can we talk inside?"

He hesitated. "My parents aren't home today. You sure you want to come in? It'll be just us, you know."

Jenn's instinct told her that he wasn't faking his uncertainty about having her in his house when his parents weren't home. This was a good indicator that, albeit he was now a flirt, he rarely brought girls home. She sighed inwardly, wondering if he was deceiving her with his innocent reaction. She feigned another friendly smile. "It's okay. I don't mind."

"If you say so." He mumbled and stepped aside.

She entered his house and went to take a seat in his living room. Shutting the door behind him, Ray asked, "So how can I be of your assistance?" He walked into the living room, wearing a curious look.

"Have a seat first." She watched him as he sat down on the couch opposite her. Zipping open her backpack, she took out a few photos and arranged them on the coffee table. They were the victims' photos. She studied his demeanour as his eyes scanned the pictures. Almost immediately, she observed his eyes glazed over – again.

Bingo.

Ray gave her a stiff smile, his body rigid. "Why are you showing me these?"

"Do you know who these girls are?" Jenn asked, ignoring his question.

He frowned, keeping his eyes on the photos. "No ..." he said slowly, shaking his head.

She saw through his feeble pretence of puzzlement. "You're lying," she stated flatly.

Ray clenched his hands into fists on his lap involuntarily, his eyes flashing between the photos and Jenn. He attempted to smile at her calmly. "What makes you say that?"

"You were avoiding eye contact, which meant deceit. Your eyebrows rose slightly when you saw the photos, implying recognition. You were rubbing your palms on your laps, which is a display of insecurity – aftermath of lying. Your clenched fists show that you're nervous." Jenn paused to take a breath. "Shall I continue?" She gave him a pointed look.

Automatically, Ray unclenched his fists, only to cross his arms in front of him. He exhaled a long breath. "Are you really Jenn?"

"That's beside the point," she merely said. "So tell me, how did you know these girls?"

"I don't." He shrugged. "Am I lying again?"

"No," Jenn observed. Something was off about the way he was acting, even for a killer. She studied him closely, maintaining a relaxed pose. His behaviour was too inconsistent for a normal person. Unless he was a sociopath, there was no way he could jump from panicking to being composed within just a few seconds. Finally, she noticed the way he was looking at her. Something was definitely not right.

Sighing, she leaned forward. "All right. I'm not going to beat around the bush anymore. Did you kill them?"

Surprisingly, Ray merely raised his eyebrows at her question. Jenn saw this, and she was sure that Ray had given up covering himself. Sure enough, an eerie smile crept onto his face, giving himself away immediately.

"Bravo, Jenn. You solved the mystery."

There was not a hint of anxiety in his voice. It was almost as if he was glad that he was discovered. She looked deep into his eyes, searching.

"Why did you kill them?" she prodded.

The smirk on his face morphed into a grimace. "They deserved it."

"Why did they deserve to die?" she pushed on, determined to get to the bottom of this.

Uncertainty displayed on his face. "They ..." Ray shook his head and tried again. "They were ..." He choked on his own words.

Just as she had predicted, he didn't know. How could he?

He made an exasperated sound, frowning at the floor. "Why does it even matter?" His eyes flashed to her, and a hint of desperation flickered across his face. "I killed them. You already have my confession. Just cut the crap and cuff me already."

Now this was getting interesting. Ray was afraid that she wouldn't bring him in.

"I don't believe you." She cocked her head at him. "I don't think you killed them."

"What?" Ray stared at her, clearly dumbfounded. "Are you kidding me?"

She sighed. "Sorry to burst your bubble, Ray, but you're not a killer. What I see in you is just a person who is desperate to take the blame."

"But I did kill them." He sounded pretty sure of it, but his wild eyes said otherwise.

She could see that he was getting flustered. It was time to change her approach.

Jenn stood up and walked around the coffee table, her eyes never leaving Ray. She stopped right in front of him and knelt down. When he tried to back away, she took hold of both his wrists and held him in place. She locked her gaze with his. "Ray, you are not a killer," she murmured gently. "I know who you really are, Ray. You are a good guy. You care about your friends. You love your family."

His gaze softened as her words filled his mind. "But—"

She shook her head, silencing him, but she kept her expression calm and tranquil. "You remember who you are, how you treat others." His breathing started to slow down.

"You rarely get upset," she continued, keeping eye contact as she slowly released his wrists. "You smile at almost everyone you see." Her hand went to his shoulder and gave it a light tap. No response. "You love to help others." She slid her hand down to his elbow and tapped it lightly again. Again, nothing. "You feel happy when your loved ones are happy." She lowered her hand and held his hand, squeezing it gently. When his body didn't respond, she moved on to his leg, resting her palm on his knee and patting it. "You know it, Ray. You did not kill the six girls."

Suddenly, he snapped out of his trance. "No, I did." His glazed eyes started to go wild again, and he brushed her hand off him.

Jenn was losing her grip on his mind, but she was already halfway through this. She couldn't stop now. So Jenn did the first thing that entered her mind. She leaned forward and kissed him.

How to distract a flirt? Play his game.

Immediately, Ray responded. He kissed her back as his hand went to her face, caressing her cheek. Jenn placed a hand at the back of his neck, squeezing it gently, and moved her hand down his back slowly, sending shivers down his spine. He groaned in pleasure at her skilful touch. She smirked against his lips as she grabbed his thigh and tightened her grip, causing him to gasp. Ray wrapped his arms around her waist and pulled her closer to his torso. She realised that it was time to stop this. She had done what she could to distract him, so now was the time to proceed with her plan.

Gently, she pushed him back, ending the kiss. Ray stared at her in wonder, looking out of breath. Jenn looked down and bit her bottom lip, feigning embarrassment. A blush would have perfected her façade, she thought.

Ray started to speak. "What was …?"

She took his hand and squeezed it lightly, managing to cut him off. "Come with me."

He blinked twice, and she saw his wide eyes glaze over. "Okay," he mumbled, staring at her with dilated pupils.

Relieved, she quickly put the photos back into her backpack. Then she took his hand once again and led him out of the house. In a daze, he followed her obediently. Her taxi was waiting for them outside the house. Together they got in the car, and she gave the driver instructions to go to her hotel.

"Where are we going?" Ray asked as the car started moving.

Jenn took a glance at him and saw that he was still stupefied by the whole incident just now. It would be very easy to lie to him right now. He was gullible and credulous, so even if she told him that the president was his father, he would have believed her without a doubt, not that she was going to do that.

"We're going over to my place," she answered, smiling at him.

"Huh?" He looked confused. "What's wrong with my house?"

She laughed gently. "It's not safe for you to be there anymore. That's why I need to bring you somewhere safe." From a corner of her eye, she saw the taxi driver watching them in the rear-view mirror. She ignored the driver's weird stare and focused on Ray. The trance that she had put him in wasn't deep enough to fully hypnotise him. She could easily lose him again if she became distracted.

Jenn continued to lull him, stopping him from coming out of the trance until they reached the hotel. After paying the driver, she brought him back to her suite.

"Wow," was the first thing Ray said when they entered the suite.

He settled down on the couch in the living area, glancing around her place. Jenn closed the door behind her and locked it while she watched him closely.

"You actually live here?" he asked, turning around to look at her.

She simply moved towards the couch, sat down beside him whilst setting her backpack at the side of the couch, and subtly placed her hand on his. Then Jenn squeezed his hand lightly, breaking his trance. "Wake."

Ray's eyes went blank for a moment. Then he blinked at her and took in his surroundings once again.

"What is this place?" Confusion coloured his face and he touched a hand to his forehead. "And how did I get here?"

Ray was frowning to himself, plainly trying to recall what had happened. "The last thing I remembered was …" His eyes widened in disbelief as he raised his eyes to meet hers. "We were … kissing?"

"You remember?" she asked warily, observing his face.

"Barely – just bits of it." He scratched the back of his head.

"Huh," Jenn merely uttered. Staring at the pink tinge on his cheeks, she realised that Ray wasn't actually a flirt. If he were, he would have looked anything but shy. This flirtatious side that he had been displaying the past few days must be a side effect of being hypnotised by the real killer. It was a mask to hide his guilt and probably to carry out his commands from the hypnotist – whatever they were.

Jenn knew that Ray remembered much more than he was letting on. Well, it did make sense. After all, to put someone in a trance was nearly impossible after a kiss, much less to suppress his memory. She did quite well for herself, Jenn thought.

Ray avoided her gaze, pushing away the images in his head. "Where am I?" he asked in a clear attempt to fill the awkward silence.

"My suite." She got up from the couch and went to the kitchen. It was a good thing that she'd prepared some hot water with the electric water boiler this morning before she left to visit Ray. "We'll be staying here for the time being." She explained as she made a cup of tea.

"Oh," Ray muttered, glancing around again. When her words finally registered, he stood up immediately. "Wait – what?"

Jenn came back into the room and set the cup of tea that she had made for him on the coffee table.

He stared at her, incredulous. "We? As in you and me?"

"There's no one else here, right?" She pretended to look around. "So yes, you and me."

There was a sudden look of remembrance on his face. Then Jenn saw his eyes flashing around, looking for a way to escape, and she knew that Ray must have recalled the confrontation that took place this morning.

"Sit down," she commanded, eyeing him with such intensity that it made him obey her. Then she sighed. "You're confused," she stated.

He regarded her with wary eyes. "Well, let's see. You came over to my house and confronted me about the girls. And I also gave you my confession. You could have handed me over to the police and closed the case. Then suddenly, despite my confession, you decided that I'm not the killer. Instead, you kidnapped me. How can I not be confused?"

She exhaled deeply through her nose. He should know the truth. "You might want to have some tea first before I start explaining," she said with a stoic expression on her face.

As Ray hesitantly took a sip of tea, she slid her hand into her pocket. She took out her badge and showed it to him. "The truth is, I'm not Jennifer Cole anymore. My new identity is Catherine Nelson, special agent of the National Security Secret Service. I'm assigned here to investigate the murders of the six girls in this town." She paused, letting her words sink.

Ray's eyes widened at the sight of her badge, and an expression of shock was frozen on his face. Ray opened his mouth to say something, only to close it again when no words came out.

Jenn continued. "The day you first saw me back in town was the day I arrived. I have been investigating the case since then. At the moment, you were not on my suspect list. It was only when I went back to the crime scenes to look for evidence that I started to think that the culprit was you. Your name was carved into a wooden chair to which the first victim was tied.

"After that, I went to see a few witnesses who claimed that they saw one of the victims leaving a party with you the night before she died. That was how I confirmed you as the killer. But then when I went to your house this morning, I observed you while I confronted you about it. You were too eager to confess your crime, and you had no idea at all about your motive for committing the murders. You displayed no signs of psychopathy or mental disorder, which could have explained your lack of motives. You also made it obvious that you are not a thrill killer, so you made it quite hard for me to actually pin you down as a serial killer.

"Also, your pupils were dilated the whole time we talked. Your pulse was considerably steady for someone who had just admitted to committing a murder. So it led only to one explanation: hypnosis."

At this point, Ray looked totally flabbergasted. He started shaking his head, denying her words. "It couldn't be. It's not true. I am not hypnotised, okay? You've got it all wrong. I feel perfectly normal."

"So you feel normal too, being a serial killer?"

"I ..." He frowned, biting his lip, looking as if his thoughts were in a jumble.

She kept her voice firm. "Have you ever thought about stopping after killing so many innocent young ladies?"

"They deserved it. They deserved to die." He repeated the words to himself like a mantra. "They deserved it."

"What did they ever do to deserve such punishment?" she pushed on, finding a crack in the barrier in his mind. "Why did they deserve to die?"

Once again, he was stuck at this question. His hands were tightly clenched into fist while his eyes went wild, searching for answers.

She started over. "So tell me again: did you really kill them?"

"Yes," Ray answered automatically.

"Then tell me how you killed the girls," she challenged.

That shut him up quickly.

"As you can see, you have no idea why or how you killed those girls. How can you expect me to believe that you're the culprit? It was obvious that the hypnotist – whoever that is – put that idea into your head. Believe it or not, the flaw to this ingenious plan of the real killer is you."

When she saw that he was still unconvinced, she explained further. "Ray, the killer simply used you as a bait to bring the victims to him. He used you to charm the victims so that they would follow willingly when you brought them to him. With your good looks and sweet words, it's not hard for you to get them to fall for you."

"But I'm not a player. I don't even flirt!" he blurted out, plainly incredulous. Then, as if he'd just realised what he had said, he blushed. "Well, it's not that I can't do it; I just never tried to flirt." He scratched the back of his head.

Jenn let out a chuckle. Only Ray could manage to feel embarrassed over something as trivial as this during such a crucial moment. Then she composed herself. "Then how did you convince them to leave the parties with you?"

"I just chatted with them ..." he answered, but he started to sound doubtful of himself.

"That's what you thought you were doing," Jenn stated calmly. "But what really happened was an entirely different thing."

When Ray didn't argue with her explanation, she carried on. "He was preparing you as his escape plan. You were meant to take the blame all along. Your name was carved by the victim on the chair because she knew that you were the one who abducted her.

"She was blindfolded when she woke up, tied to a chair. She couldn't see who the captor was, so she assumed that it was you too. Hence your name on the chair." She paused to see how well he was coping with all this. He seemed to be doing okay. "You know, it kind of surprised me that the killer managed to hypnotise you to believe that you are responsible for all this. After all, a subject cannot be hypnotised to do something against his morals or values. Though in your case, you were hypnotised to believe something and not actually do it all the same."

A strange look flickered across his face, disappearing as soon as it appeared. But Jenn caught it nevertheless. "Unless, of course, deep down you don't believe it," she said suggestively.

Ray looked torn. He squeezed his eyes shut, holding his head in his hands. "Look, I had no choice," he finally confessed, sounding desperate. "I have to believe it."

"You don't remember anything during the time when the murders took place, do you?" She spoke calmly, figuring it out all by herself.

His eyes snapped open. "How did you …?"

"The first step to insert falsified information in one's mind is self-doubt. "How else would the killer have you convince yourself that you are guilty?"

Ray nodded in comprehension. Then he proceeded to explain his situation. "At first, all I knew was that I brought those girls away from the parties. I wasn't sure why I did so. I just had to, you know." He looked up as if to be sure she understood his meaning. Jenn gave him an encouraging nod, so he went on. "I assumed that I was drunk, considering the fact that I didn't know what I was actually doing or why I did any of the things I did. Well, I did bring them out of parties without any particular reason," he muttered. "Anyway, after I left with the girls, I kind of blacked out. And when I woke up, I was already back at my house.

"The day after each party, I woke up to the news of a girl's death. I had no idea what I had done to her. I thought that I was losing it, you know. I tried to stop myself from attending parties, but it didn't work. I didn't even realise what I was actually doing until after the parties, when I woke up to headaches. It kept happening again and again, but I didn't know how to stop it. It just happened, you know. I felt so bad to think that I'd killed them without even realising it. It was so disgusting." He pressed his fist to his mouth as if to stop himself from screaming aloud.

Jenn continued where he'd left off, speaking slowly, making sure he heard every word she said. "But after a while, you got used to it. You convinced yourself that the fault wasn't entirely on you because you were drunk every time it happened. Deep down, you felt bad for their deaths. But since you couldn't stop it from happening again and you were afraid to turn yourself in, you figured that accepting who you are would probably hurt less, so you turned off your conscience and kept quiet.

"That is, until just now. When I confronted you, you jumped at the chance to confess what you thought you had done. You had never had enough courage to go to the police, so when I came to you and gave you a chance to confess, you were more than happy to do it," she concluded. "So in a way, your conscience still exists inside you. You just need to believe it."

He nodded in resignation, finally accepting the truth. "You got it all correct this time," Ray muttered. Then he laughed dryly. "Hypnotised, huh? But I feel so normal."

"That's what every person under hypnosis thinks. It is a tough fact to accept." Jenn shrugged. "But now that I have clarified the situation to you, I suppose that you would rather believe that you're hypnotised rather than think that you're a serial killer." She gave him a pointed look.

He sighed. "Yeah, I guess so." Then he met her gaze. "You really have changed." He said suddenly, catching her off guard. "The Jenn I used to know could never be as sharp as you are right now."

She chuckled, but there was a hint of sadness in her voice. "Time changes a person."

"I suppose so," Ray said, mostly to himself. Then his eyes focused on her again. "For a moment, I almost thought that you're psychic."

His words made her laugh. "There's no such thing as psychic, though people do say I'm one. I don't really see myself as psychic; instead I think it's just a gift – or sometimes a curse. Sometimes it's annoying analysing idiotic or spiteful people. It makes me feel that I'm like them too, being able to understand their thoughts."

"You read minds?" he asked in awe.

"No." She frowned. "That would make it a whole lot worse." She shuddered at the thought. "I study people. I can analyse a person instantly and anticipate his thoughts and actions based on his behaviour. That's all."

"Cool." He raised his eyebrows with a hint of amazement.

"Not." She made a face. "It is useful during my missions and cases, but at other times, it's just plain irritating. Period. That's why I switch it off most of the time."

"You can ... switch it off?"

She paused to think of an understandable explanation. "Actually, it's more like reminding myself not to pay too much attention to body language and micro-expressions, or something like that. I focus on certain thoughts rather than my surroundings and ..." She trailed off and sighed. "It's complicated." She waved her hand, dismissing the topic. Right now, she needed to make sure that Ray had really accepted the fact that he was under hypnosis. "So—"

Her cell phone rang, interrupting her. Much to her chagrin, it was Ben.

Seven

"Warner, what do you need now?" Jenn asked when she answered the call.

Ben greeted her in a low, urgent voice. "Catherine. Did you kidnap a suspect?"

She frowned in surprise. How did he know that? Not that she really did kidnap anyone, technically speaking. "Get to the point."

"Okay, okay," he said, much to her surprise. Usually he would have responded differently, more sarcastically. "Your town agent, last name's Turner, if I'm not mistaken, called the general."

Damn it. She realised now what was going on. Agent Turner must have gone to Ray's house after she had brought Ray to the hotel. He assumed that she'd help Ray escape because he was her friend. Ugh, this was going to be ugly.

"Hello? You still there?" Ben's voice brought her back to the present.

"Yes," she replied curtly. "So your dad is going to call me?"

"Um, that's a given, isn't it?" Ben said, chuckling nervously. "Look, I'm not sure what the general has in store for you, but it's not going to be pleasant."

"It would take an idiot to not figure that out." Then her tone softened a little. "Thanks for the tip. Bye."

She didn't wait for his reply before hanging up. Jenn turned back to Ray, who was giving her a questioning look. Before she could say anything, her cell phone rang again. "Sorry," she muttered to Ray. She wanted to answer the call in her room, but Ray still needed supervision. So she walked towards the kitchen, where she would be out of earshot and Ray would still be within her sight. Then she answered the call.

"Sir."

"Agent Nelson." His voice sounded calm. "I suppose that Agent Warner has briefed you on the details, so I'm getting straight to the point. Did you kidnap a suspect?"

Like father, like son, she thought, recalling Ben using the exact words. "Yes." What else could she say? She did bring Ray over to her place without his consent.

The general heaved a sigh. "Why did you do so?"

At least he gave her a chance to explain. In a low voice, she explained everything to him. "Yesterday I found evidence in one of the crime scenes. A name was carved onto the handle of a wooden chair where the first victim was supposedly tied. Later, I met with a few witnesses who saw one of the victims leaving parties with a guy named Ray Darce – which is the name on the chair – the night before she was found dead. So I gave Agent Turner and his partner an update about my progress so far.

"The next morning, I went to Ray's house to confront him about the case. He confessed to the crime but when I prodded him for more details, he couldn't answer. He had no idea why or even how he did it. He showed no signs of deceit and mental disability, so the most possible explanation was that he was hypnotised.

"Then I decided that he was off the suspect list. I figured that it would be best for him to be under my supervision until the real serial killer is caught, so I brought him back to my place. Agent Turner must have made assumptions about this whole thing." It was a long-story-short version of the whole incident, but Jenn thought that it would do trick.

The general remained silent for a few moments before speaking again. "You take the next flight back to HQ. You'll be assigned to a new case."

"No." She was taken aback at his irrational decision. Obviously, he thought that she was letting her personal feelings get in her way. "Sir, with all due respect, you have misunderstood my actions."

"Have I now?" the general said coolly.

"I have checked twice before I confirmed that Ray has been hypnotised. I did not assume anything just because he is my friend. I did not allow my personal feelings to affect my decisions in this case."

The general was silent, reconsidering his decision, perhaps.

"You sent me here because of my ability so please trust your decision, even if you don't trust me," she said steely.

He sighed in resignation. "I can see where you're going with this." He cleared his throat. "Fine, I'll give you the benefit of the doubt." She smiled victoriously. "You have two weeks to solve this case. If you fail to do so, you will be withdrawn from this mission."

Okay, she could handle that.

"One more thing: I'm assigning two more agents to this mission."

This wiped the smile off her face. "I do not need supervision," she objected. Two agents? Did he find her that distrustful?

"This is not up to you," he retorted, finalising his decision.

She groaned inwardly. "Then can I at least choose my partners?" she asked, feigning submission.

The general considered her request for a few moments. "You'll choose one. I'll choose the other."

"Fair enough," she conceded. "I want Dolphin on this one."

"Dolphin?" Obviously he was momentarily confused. "Oh, right, Agent Leon," he mumbled to himself. "Catherine, you do realise that Dolphin is just a nickname, don't you? Her code name is Falcon. You should stop using nicknames at serious moments like this. It's really confusing." For a moment, he was clearly distracted.

"But she dislikes it. She thinks that Dolphin suits her better – intelligent, brainy," Jenn replied, thrilled for the distraction.

But then he got back to business. "Okay, then, it's decided. Falcon and Cougar will assist you in this case."

What!

"They'll arrive tomorrow."

No! The word was stuck in her throat.

"Good luck, Agent." The line went dead.

"No," she mumbled belatedly, suppressing the urge to scream aloud. Her emotions were in turmoil right now. She tightened her grip on the cell phone. Out of all the agents, the general had to choose his son. He did this on purpose, didn't he? She should have seen this coming.

Ray spoke hesitantly, breaking her train of thought. "Uh … Jenn? Oh, I meant Catherine."

Her eyes snapped to him, causing him to flinch involuntarily under her stony gaze. "Your phone is ringing again," he said gingerly.

"Sorry, it's not you that I'm mad at." She apologised curtly before answering her phone.

She didn't have to check the caller ID to know that it was Ben again.

She answered the call immediately. "Did you do it on purpose?" she demanded, not bothering to lower her voice.

"It wasn't me." He was plainly trying to suppress his laughter. "I swear it wasn't, though I'm not really surprised that he chose me."

She scoffed and hung up, pressing the END button a bit too forcefully.

She strode towards the couch and stuffed her cell phone into her backpack. Then she threw herself onto the couch in a huff. She turned to Ray, only to see him struggling to contain his smile.

"What?" she asked, blatantly puzzled at his amused expression.

"You look really cute when you're angry," he answered, laughing.

She put her frustrations aside and raised an eyebrow at him, ignoring the fluttery feelings in her stomach when he said that.

"That came out all wrong." He made a weird face. "Wait, let me rephrase that."

Now it was her turn to be amused. "Don't worry. I got what you meant. I was just messing with you."

"Oh." He chuckled, embarrassed.

"A piece of advice from me: think before you speak." She could barely suppress a smile. "You're going to break many girls' heart if you keep that up."

His sheepish expression turned into a playful grin. "Should I take that as a compliment?"

"Up to you." She shrugged before getting all serious again. "Ray, are you still confused about the case now?"

He thought about it for a few moments. "I think not," he said slowly. "But it's still kind of hard for me to accept the fact that I'm under hypnosis." He frowned.

"Don't worry. You'll get used to it." She replied, finding his muddled expression amusing.

He glanced up at the ceiling and muttered to himself, "Believe it, Ray. You are under hypnosis. You did not kill those girls. You were framed by the real killer." He repeated the whole thing a few times like a mantra.

She chuckled, shaking her head. "You should not have any contact with the outside world too, you know. Add that to the list."

He turned to her with wide eyes. "I'm basically a prisoner here," he exclaimed. Then he added cheerfully, "Well, a willing prisoner." He laughed despite himself.

Even at a time like this, he could still manage to be funny. She rolled her eyes at his silliness and stood up. "Come on. I'll show you to your room. By the way, just call me Jenn."

~

That night, Jenn and Ray were both sitting in the living area. The television was turned on, but neither of them was watching it. Ray's eyes were glued to the television, but his mind was plainly elsewhere. Jenn paid no attention to him as she feverishly clicked and typed away on her laptop, searching for whatever information she could find about breaking a hypnotic trance.

Ray spoke suddenly. "Jenn?"

"Yes?" Jenn mumbled, her eyes never leaving her screen.

"Why did you leave in the first place?"

Her fingers froze over the keyboard, and she slowly turned to look at him. His expression was a mixture of curiosity and hesitation. She was sure that he saw her rigid posture, for he quickly added, "You don't have to answer my question if you don't feel like it."

"I wasn't planning to."

"Okay." Ray blinked and pursed his lips, seemingly taken aback by her bleak tone. He went back to staring at the television.

Jenn had turned back to her laptop, but she could no longer focus on her current task. After a few moments, she spoke again.

"My parents were killed."

Ray's eyes went back to her face, observing her emotionless face. He remained silent, waiting for her to open up more.

"They were assassinated, to be exact," she said in a quiet tone. "When the government learned about my ability, they wanted to recruit me." She continued, her tone mirroring her expression, void and empty. "At first, I turned down their offer because I never wanted to leave town. But then one of the agents – the one who discovered me in the first place – approached me with a case, asking for my assistance. He promised that I did not need to leave town for the case and it was just a one-time deal. He said that he needed my extraordinary perception – his words, not mine – and I thought it harmless enough that I agreed to it.

"I helped him solve the case. We investigated a corrupt firm and took down several high-profile figures. I made it clear that I didn't want any credit in solving the case, but someone must have leaked my name. Terrence Anderson, the big gun in the firm, whom we haven't yet managed to bring in at the time, put a hit out on me and the agent I was working with … as well as our families.

"Within three days, our families were wiped out by assassins." Her voice turned cold. "The agent and I were brought into protective custody. A letter was left behind to cover my tracks so that my sudden departure wouldn't raise alarms. When I heard about my parents' death, I snapped. I requested to join the NSSS right after I left Tirjuan to hunt down the bastards myself. They were more than happy to recruit me. I wanted to keep this whole thing silent. My parents were killed during their business trip to Hawaii, so the news never managed to travel back here. The government had to pull some strings to cover up the whole situation, but they managed to make it look as if my parents had spontaneously decided to move overseas, so that's that."

Now everything made sense to Ray. He had always thought it weird for the Cole family to move away just like that. And now the mystery had finally been uncovered. However, the truth was nowhere near his previous assumptions.

"In the end, I did succeed in taking down every single person involved in my parents' murder, including Anderson, but it never felt enough. I made myself forget about it. I got a new identity, a new life. I never looked back." A ghost of a smile touched her lips, but then it vanished as soon as it appeared. "Until now."

Ray kept his eyes on her, clearly absorbing everything she had just told him. Jenn began staring off into space, immersed in deep thought.

A part of her wondered why she had told him about her parents. It puzzled her that she would open up to him so easily. But more than that, she was surprised at herself for not breaking down after all that. There were traces of sadness and grief inside her, but the feeling of relief overpowered those melancholy feelings. It felt good to finally get it out of her. It was amazing how talking about her parents could make her see how foolish she had been for running away from her past all this while.

"You okay?" Ray's voice pulled her back to the present. He gently laid his hand on hers as an act of consolation. "If you need a shoulder to cry on, I am more than honoured to be of service," he said jokingly.

"Do you see tears in my eyes?" Jenn asked him rhetorically, and then she surprised him by laying her head on his shoulder. "But thanks."

"You're welcome. I'm glad that you trust me enough to give me the truth."

"Feels good to have someone who understands." Jenn sighed.

Ray felt something inside him stir at her words, and he couldn't help but feel sad for her. It must have been really hard for her to not speak of it for four years. For a moment, he wanted to embrace her in his arms and let her know that he would always be there for her. But then he pushed away the silly thought. How could he take advantage of her at a moment like this? Instead, he simply asked, "So you're really okay now?"

She lifted her head from his shoulder and turned to meet his gaze, smiling softly. "Never better."

Eight

The next day, Jenn woke up earlier than she usually did. It was only four in the morning, and she couldn't go back to sleep. She was fully aware that she was all too nervous about her partners' arrival. Okay, to be honest, she was nervous to see him again after all the effort she had put in to avoid him for the last six months.

She knew that she was overreacting, but she couldn't help it. As ridiculous as it sounded, Ben was her weakness – not the mushy romantic kind which people would assume. It was just that Ben was the only person who knew her so well that she felt like an open book sometimes when he was around. He knew exactly how to deal with her, even when she was upset. Most of the time, he would see through her thoughts and intentions behind her actions. He was a weakness she would never admit to anyone.

And now with him around, she was going to have loads of headaches if she wanted to do things her way. For a fact, Ben would surely choose not to trust Ray because Ray had been in contact with the killer. Groaning, she pushed herself up into a sitting position.

"Stop thinking about him, will you?" she scolded herself, annoyed.

She tried to clear her mind as she got off her bed. Tying her hair into a loose ponytail, she headed to the kitchen to get a glass of water. Then she went into the office to study the case files. She had to find something to do to pass the time somehow.

About fifteen minutes had passed when she heard a strange noise coming from outside the room. Immediately, she left her files on the table and made a dart for her pistol back in her room. Clutching her pistol now, she went back into the living area, scanning the room. The noise came from the door. Apparently, someone was trying break into the suite.

Quietly she approached the door and wrapped her fingers around the doorknob. She heard the intruder whispering from the other side of the door, arguing with someone else. She figured that there must be two of them, then.

Bracing herself, she opened the door in a flash and pointed her pistol at the intruders. She frowned when she saw who they were.

"Ben? J. Lee? What the hell are you doing?" she asked in bewilderment. "Are you actually trying to break in?"

"Uh …" Ben eyed her pistol warily. "Can we talk without waving guns around?"

Jenn rolled her eyes at him. She lowered her pistol and stepped aside for them to enter. Ben and J. Lee carried their bags into the suite, and she shut the door behind her.

"Now talk," Jenn demanded, crossing her arms in front of her chest.

Ben spoke first. "We reached here a bit too early. We thought that you were still sleeping, and we didn't want to wake you up, so we decided to let ourselves in first." He grinned sheepishly and glanced around the room. "Nice place."

She ignored his last comment and gave him a grim look before turning to J. Lee, raising her eyebrows. "What do you have to say about this?"

"He wanted to take the first flight so that he could see you sooner," J. Lee stated bluntly, wearing her usual flat expression. "Then he wanted to let ourselves in first to give you a pleasant surprise when you woke up."

Ben gaped at her, incredulous. "Did you have to quote everything I said?"

J. Lee turned to him, still expressionless, and said, "She asked."

He gave her a look of dubiety. "Can't you at least edit it a little?"

"Doesn't matter. She would have guessed it too," she stated.

Jenn laughed suddenly. "You haven't changed much, J. Lee."

"Good to see you again, Spider." J. Lee gave her a tiny smile. For her, it was considered a huge hello gesture.

"Likewise." Jenn smiled.

"Don't you feel good to see me again too?" Ben cut in as if feeling left out.

Jenn sighed. "Not really, especially when you're being unusually ridiculous right now." She wanted to call him childish for what he had said to J. Lee about arriving sooner, but she decided that she didn't want to give him the impression that she was fine with him around now. So she turned back to J. Lee. "Have you taken your breakfast yet?"

"No," J. Lee replied, throwing a quick glance at Ben. "We were in a hurry."

Hearing this, Jenn shot Ben a scowl. "You are such an inconsiderate … person."

"Sorry, it sort of slipped my mind." He raised his hands in defence. "Plus, she didn't mention anything about being hungry just now."

Jenn decided to ignore him. Putting on a smile, she said to J. Lee, "You must be starving. Come on. I'll get you something to eat."

"Okay. Let me help you." The two girls went into the kitchen, leaving Ben alone in the room.

J. Lee offered to make toast and fried eggs, and she insisted that she could handle it alone. Jenn knew that arguing with her was pointless – her friend could be quite stubborn when she wanted to – so Jenn prepared some fruit juice and a pot of coffee. When they were done, they brought the food and drinks out to the dining table.

Ben was already seated at the table, studying a flower painting on the wall behind him while he was waiting.

"Breakfast is ready," Jenn announced as she sat down. There were only four seats around the square table, so she did not have much choice. She could choose either to sit beside Ben or opposite him. She chose the latter.

Her quiet friend settled down between them. She put a few slices of toast on her plate and started eating immediately. Within seconds, she managed to devour a whole slice of toast. Then she moved on to the next one, munching away.

Ben stared at her with wide eyes. "With such small bites, I'm surprised that you actually managed to finish that whole thing so fast. Are you really that hungry?"

J. Lee chewed quickly and swallowed before saying, "I'm a fast eater." Then she turned back to her toast.

"No kidding," Ben tittered. "But you're ridiculously sophisticated for a fast eater." He took a sip of his fruit juice. When J. Lee didn't make any response, he added, "I was just kidding."

J. Lee didn't take her eyes off her food. She simply replied, "I know. I don't get the punch line. That's all."

"Okay, I get it. You don't like to talk while eating. Message received," Ben said, giving up on making a conversation with her. He glanced at Jenn and made a face. In return, he earned a disapproving look from her.

Meanwhile, J. Lee merely said, "I don't like to talk. Period."

Jenn snorted. That was why she liked J. Lee so much. Her friend's bluntness could not be found in anyone else. She was truly one of a kind. Jenn took a bite of her pancake, trying to suppress the amused smile on her face but failing terribly.

She could see that Ben was trying to get along with his new partner, but he was trying way too hard. What he didn't realise was that J. Lee was very different from most people he knew. If he could just be himself, they would get along just fine.

After that, they finished breakfast in silence. There were a couple of times when Ben tried to initiate a conversation with Jenn, only to be silenced by her cold gaze. After breakfast, Ben volunteered to wash the dishes while the two girls stayed at the table, chatting for a while.

"So what were you working on before this?" Jenn asked out of curiosity.

"You mean before you summoned me here?" J. Lee muttered, causing Jenn to laugh at her choice of word. "Well, I was tracking down a couple of missing meteorites for a scientist. He claimed that they were stolen."

"How did it turn out?" Jenn asked, raising an eyebrow.

"I recovered a few of them in the basement of the national museum. The rest are still missing."

"That ought to be fun." Jenn grinned, guessing what her friend would say to that.

J. Lee stared at her. "They're just stones," the junior agent stated, still expressionless.

"From outer space," Jenn added.

"Destructive stones, then. What's your point?"

Jenn laughed, amused at her friend's perception. "Never mind."

"What's going on here?" Ray's voice came from behind them.

Jenn turned around and saw a puzzled Ray blinking at the stranger who was talking to her. Seeing his tousled hair, she guessed that he had just awakened up. Reflexively, Jenn stood up and her friend followed suit.

"Ray, remember I told you yesterday that two more agents would be coming to assist me in the investigation?" Jenn asked. Ray nodded at her, and she continued. "Well, this is Agent Leon." She gestured towards J. Lee. "The other one, Agent Warner, is in the kitchen. They'll be with us from today onwards."

J. Lee stepped forward to formally introduce herself. "I'm Agent Justine Leon, Criminal Investigation Department detective. You can address me as J. Lee or Dolphin." She extended her hand for a handshake.

Ray raised his brows at her choice of nickname. "J. Lee it is, then." He accepted the handshake hesitantly, obviously not used to this level of formality. "Uh … I'm Ray Darce, fresh graduate from college, no title, no job – for now. You can just call me by my name, Ray." He introduced himself in a stiff voice as he let go of her hand.

Jenn covered her mouth to muffle her laughter, and even J. Lee cracked a smile. Ray, oblivious to the mirth he had caused, kept his face serious and stood straight, mirroring J. Lee's stance.

At that moment, Ben came out of the kitchen. He raised his eyebrows at Ray and gave him a once-over. "Who's this?" he asked Jenn.

Jenn sighed quietly as she detected the slight disdain in his tone, hinting that he'd already guessed who Ray was. She turned to Ray and said, "Ray, meet Agent Warner."

Ray was already coming forward to greet him when Ben said, "Ah, the prime suspect." He spoke coolly, making no effort to hide the derision in his eyes. "I'm Special Agent Bennett Warner from the National Security Secret Service. How nice to finally meet you."

Ray's eyes narrowed at his unfriendly tone. Jenn decided to step in before it could get any worse. "In case you weren't informed by the general, Ray is no longer on the suspect list."

"Huh," Ben uttered indifferently. "Perhaps the general left out that part during the briefing. Sorry about that." He did not sound the least bit apologetic.

Jenn shot him a warning look before turning back to Ray. "Okay, now that you've met the both of them, why don't you go have some breakfast? J. Lee made some toast and fried eggs."

Taking the hint, her friend moved towards him. "There's fruit juice too," she said, steering Ray towards the dining table. "Let me know if there isn't enough food. There's still some bread in the kitchen."

In the meantime, Jenn turned to Ben, wearing a grim look. "You come with me," she instructed in a low voice, striding towards the office.

"Your wish is my command," he replied smoothly, following her into the room. He shut the door behind him while Jenn started to speak.

"Mind explaining what that was all about?" she asked, crossing her arms in front of her. She had walked to the other side of the conference table, putting some space between them.

Ben let out a small sigh, dropping the arrogant façade. "Look, Catherine, Ray Darce might not be on your suspect list anymore, but he's still on mine. He has been in contact with the serial killer for more than three years," he explained, grimacing. "For all we know, his mind could have been twisted by the killer. I just thought that it would be better if we keep our guards up around him."

Jenn's eyes were on the floor as she slowly nodded, showing that she was listening. Then she looked up, meeting his gaze with a frown. "First of all, in this town, I'm Jennifer Cole, not Catherine Nelson. Do not address me by my alias here." She gave him a pointed look. "Second, Ray was under the influence of hypnosis and tricked into believing that he is the killer. He has no knowledge of the motive or method of killing of the serial killer. This means that he is actually innocent so we don't have to worry about him being a mole." She paused to let the words sink in. "Third, your attitude just now was not you being cautious around him. You were just being mean to him." She hardened her gaze, daring him to disagree with her.

Ben made a disgruntled sound. "Fine, I'll be frank. I don't trust him, okay? I don't know where this feeling come from, but I just don't like the guy." He was clearly trying to hide the confusion in his voice, but it sounded obvious to Jenn anyway. "And you can never know what he could be hiding from us. Better be careful," he added.

"I've talked to him about the murders – very thoroughly," she stated, exaggerating a little. "I would know if he is lying or holding back any information." She was trying her best to be patient with him. "If only you'd put your ego aside just now, you would have noticed how naive of a person Ray is. His credulity made him the perfect subject for hypnosis. That is exactly why the killer chose to hypnotise him."

"You hypnotised him too, didn't you?" Ben asked, frowning.

"Yes, but I did it to bring him here, not for the reasons you've implied," she replied calmly. "His mind wasn't under my influence when I questioned him."

"Then you can never be too sure if he's speaking the truth," Ben reasoned with her. "Subjects under hypnosis tell you what they believe. Ray Darce could be feeding you with lies or misleading half-truths from the killer. As long as they're commands from the killer, he could not disobey. For all we know, he's just a puppet of the hypnotist." Jenn held on to her point. "A subject cannot be hypnotised to do something that is against his moral values. And I can assure you that Ray is a good person."

Ben was silent for a few moments, his green eyes staring at her intently. Then he spoke again in a calm manner. "Jennifer, time changes people, you know that? No matter how close you both were or how well you knew him four years ago, he can never be the exact same person now, especially when his mind has been twisted and toyed with by a psychopath. God knows what he has been through these years under the influence of a cold-blooded serial killer. He might have been brainwashed or gone through torture when the serial killer dealt with him."

"I know," she answered. "But I've talked to him, really talked to him, about the case and his situation. I can assure you that he really is innocent."

Now that he was being his true rational self again, Jenn found it much easier to talk to him without getting irritated. This was who he really was, calm and sensible. He could be playful, humorous, and sarcastic at times, but personally she preferred it when he was just being himself.

"Okay," Ben said, breaking her reverie. "I trust you."

Dismissing the trail of thought inside her head, Jenn mentally kicked herself for being so careless. She shouldn't have let her mind wander like that. She gave him a diplomatic smile, trying to maintain her cool. "It's settled."

"I hope that you can extend the same courtesy to me. Just try to trust me like before." he slowly said, starting to move towards her.

Jenn could see where he was going with this. "Stop right there." There was an edge to her voice now. Squaring her shoulders, she continued in a business-like tone. "Let me make things clear. We're here to solve a case, nothing more. As high-ranked agents, we keep things professional between us. Period." Then she added, "When you learn how to behave, then we'll talk about my extending the same courtesy to you."

With that, she swept out of the room.

Nine

After her little chat with Ben, Jenn decided that it was time to get things back on track. She gathered everyone, including Ray, in the office to brief them on her progress on the case so far.

She started by sharing the information which she had managed to dig up in town during the last few days. She went into details about her visit to the crime scenes and what the witnesses had told her. Then she moved on to the confrontation at Ray's house. When she came across the part where she kissed Ray, Jenn saw a hint of s blush on Ray's face and Ben's lips were pressed into a thin line. Only J. Lee seemed unaffected after hearing about the incident.

She ignored their reactions and proceeded with the briefing. After all, they were a team, so nothing concerning the case should be kept hidden from each other. When she broached the topic about how the victims were killed, she made sure the others fully understood what she was talking about.

"Based on the autopsies, none of the victims had physical traumas, nor were there any drugs in their systems. The examiners couldn't find any cause of death after examining the bodies. However, I have an idea of how the killer did it, but it's just a hunch."

"Are you saying that you know the cause of death in the murders?" J. Lee asked.

Jenn answered with a nod. "Just a hunch, but I'm pretty sure that I'm right on track."

"Do share, then." Ben leaned forward in his seat with his elbows on the table, entwining his fingers as he stared at her expectantly.

Jenn smiled thinly. "Hypnosis."

At this point, Ray was completely dumbfounded. "H-how does that work?" His eyebrows furrowed, uncomprehending.

Ben and J. Lee seemed slightly confused, but they waited for her explanation.

"Okay, I'll try my best to explain this," she said calmly. "You see, the killer hypnotised Ray not only to let him take all the blame; he was also using Ray as bait to bring the victims to him. That was why the victims were seen leaving parties with Ray. When Ray got the victims alone, I believe that he chloroformed them, as suggested by the killer beforehand."

Ray was listening intently, fighting the doubts in his mind. A deep frown appeared on his forehead.

"After that, the victims were brought to the killer and Ray was dismissed immediately, so he would not know anything about the actual murders. Now the real thing begins. First of all, the girls were blindfolded so that they wouldn't see what the killer would be doing to them. Then the killer woke them up somehow and started putting them into trances," Jenn continued, keeping a close eye on Ray.

"If we look at the spots the killer chose to commit these murders" – she gestured to the map that she had put up on the board – "we can see that all the locations chosen were found in secluded and deserted areas. The killer took these spots and created the perfect environment for hypnosis, so it wasn't hard for him to reach into their minds. What the killer would mainly focus on was inserting negativity into their heads, convincing them that it was the end for them. When the girls had lost any hope of surviving, they would beg him to end their lives quickly." Her voice turned cold.

"At this point, the killer simply needed to trick them into believing that he had done it. I believe what the killer did was graze something against their skin. He must have used something hard with a rough surface but not rough enough to leave any mark on the victim. I think that he did this on their wrists because when the victims' bodies were discovered, the ropes that tied them to the chairs were too tightly tied around their wrists. This meant that the blood circulation at their wrists was mostly cut off so they could not detect his trick.

"In the end, all the killer had to do was to create a water dripping sound near them so that they would get the idea that they were bleeding to death. This was the critical moment of the murder. If the girls realised that the whole thing was a hoax, then they would be totally unaffected by the ruse. However, if the subjects were too deep in trance, they would only be immersed in the thought of losing their lives. Once they lost their will to live, their bodies reacted accordingly. Their hearts weakened, and their breathing became shallower." Jenn ended her speech.

"So the killer made the girls kill themselves," J. Lee stated flatly, but her expression was quizzical.

"In a way, yes," Jenn replied slowly, after a moment of consideration.

"Is that even possible?" Ben wondered aloud. "To use someone's mind against her in such a way?"

"You'd be surprised what humans are capable of."

"Huh," Ben uttered, plainly trying to wrap his mind around this.

"So basically, we know that this serial killer is completely obsessed with hypnosis," Jenn concluded. "Noticing the patterns in his choice of victims, we know that he aims for redheads around the age of twenty. Perhaps it's because red hair is by far the most common hair colour in this town so the police can hardly narrow down the possibilities of the next target. It's also possible that the killer has a personal grudge against redheads. So we can't be sure of his motive yet.

"I have come up with a list of suspects based on what I've learned in this town so far. Ray is the key point. The killer could only hypnotise him if Ray trusted him. So I figured that the killer must be someone he's close to. The names on my list are—" The sound of her cell phone ringing cut her off. She saw Ray's tense body visibly relaxed at the interruption. That was odd.

Muttering an apology, she fished out her cell phone from her pocket and checked the caller ID. It was Agent Turner. What impeccable timing he had. She spoke smoothly as she answered the call. "Agent Turner." Ben cocked an eyebrow at her at the mention of the name, but Jenn kept her expression neutral.

"Jumping Spider," Agent Turner greeted back, his voice stiff.

"How can I help you, Agent?" Jenn asked as she stared ahead, not meeting anyone's gaze.

"I … uh …" As he hesitated, she heard him taking a deep breath. "First things first, I'd like to … apologise for the misunderstanding that I caused yesterday. I … I sincerely did not mean to complicate things for you."

Something told her that the general had given Agent Turner a call after she had explained the situation to him.

"And, uh," Agent Turner uttered awkwardly, "I promise not to make the same mistake again."

Her eyes were filled with mild surprise. Though she knew that he must have rehearsed his apology a few times before calling her, she could hear the sincerity and respect in his tone. Perhaps the general did trust her after all. And judging by his attitude just now, it seemed as if the agent was really trying to patch things up with her.

"Okay, I accept your apology," she said at last. Jenn heard him heaving a huge sigh of relief, and she laughed quietly, shaking her head. "But from now on, if we're going to work together, your lack of trust has to be dealt with. Understood?"

"Crystal clear," he replied instantly.

"Good. Now, get to the main point, why did you call me?"

"Oh, the main point – right." Agent Turner stumbled over his words. "I think it will be easier to explain things after you get here. I'll text you my current location."

Her ears pricked at his words. "What happened?" she demanded.

"We've got another murder."

Getting out of the black sedan that Ben had rented when he arrived in town, Jenn saw Agent Turner and his partner coming out of the deserted storehouse to meet them. Ben got out of the car a few moments later, taking a good look at the building before them.

"Jumping Spider." Agent Turner and Agent Potts said in unison. Then Agent Turner caught sight of Ben behind Jenn and said, "I'm sorry, sir. This is a crime scene—"

"And I'm here to help with the investigation," Ben interrupted. He looked the agent over, sizing him up. "NSSS. Special Agent Bennett Warner." He flashed his badge.

There was a surprised look on the agent's face. "Oh, I see. Special Agent Bennett Warner, huh?" Agent Turner muttered the name to himself. "Major General Warner's son, I assume. My partner, Agent Potts." He gestured towards his partner behind him. "Agent Turner," he said by way of introduction, extending his hand for a handshake.

Jenn saw a glint in Ben's eyes. Ben didn't like people referring to him as the major general's son. This was going to be bad.

"Ah, the snitch." Ben said dryly, shaking the agent's hand briefly. Behind Agent Turner, his partner's eyes grew wide.

Agent Turner frowned. "What did you just say?"

"Snitch." Ben pronounced the word in an exaggerated manner. "Look it up in the dictionary if you don't know what it means."

Seeing the puzzled and offended look on Agent Turner's face, Jenn couldn't help but feel sorry for him, but he had brought it upon himself. However, she had to give him credit for figuring out Ben's identity that fast. Jenn gave Ben a sharp nudge in the ribs. "Okay, we can bond later. For now, we have a crime scene to investigate." She started walking towards the storehouse. "Agent Turner, what do we have here?"

The agent fell into step beside and started to brief her on the situation. "The victim was Gina Lee, age twenty-three, worked as a manager in a bank not far from here. She was reported missing after attending a party at her colleague's place last night. She lived with her parents and a sister. She didn't return home or answer any phone calls, so her parents put in a missing person report this morning. Then a couple of teenagers found her dead in the building shortly after the report was made."

Jenn frowned. "What were the teens doing in a deserted area like this?"

Agent Potts spoke for the first time before dissolving into the background again. "They said they were taking photos of the building for a school assignment."

"So you've brought them in for interrogation?" Jenn asked.

"Yes, Agent Potts handled it," Agent Turner stated stiffly, his tone tinged with annoyance due to his partner's interruption. "I was here, searching the area for the killer."

Ben snorted. "You were expecting to catch the killer here, at a crime scene filled with cops? No wonder you couldn't solve the case even after three years."

Jenn had to bite back a laugh stuck in her throat. She had thought the exact same thing Ben had just said. Agent Turner truly needed to go over his homicide investigation guidelines again. She gave Ben a stern look, hoping that he would just let it go. He was being childish. Agent Turner hadn't intentionally offended him in any way. Then she turned to Agent Turner. "Did you find any evidence at the crime scene?" she asked.

"Useful evidence." Ben emphasised the first word, earning himself a glare from the agent.

"Actually, I did," Agent Turner said with apparent irritation. "This time, there was a significant difference in the murder. The serial killer left a short note behind. The paper he used gave off a distinctive fragrance. My people are ID'ing the smell now."

They stepped into the building. Immediately, the smell hit them. Jenn came to a stop, confused. She knew this smell. She was sure of it. But what she couldn't be sure was where she had smelled this fragrance before.

"What's wrong?" Ben asked, eyeing her with concern.

"I know this scent," Jenn replied. She continued walking. "I need to take a look at the note you mentioned just now," she said to Agent Turner.

"Got it." He nodded once at her before taking the lead. "This way."

He led them into a small room in the building. In the middle of the room was their victim, tied to a chair. One look at the victim and Jenn noticed something odd. The victim wasn't a redhead. Instead, her hair was raven black.

"Here's the note." Agent Turner pointed at a small piece of paper on a table at the corner of the room.

Jenn put on her gloves and went to take a look at the paper. The smell was getting stronger now. "Why haven't you bagged it?" Jenn asked as she picked up the paper to examine it.

"I thought that you might want to take a look at everything as it was, so I asked forensics to leave the crime scene untouched, including the victim," Agent Turner answered uncertainly.

"That's wise of you," she said. She started reading the note. "What goes around comes around." At the corner of the note, it was signed *K*.

"Karma?" Ben guessed.

"Most likely." Jenn took a whiff of the smell covering the paper. "It seems our killer finally decided on a name." The smell was really strong. It was almost as if … In sudden realisation, she said, "The killer left this fragrance on purpose. Judging by the intensity of the smell, the killer must have soaked it in some kind of fragranced liquid."

"You mean it's another dead end?" Agent Turner asked, disgruntled. "Great."

"Yeah, great job, snitch," Ben muttered.

Agent Turner turned to Ben in a huff. "Look, I know that you're mad at me for causing such big trouble for your girlfriend, and I accept that it was entirely my fault. I even got a lecture from the general himself," he said, confirming Jenn's earlier suspicion. "But I have apologised to her personally, and she has accepted my apology rather graciously, so can you just get over it already?" He was fuming, but it was obvious that he was still trying to hold back most of his anger. Probably due to her watchful eye on them, Jenn supposed.

Ben stared at the red-faced agent for a moment. Then he smirked, turning to Jenn. "Girlfriend, huh?"

In return, she grimaced at him. "We're investigating a murder here. You're a special agent so start acting like one." Then she swung her steely gaze to Agent Turner. "I understand that you're upset. But that doesn't mean that you can throw insults around here. Agent Warner and I are just partners."

"Sorry," Agent Turner mumbled sheepishly, shooting Ben a dirty look.

Jenn heaved a sigh, calming herself. "Now back to the case. The fragrance on this paper might not be a direct lead to finding out who the killer is, but I believe that it has something to do with his motive … or the next target."

"Next target?" Agent Turner repeated her words, looking puzzled. He seemed to have recovered from his outburst.

She handed the paper over to Agent Potts and asked him to bag it. Then she started to explain her theory. "If you take a close look at the victim, you will notice something different. Instead of choosing a redhead, he aimed for a brunette. And according to his time pattern, this is not carried out according to his schedule."

"Okay, the killer broke the pattern. Perhaps he made a mistake about the date," Agent Turner said slowly, plainly still not getting her point. "So what?"

"Mistake? It's highly impossible, don't you think?" she asked dryly. "Given that he's quite the experienced and careful killer after all these murders he's committed, it's unlikely for him to make such a silly mistake. Something must have changed his course of action. 'What goes around comes around.' It means payback. So the killer must be seeking some sort of revenge. All the girls that he killed before this were merely like drugs as to relieve his pain, substitutes for the real target." She frowned, her eyes inadvertently moving to the victim in the chair. "And this is a warning. He will kill again soon."

"When?" the agent asked in an alarmed tone.

"We can't be sure." She shook her head. "Right now, the killer is almost unpredictable." She was still staring at the victim, and suddenly something stood out. There was a bruise on the victim's cheek. The killer was sloppy this time. Something must have agitated the killer to act so rashly. "But one thing we know for sure is that the fragrance on the paper is not a dead end, rather a clue the killer left for us. It could be some sort of perfume. Perfume usually relates to romance. Perhaps it's a relationship-gone-wrong murder."

"Why can't it be that this girl's the killer's real target? After all, she stood out the most among all the victims," Agent Turner mused.

"There's a possibility that you might be correct." Jenn said thoughtfully. "But we have to take precautions. Check to see if you can find any connections between this victim and the previous ones – similarities or differences that stand out the most."

"Got it," Agent Turner said, nodding. Then his tone turned hesitant. "About the hair colour thing … Do you think that it could be just a coincidence that the previous victims were redheads?"

"That is a possibility, but we have to make the most out of what we have right now." She moved closer towards the victim, not taking her eyes off the body as she spoke. The victim was still in her working clothes, so she clearly hadn't had time to change for the party when she was abducted. "So we have to consider the change in hair colour preference as one of our leads in finding the next target."

"You could be next," Ben said suddenly, expressionless.

"Shut up." She glared at him. "If you're not serious about this, then get into the car." She could see that he was still upset at her words earlier. Well, he should take some time to cool off then, she figured. Behind her, she heard a muffled laugh from Agent Turner.

"Fine. I can see that I'm not wanted around here," Ben muttered as he strode out of the room.

A pang of guilt pulled at her chest as she watched his retreating figure. But then she pulled herself out of it. Now was not the time to dwell on all this drama. Turning her attention back to the task at hand, she looked at Agent Turner and said, "You mentioned earlier that the victim went missing after attending a party at her colleague's house. Who's the colleague?"

"If I'm not mistaken, his name is Nick Jefferson," Agent Turner replied.

"Nick Jefferson," Jenn repeated, feeling surprised that his name turned up.

"Yes," he confirmed. "Do you want to talk to him?"

"No, it's okay." She couldn't risk letting another person from her past know her identity as a special agent, plus she was quite sure that he wasn't the killer. Nick was a softie, and even if he was the killer, he wouldn't be dumb enough to draw attention to himself by abducting someone from his own house. So it would be a waste of time for her to talk to him anyway.

"I think you can handle this one." She gave him a pat on the shoulder. "Bring him in and ask him if he remembers anything odd at the party."

"Yes, boss," he joked. He started to leave, but Jenn stopped him.

"Have you determined the cause of death?" Jenn asked, testing him. "For the previous victims, I mean. What caused their heart failure?"

"Uh …" His face showed his answer.

She sighed. "Don't worry. I have a lead. Hypnosis."

Puzzlement coloured the agent's face. "What? How?"

"That I'll leave to you to find out for yourself."

He cocked an eyebrow at her. "My punishment?"

She gave him a look. "I'm not that childish, okay? I'm so over the whole misunderstanding yesterday. It's time you move on too."

"Glad to hear that." He laughed, looking embarrassed. "Speaking of which, I heard from the general that two new agents will be in town. Where's the other one?"

"Agent Leon stayed behind to babysit Ray Darce," she explained. "We can't risk having the killer contact Ray anymore."

"Oh, okay." The agent nodded. "I certainly hope that the next time we meet, Agent Leon will be around."

"You're not really looking forward to meeting her. You're just not looking forward to seeing Ben …" She quickly corrected herself: "Agent Warner again." Her heart thudded with relief when she realised that Agent Turner didn't notice her mistake. That would have been awkward. She then gave him a brief smile and turned around. "Update me if anything new comes up," she said over her shoulder before stepping out of the room.

Ten

Jenn stared out of the window, immersed in her thoughts as Ben drove silently beside her. She kept thinking about the fragrance left by the killer at the crime scene, trying to figure out the mystery behind it. It was just a refreshing vanilla peppermint scent. What made it so special and familiar to her? She had never used perfumes with this scent in her life – she was very sure of that – so where had she come across this scent?

"You hate me so much, huh?" Ben said suddenly, pulling her out of her thoughts. He was staring ahead, but somehow Jenn knew that he was observing her.

"I don't hate you," Jenn answered flatly.

"Well, your insult earlier suggested otherwise," Ben replied sourly.

"Honestly, I don't hate you. I don't have time for that." Jenn simply said, keeping her face void of emotions.

Suddenly, Ben pulled the car over to the side of the road, surprising Jenn. He turned to her with a look of frustration. "Why don't you just spit it all out right now? Insult me as much as you like. Call me names if you want. Even better, hit me. You have your gun, right? Shoot me too if you want. Let it out. I promise I won't defend myself or anything."

"What's the point?" She laughed dryly, staring at the road in front of her.

"At least you'll stop acting like this if you release the anger inside you," he reasoned with her.

"Acting like what?" She still refused to meet his gaze.

"Like you're disgusted with me or something." He was clearly trying to hide the hurt inside him, but it was still apparent in his voice.

His tone stirred up something inside her. Finally, Jenn sighed quietly and turned to look at him. His poker face mirrored hers, but she caught something in his eyes: traces of hopefulness. Seeing this angered her.

"The damage has already been done. Insulting or hurting you doesn't change anything." The words were out of her mouth before she could stop them. Her hands inadvertently balled into fists on her lap as her own words floated around in her head.

Damn it. Of course, Jenn was well aware that Ben was trying to push her buttons, but she couldn't believe that she actually said those things to him. Openly admitting that he had managed to hurt her was probably the stupidest thing she could've said to anyone, especially to Ben.

A frown appeared on his forehead. "I don't—"

She cut him off, her voice shaking a little. "Drive." She turned away from him and stared out the window.

"Listen—"

"*Just* drive." This time her voice was firm.

"Catherine, please just—"

"Jennifer," she corrected him, cutting him off again. "And if you don't start driving now, I'll go back to the hotel by foot."

Ben said nothing more after that. He drove them back to the hotel in complete silence. Even after they reached her suite, the tension between them hung in the air like a dead pheasant.

When they arrived, Jenn went straight into the office and shut the door. In her file, she started writing down all the information that she'd gathered at the crime scene. She heard the door open. "Not now," she muttered, not looking up from the file.

"Okay, just remember to take your lunch," J. Lee said before closing the door, leaving Jenn alone.

Jenn finally raised her head and saw the food placed in front of her. She closed her eyes and sighed tiredly, pinching the bridge of her nose. This was way harder than she expected it to be, and it was only her *first* day with him.

Her eyes strayed back to her file. She recalled the note at the crime scene. Another girl was going to be added to the list of victims soon. No, she shouldn't be absorbed in her own little world right now. She had far more important matters to focus on. She had to stop the killer. She must.

Pushing away all the distracting thoughts in her head, she continued with her report. She would get this over with as soon as she could, and then she would not have to face all this crap anymore, she thought to herself as she scribbled away in the quiet little room.

In the evening, Jenn finally finished her report. She glanced up at the food that she had not yet touched. Yawning, she got up and went out of the office, taking her food with her to the kitchen. The others were in the living area, watching her as she walked by, but she ignored them. She put her food in the microwave and turned it on. As she waited for the meal to get hot, she brought up a hand to cover her mouth, yawning again. All the writing and thinking were really wearing her out.

The microwave beeped twice, signalling that her food was ready. She swiftly took it out and scarfed down the entire contents of the plate. Just as she finished washing her plate, her cell phone rang. She wiped her wet hands on her jeans before taking her cell phone from her pocket. It was the general again. What was going on now?

She answered the call warily. "Sir."

"Agent Nelson." The general spoke in his usual calm voice. That was a good sign. "How's the case going? Coping well with your new partners?"

Her eyebrows rose at his questions. "You're calling to check on me?"

"Calm down, Agent." he soothed. "I'm just concerned about the case."

Her lips twitched. "What? You trust me now?"

"I never said that I don't," he replied smoothly with a smile in his voice. "It was just you assuming all along."

She let out a laugh. He did have his way with words. "Okay, my fault, then," she said. "About the case, I have some bad news." Her voice turned serious. "Apparently, the killer struck again last night. The victim was discovered in a deserted building this morning."

"What?" The general sounded puzzled. "But the killer was not supposed to kill again until next month, right?"

"He broke his pattern." She gave a few details about what she had observed at the crime scene. "So I believe that this is just a warning. Another girl will die if we don't solve this case soon."

"If *you* don't solve this case soon," He corrected her. "Cougar and Falcon are there to assist you, but you know this case and town better than anyone. I'm afraid it's only you who can solve this case."

"Right," she uttered, biting the inside of her cheek. Yesterday the general was all upset and grumpy with her, and now he was suddenly back to his trusting self again. It made her wonder if yesterday was merely an act to get her to be stuck with his son ... "I will bring this serial killer to justice." She adopted a mock-serious tone. "Even if it means dying to get the case solved."

"You have a wicked sense of humour," the general remarked with a slight chuckle. "All right, then. I won't be a bother anymore. Good luck, Agent." The line went dead.

She stared at her cell phone and sighed. "If only luck could break a hypnotic trance," she mumbled to herself as Ray's face entered her mind.

Stuffing her cell phone back into her pocket, she left the kitchen and noticed that J. Lee was sitting on the couch alone, reading a book.

"Where are the guys?" she asked.

J. Lee looked up from her book. "Don't worry. They haven't gone out. They're just in the room, bickering about where they'll be sleeping tonight." She said this in a flat tone. "You okay?" She cocked her head to the side, her hazel brown eyes staring intently at Jenn.

"Yes." Jenn nodded, giving her friend a tiny smile. "By the way, thanks for lunch."

"No problem," J. Lee muttered as she turned back to her book. "You might want to go check on them. Ben isn't really himself since he came back."

As if to prove her words, a long string of profanities echoed from the bedroom next to hers. Muttering under her breath, Jenn strode towards the room and threw open the door to find a flustered Ray scowling at Ben, who was sitting on the bed smiling triumphantly. As soon as they saw her entering the room, the two guys quickly rearranged their expressions into composed looks.

She gave them both a grim expression, hinting to them that she knew exactly what was going on in the room just now. "There's no need for a fight. You will both be sleeping here. The bed is big enough for the both of you. No one is allowed to sleep on the couch," she stated bluntly. "Now stop acting like you're three."

"Yes, ma'am," Ben muttered sarcastically in a low voice, obviously not satisfied with her decision, but she knew that he knew better than to pick another fight with her. Ray simply kept silent, his eyes fixated on the floor. He wore a frown on his forehead, mirroring Ben's emotions.

Jenn forced herself to meet Ben's eyes, keeping her face blank. "You can unpack now. Briefing continues after dinner." Then she turned to Ray. "You come with me."

Ray raised his eyebrows, giving her a questioning look. "Where to?"

"Your house," she simply replied, tapping her foot impatiently. "You need to bring over some of your clothes. Now come along." Then she spun around to speak to J. Lee. "You might as well start unpacking too," she said, her tone back to normal. Then she left with Ray, hoping that their short trip to his house would go smoothly, without any more complications.

Much to her contentment, they managed to reach his house and leave without bumping into anyone they knew. Ray seemed to be in good mood right after they left the hotel, which made Jenn wonder if he was glad to be away from Ben or if he just wanted to get some fresh air.

She did raise the question on their way back to the hotel. Ray didn't reply, but the twinkle in his eyes told her enough about what he was thinking. She regretted bringing up the topic. It had totally escaped her mind that Ray had romantic feelings for her. However, she was puzzled about Ray's behaviour in showing his feelings. Of course, she figured that this flirtatious side of Ray could just be a side effect of him under the influence of hypnosis, but now she wasn't so sure.

Sometimes when Ray was being serious and focused on something important such as the case, it felt almost as if there were nothing but friendship between them. At other times, when he was relaxed and casual, he would start showing interest in her all of a sudden. She certainly wasn't planning to get involved in any romantic relationship with him, but it still bugged her somehow.

It bothered her that she could not be sure about how he really felt about her. What if Ben was right? What if Ray's mind had been so thoroughly twisted by the killer that he wasn't feeling anything at all? What if this was just a mask Ray had put on to protect himself? No, this couldn't be it. She must have been too concerned about Ray to be coming up with these absurd thoughts.

Wait, why was she even thinking about this? Jenn shook her head to clear her thoughts. Gosh, she really needed to get herself together. First Ben, now Ray. This was not how she should be acting as a special agent.

She said nothing more to him until they reached the hotel. She could feel Ray's eyes on her much of the time they were in the car, but she tried to be oblivious to his constant staring.

"We're back," she announced as they entered the living area. No one replied. Then a piece of paper on the coffee table caught her eyes. She went forward and picked it up. Behind her, she heard Ray closing the door.

On the paper was J. Lee's neat handwriting: "Grocery shopping," it read. Great, it was her turn to babysit Ray, then.

"Where are your partners?" Ray asked, looking around.

"At the grocery store," she replied, sitting down on the couch.

"So it's just the two of us then." Ray plopped down beside her. The room was silent for a few moments before he sighed. "Can I ask you something?"

"Sure," she said nonchalantly, covering the wariness inside her. She met his gaze and saw the troubled look on his face. "Is something wrong?"

He hesitated before answering. "This morning during the briefing, something weird happened. When you were explaining about how the victims were killed, I uh ... sort of heard someone else's voice while you were speaking."

Jenn scrunched her eyebrows together in confusion. "Do you mind explaining further about that?"

"Well, the way you spoke, your tone, it somehow reminded me of another person's voice." He said this slowly, trying his best to put his thoughts into words. "I'm not sure whose voice it was, but it sounded really ... eerie."

Jenn remembered the way his rigid stance relaxed when Agent Turner's phone call had interrupted the briefing this morning.

"And then I kind of just froze right there in my seat," Ray continued as he shifted uncomfortably on the couch. "It was as my body were detached from my mind ... I could hear you talking, but I didn't understand a word you said. All I knew was that my mind went blank too. It was almost like ..."

"You were in a trance," she finished for him.

He stared at her in surprise. "Yes. How did you know?"

"Well, it wasn't really hard to guess after you said that your mind went blank. Do you remember the voice now?"

"Vaguely," he replied, still looking troubled. "What's going on with me?"

"I think the voice you heard was the person who had hypnotised you to believe that you're responsible for the six girls' deaths." She spoke calmly, gauging his reaction.

Ray widened his eyes. "You mean it was the killer's voice?"

"Yes." She nodded. "Can you describe how the voice sounds?"

He looked away from her eyes, trying hard to recall the voice he had heard. "Well, he sounded … calm but cold … dark … and uh …" As he struggled for words, his eyes started to go wild.

Jenn saw that he was getting wound up by the memory of the voice. Gently, she laid a hand on his shoulder, pulling him back to the present. "It's okay. Calm down. Just take it easy," she said soothingly. Ray had already given her critical information. The killer was confirmed to be a guy.

"I'm sorry. I'm not helping much here, am I?" He laughed weakly.

"Actually, you did quite a good job." She smiled gently. "You're finding it so hard to recall his voice because the killer had already suppressed your memories of him when he put you in trance. It's quite impressive that you're able to break through the barrier inside your mind, but don't push yourself too hard. Let it come to you naturally."

"What if it doesn't?" Ray asked, plainly unconvinced.

"Ray, your memory of him has been suppressed for more than three years." Jenn stressed the last two words. "Being able to break through such thick barriers is already a miracle. Take it easy, okay?"

He nodded, wearing a resigned look on his face. "I suppose you can't break the trance, then?"

"I'm still trying." She gave him a tight-lipped smile. "A trance can be triggered by a touch, pressure point, or word. The trigger could also be a specific view or sound." She shrugged. "It could also be a mixture of physical, visual, and auditory factors. So it really isn't that simple to break a deep trance like yours."

"You make it sound so complicated," he muttered, seeming to be lost.

"It is complicated," she said in a lighter tone, laughing at his confused expression.

He sighed, looking up at the ceiling. "Why am I born with such a slow brain?" he said with mock anger. Then he laughed along with her, dropping the subject.

"Having a slow brain isn't that bad sometimes."

He made a weird face at her. "You think so?"

"I know so," she stated, feigning seriousness. "It's entertaining to me. That's good, isn't it?"

His eyes twinkled with amusement. "So I'm an amusement to you, huh?"

"Sure, if you prefer to interpret it in that way." She wore a playful grin, deciding to put her task aside for now. Her being Catherine around Ray wasn't really going well anyway. After all, she would always be Jenn to him, even though he knew of her new identity now, so she might as well enjoy playing Jenn around him.

Ray had his trademark goofy grin on his face as he responded, "How else would you interpret it?"

She pretended to think for a moment before saying, "Well, that's for me to know and for you to find out." She put on a smug look, knowing that he would be speechless at her reply.

Ray pursed his lips, suppressing a smile. Cocking his head to one side, he studied her closely, his blue eyes filled with curiosity. "You know, I sometimes wonder if you'll ever be truly honest with me."

"What makes you doubt my honesty?" she asked smoothly, adjusting to the sudden change in their topic.

"For starters, you are now a special agent, so I suppose that you're not allowed to give out too much info about yourself," he said in a matter-of-fact tone. "Next, I've noticed the way you evade my questions when it comes to talking about your life now or your thoughts and feelings about something." He wore a knowing look.

She raised an eyebrow at his reasoning, showing that she was impressed with his scrutiny. "Indeed, I have been evading some of your questions," she admitted calmly. "But I have not told you anything false about myself."

"So you do admit that you're hiding things from me," Ray stated, keeping the conversation casual.

"There's a difference between protecting one's privacy and hiding things from you," she remarked. "Some things are better left unsaid."

"True," he agreed with a nod. "Yet there's no harm in sharing some of your thoughts with me."

"True," she mimicked him. "Yet there's no point in doing so either."

He made an impatient sound, dropping his calm exterior. "Come on. I'm just being curious about you," Ray whined, pouting at her.

Something fluttered inside her. She ignored the unsettling feeling and kept calm. "What exactly are you curious about?" She could already guess his question.

He fired his question right away. "What's going on between you and Agent Warner?"

Jenn was expecting that he would ask if she and Ben were a couple, but it was close enough. She debated whether she should tell him the truth or not. In the end, she decided that a short version of the truth would be enough.

"We used to be together." She kept her tone nonchalant. "But it didn't really work out between us, so we ended it. The breaking up part got quite ugly. That's why we couldn't really get along after that." She had given him the simplest version of the truth without much detail, but she still felt a pang in her chest when she talked about it.

"Oh, sorry about that," Ray muttered with a hint of regret.

She laughed half-heartedly. "Well, don't be. I certainly don't feel sorry at all." Now that was a lie, a big fat lie. But how else was she supposed to respond to such a comment? Say that she was sorry that she had lost Ben? No way.

Just then, the front door slammed open. Jenn turned around to see Ben stalking into the kitchen with bags of groceries in his hands, his face dark. Her eyes then went to J. Lee, who stood at the doorway with a blank expression, staring after Ben and muttering, "I suggest that the briefing tonight be postponed till tomorrow morning. Give him some time to cool off first." Then J. Lee shut the door behind her and proceeded to the kitchen too.

"They heard everything, didn't they?" Ray said in a small voice.

Jenn simply groaned in response. And she'd thought that today couldn't get any worse.

Eleven

The next morning was rather uneventful. Ben was up before anyone else was, and he went out quietly, leaving a note saying that he was out for a morning run. Jenn and J. Lee woke up next to find the note he had left on the coffee table in the living area.

"Do you think he'll be back for the briefing?" J. Lee asked after she had read Ben's note.

Jenn scrunched the paper into a ball and threw it into the bin near the couch. "Don't worry. He's not one who skips important meetings, especially when it comes to a case," she answered in an indifferent tone.

Her friend nodded and went into the kitchen. "Coffee?"

"Yes, please," Jenn said as she took out her cell phone to inform Ben when the briefing would start. She saw that she had two voice mail messages from the night before and one unread text message from earlier this morning. The voice mails were from Agent Turner, while the text message was from Ben.

She decided to listen to the voice mails first.

"Hi. I've just finished talking to Nick Jefferson. He said that he didn't notice that the victim was missing at the party because he

was drinking with a bunch of his guy friends at the courtyard almost throughout the whole party. Talked to the friends he mentioned and his alibi checks out. I'll come back to you with more updates. Bye."

She moved on to the second one:

"Hi. So we've talked to all the people who attended the party. According to them, Nick Jefferson and Jack Giller held the party spontaneously. Most said that it wasn't a big event. It was more of a gathering than anything else. Apparently, none of them had seen the victim at the party. Possibly the killer got his hands on her before she reached the party. A few of the people who were there early said that they had seen a strange guy leaving Nick Jefferson's backyard just before the party started. Looking into the new suspect now. That's all. Goodnight."

It seemed she was right about Nick, then. A thought occurred to her suddenly, and she quickly replied with a text message:

Give me a quick description of the new suspect. Do not speak to the suspect first. I'll be at the department in the afternoon for further discussion.

She hit the SEND button. After that, she reluctantly opened the last text message:

You won't talk to me about what happened between us. You won't even listen to my explanation. And yet you're willing to talk to a stranger about us. All I want from you is to give me a chance to clear things up between us. Is that too much to ask?

She scoffed and rolled her eyes. Had he not made things clear six months ago? Insulting her on the phone wasn't enough for him? Must he say it to her face to make it clear that it was over between them?

She balled her hands into fists, gripping her cell phone tightly. Did he have to be so particular about this? She had already gotten his message when he decided to cheat on her. Man, she had even heard the girl laughing at her while he repeatedly insulted her. Wasn't that obvious enough?

Uh-uh, there was no way she would let herself be humiliated again by allowing him to toy with her emotions like this. Furiously, she typed a reply:

> *Ray is not a stranger. He is my friend – a good friend. As for your explanation, I don't see any point in listening to it. You already made things clear six months ago. There's no need to complicate things now. Let's just keep things the way they are right now and stop bugging me about this. Stop wasting our time and move on.*

After hitting the SEND button, she threw herself on the couch and sighed exasperatedly, staring at her cell phone with annoyance.

"Your coffee."

Jenn snapped her head up from her cell phone to her friend's sudden appearance beside her. "Oh, thanks." She took the cup of coffee from J. Lee and smiled at her gratefully, putting her cell phone aside.

"You want to talk about it?" J. Lee asked bluntly as she sat down beside Jenn.

Jenn turned to give her a funny look, surprised at her friend's question. "You want to hear about it?"

"No ..." J. Lee replied, staring at the cup of tea in her hands. She turned to Jenn and made a weird face. "Not really."

Jenn chuckled lightly. "Thought so. But thanks for asking anyway." She took a sip of her coffee. Mmm, it was *heavenly*. "You always make the best coffee." She took another sip from her cup.

J. Lee mumbled thanks in reply before taking out her book and starting to read. The next hour went by slowly. Jenn simply sat there, drinking her coffee and enjoying the comfortable silence in the room. For once, her mind was free of disturbing thoughts about her messed-up relationship.

When it was almost seven thirty, J. Lee automatically got up from the couch and went into the kitchen to prepare breakfast. Jenn offered to help, but her friend turned down her offer, saying that she liked to cook alone. But of course, Jenn knew that the real reason was because she wasn't much of a cook. So she went to wake Ray up instead.

Jenn knocked on the door softly before letting herself into his room. Ray slept soundly, oblivious to her presence in the room. She walked over to his bed, watching the serene expression on his face as he continued to snore lightly in his sleep.

He looked so innocent, so vulnerable. A strong wave of emotions flowed through her as she thought of his words yesterday. It must have been quite hard for him during the past few days – having to be confined to this hotel and to cope with the idea that his mind had been tinkered with.

He wouldn't even be here if it weren't for the killer. She exhaled deeply through her nose, her eyes never leaving him. She vowed to herself that she would find the trigger to break his trance. Considering the fact that his mind had been in a trance for more than three years, he would most likely experience a large magnitude of post-hypnotic amnesia when the trance was broken. He would lose most of his memories that took place while he was under hypnosis, but that would probably be the best for him.

Putting those thoughts aside, she touched his shoulder and shook him gently. "Time to wake up, Ray," she said in a hushed tone.

Ray stirred slightly, mumbling incoherent words before his breathing evened out as he slipped back into sleep.

She shook him again, inserting more force into it this time. "Come on, Ray. Get up."

He moaned sleepily. "Five more minutes."

"Uh-uh," she uttered sternly, placing her hands on her hips. "No sleeping in today. Wake up."

Ray opened his eyes blearily. "You sound like my mum," he muttered, rubbing his eyes as he sat up. Then he glanced around the room. "Where's Warner?" he asked, his voice sounding groggy.

"Morning run," she replied, trying to pat his unruly hair down. "Go wash yourself up. You look like a mess."

Groaning, he got out of bed and trudged into the bathroom. Jenn shook her head at his wobbly state and went out of the room.

In the living area, Jenn saw that Ben was already back from his morning run. He was sitting on the couch, wiping off the sweat on his face with a small towel. She was debating whether or not she should greet him when he turned and saw her standing by the doorway staring at him.

"Hey," he greeted with a hint of smile on his lips.

Jenn blinked at the absence of awkwardness between them and averted her gaze from him as she moved towards the other couch. "Hey," she replied softly, sitting down and meeting his gaze again. She searched for any sign of bitterness in his emerald-green eyes, but there was none.

"This town is really something," he said. His eyes were soft, thoughtful as they stared straight into hers. "Especially the park in the centre of the town."

"Eiry's Garden." The words came out naturally. "That's what the people in town named the park," she explained, slowly lowering her guard.

"Eiry's Garden," he mused, repeating the name. "Beautiful." There was an undercurrent of emotion in his stolid voice.

The sound of plates clattering onto the table broke the peaceful atmosphere in the living area. Blinking, Jenn broke eye contact with Ben and released a shaky breath, wondering what had caused the change in his attitude.

"Breakfast is ready," J. Lee called out from the kitchen.

Ben's eyes stayed on her for a few more moments before he stood up and went into the kitchen to help J. Lee set the table. Jenn's eyes swung to her cell phone, which she had left on the couch. She had a strong feeling that the reason to his amiable demeanour was inside her phone.

Taking her time, she reached for her cell phone. Sure enough, there was a new message from Ben. It was sent half an hour ago – long after her last reply. She bit her lower lip as she opened the text message.

If this is what you really want, then I promise that I won't bring up anything about the past unless you broach the topic first. But I won't let it go this easily. I will wait until you're ready to hear me out.

The moment she finished reading the message, her cell phone buzzed, signalling a new text message. Jenn frowned and pushed aside the jumble of emotions inside her. Then she checked her phone and saw that it was from Agent Turner.

We've identified the guy who was seen leaving Nick Jefferson's backyard. His name is Tom Gallner. Jefferson said that Tom had gone to his house to borrow a book, not to attend the party. According to Nick Jefferson, he also belatedly remembered that two of the colleagues he had invited didn't attend the party, Paul Tanner and James Hendricks. Looking into that now.

"Okay, let's start." Jenn stood at the end of the conference table. She opened her file and started going through everything she had noted on her report yesterday. She explained to them about the crime scene and the seventh victim, not forgetting to add some of her opinions as to the killer's unexpected change in his killing pattern.

"In the first six murders, the serial killer didn't exactly leave any clue about his motive in committing those murders. But this time, he readily left a note and a scent behind, broke his time pattern, and killed a brunette instead of a redhead. Also, our killer has never been violent towards any of the victims before this, but this time, there was a fresh bruise on the victim's cheek, suggesting that it might have been the killer who'd hit her. From what I see, something's changed to make the killer desperate. The note could be a warning that his real target has appeared, the scent and the change in his choice of target are clues to his final target."

"How do we know that this Gina Lee isn't his real target?" Ray asked, confused. "How do we even know it's to be his final target after this murder?"

Jenn sighed, reminding herself to be patient with Ray. "Gina Lee has been around since the beginning of this series of murder. He wouldn't have to break his pattern in such desperation to kill her if she was his real target." She paused to see if Ray could follow.

Then she continued, "Next, I said that the killer's going after his final target because the note which he'd left us has his motive clearly stated for us, that is, revenge. If he planned to continue murdering innocent girls even after he's gotten his revenge, then I don't think that it would be wise of him to reveal his motive for the world to see.

"So what we need to focus on right now is finding out who his last target is as soon as possible. Based on the last seven victims, I suppose we can safely assume that his target will be a girl in her early twenties with auburn hair dyed black recently, plus she is somehow connected to a specific smell which is a mixture of peppermint and vanilla scents. It could be the perfume she wears, or her preference of fragrance, or something else." She turned to J. Lee. "You'll be in charge of narrowing down the list for the last target."

"Okay, no problem." J. Lee nodded as she scribbled down something on her notepad.

"Now, I'd like to discuss our list of suspects. Since there is a break in pattern in the latest case we've received, we might be able to narrow down our pool of suspects. Nick Jefferson has been taken off the list after Agent Turner interrogated him yesterday. So are the guys he was drinking with: Henry Winters, Jack Giller, Thomas Sawyer, and Mike Furley. Their alibis checked out." She turned to the board and crossed out their names.

"According to them, the party was held quite spontaneously by Nick Jefferson and Jack Giller, so supposedly not many people knew about it. Their words: 'It wasn't a big event. It was more of a gathering than anything else.' From this, we can safely say that only the people who were invited to the party are to be listed as suspects."

She turned to Ray and handed him two profiles. "Do you know these two guys?"

Ray took a brief look at the papers he was given and nodded. "Yes. They're James and Paul. You know them too. They used to be in VCS too."

"Yes, I remember." She nodded once. "Just checking if you still remember them."

J. Lee raised her hand. "VCS?"

Jenn let out a laugh. "It was an association called the Voluntary Community Service. VCS closed down a couple of years ago."

J. Lee nodded in comprehension and gestured for her to proceed with the discussion. Jenn then conveyed to them Agent Turner's updates about James Hendricks, Paul Tanner, and Tom Gallner.

"So now James Hendricks and Paul Tanner will be added to the list as prime suspects." She handed the suspects' profiles to Ben and J. Lee as she continued explaining. "We're informed that they were not at the party on the night of Gina Lee's murder, though they were invited. But of course, one of our top suspects is still Tom Gallner, who was seen leaving Nick Jefferson's house before the party. Jefferson told us that Tom Gallner was at his house to borrow a book, but looking at the timeline, we have reasons to suspect that he could have been there to gather information about the time of the party so that he could plan Gina Lee's murder."

At this, Ray shifted uncomfortably in his seat, pursing his lips into a thin line. Jenn's sharp eyes caught this. "Ray, I know that Tom is one of your closest friends. But we have to take into account every person who could possibly have hypnotised you. You know these three suspects, but Tom is the one you trust most, which makes him mostly likely to be the killer."

Ray tried to defend his opinion of Tom. "But he has no grudge against anyone."

"That we cannot be sure. But as long as there is a possibility of his hypnotising you, we can't take him off the suspect list," she said calmly.

Ray laughed in disbelief. "You really think that Tom has it in him to hypnotise someone?"

Jenn shook her head. "No," she admitted. "But Tom is a smart guy. He picks things up pretty fast if I remembered correctly. And you have been spending a lot of time with him during the past few years, haven't you?"

"And with Isabella and Nick too," he argued. "I've spent plenty of time with my parents too."

"You want to bring your parents into this?" Jenn raised an eyebrow at him.

"What? No, of course not." One look at his expression, you would've thought that Jenn had asked him if he was gay. "I'm just trying to make a point here." Ray sighed in resignation, leaning back against his chair. "It doesn't feel right that I am to suspect my best friend of murder."

Jenn breathed in deeply before saying, "Do you want to sit this one out?"

Ray stared at his entwined hands on his lap. "Sure." He sullenly stood up and dragged himself out of the room.

"Do you want me to go with him?" J. Lee offered.

Jenn shook her head. "We'll trust him to be on his own right now. He needs the space anyway. Let's proceed with the discussion."

"I think we're done with the suspect list for now." Ben spoke without raising his eyes from the papers laid out in front of him.

"Yes. We'll leave that aside for now," Jenn agreed. "I have something else to let the both of you know. It's about Ray's condition."

J. Lee arched an eyebrow at this. "What about him?"

Ben lifted his gaze to Jenn, waiting for her to explain further.

"Yesterday when you two were out for groceries, Ray talked to me about our briefing that morning." At this, she noticed a slight change in Ben's expression, but he listened on intently. "During the meeting, he somehow recalled a voice that I think is the voice of the hypnotist." Surprise flickered across her partners' faces. "He couldn't give much description about the voice, but one thing is for sure: our killer is a guy." Jenn paused to see if they had questions. Sure enough, J. Lee raised her hand.

"Is it possible that it's actually a memory?" J. Lee asked. "Or can it be that it was just a figment of his imagination?"

"I've tested him," Jenn replied. "It's a memory."

"How?" Ben wondered aloud. "How can you be sure?"

Jenn considered his question for a moment. "During the meeting, when I was explaining the method used by the killer to end the girls' lives, I somehow managed to replicate the tone the hypnotist used on Ray. Ray fell into a trance state. I noticed this, but I wasn't aware of what actually happened to him. When he told me later in the afternoon, it was only then that I realised what had taken place during the meeting. He was in a trance. So without a doubt, it was a memory."

Ben nodded as he digested her explanation. "Do you think we can have Ray match the voice with audio recordings from the suspects?"

"Negative," J. Lee said. "It will raise the killer's suspicion that we know about Ray as his puppet."

"Don't you think that we've already raised suspicion by keeping Ray here and cutting off his contact with the outside world?" Ben asked.

J. Lee shook her head. "It's been only less than three days ..." Her voice trailed off, and her eyes abruptly snapped to Jenn. "We need to check his phone records, house and cell phone."

Immediately, Jenn's eyes widened in comprehension. "Of course! Great job, J."

"Wait, what?" Ben stared at them in confusion.

Jenn turned to him with a pointed look. "Gina Lee was murdered when Ray was already here with me."

Understanding dawned on his face. "Got it."

"Smart," Jenn muttered wryly with a smirk. Ben merely rolled his eyes at her. A smile touched her lips as she turned back to J. Lee. "Check it out."

"Sure." J. Lee nodded, scribbling on her notepad again. "Anything else?"

"That's all for now," Jenn announced. "Meeting adjourned."

Twelve

Jenn had ended the briefing as quickly as she could. She was starting to get worried about leaving Ray alone in the living area. As soon as the briefing ended, she left her partners and rushed out of the office, only to find Ray sitting on the couch, staring off into space. Her heart skipped a beat when she noticed that he was holding his cell phone in his hands. Damn it, she shouldn't have allowed him to leave the briefing.

"Ray, were you on the phone with someone just now?" Jenn asked in a wary tone.

Ray blinked a few times before turning to her. He seemed to be coming out of a daze. "Pardon?"

Jenn saw the look on his face. Alarmed, she stepped forward and held out her hand towards him. "Can I have your cell phone, please?"

Ray frowned in response, tightening his grip on the cell phone. "Why?"

"It's just for a moment," she said in an assuring tone. A subject under hypnosis was highly suggestible. If Ray had been speaking to the hypnotist just now, he might be still in a deep trance, which meant he would be easily convinced to give her the phone.

Ray hesitated, looking at his cell phone.

"Trust me, Ray." She moved closer to him. "Just let me have a look at the cell phone."

He took a long hard look at her, but he handed the cell phone over willingly. "What's wrong?"

She ignored his question and viewed his call history. There was a phone call from an unknown phone number about five minutes ago, and it lasted for less than a minute.

"Who was it that you were speaking with on the phone just now?" Jenn asked, keeping her voice as calm as she could manage.

"My mum," Ray replied with a hint of sadness. "She called from Milan, using her spare phone. I guess she lost her phone again."

Jenn silently heaved a sigh of relief. "Why did she call?"

"She was asking for my whereabouts. My mum called the house last night, but no one answered the phone. She called to tell me that she and Dad would be staying overseas for a little longer. I guess they've met up with some old friends again." He spoke in a wistful tone as he stared down at his intertwined hands.

"You miss them, don't you?" Jenn asked softly as she sat down beside him.

"I haven't seen them since a month ago. How can I not miss them?" Ray muttered, looking downcast. "The worst thing is that I had to lie to them about my whereabouts."

Jenn handed the cell phone back to him, and he held on to it tightly. Then she said, "I'm sorry that you have to endure all this. It's tough, I know."

He gave her a brief glance before lowering his head. "Sorry, I didn't mean to remind you of your parents."

Jenn smiled solemnly, putting her hand on his shoulder. "Toughen up, okay?" she said, squeezing his shoulder. "At least you know that they'll be back. That counts as something, doesn't it?" Then she gave him a light pat on his back as she stood up. She knew that he would need some space right now to clear his thoughts, so she sighed and went back into the office to join her partners.

In the afternoon, Jenn went to the local PD to meet up with Agent Turner and Agent Potts. She brought J. Lee along, fulfilling Agent Turner's wish. The introduction was brief, and they started their discussion right away.

Agent Turner went into detail about all the information he had managed to dig up yesterday. Agent Potts simply stood aside, letting his partner do all the talking. The few times that Jenn asked for his opinion on the suspects' statement, he answered as curtly as he could manage before shutting up again.

J. Lee clearly noticed this too. At the end of the discussion, she commented on that. "Agent Potts, are you afraid of public speaking?"

Jenn raised her eyebrows, wondering what Agent Potts would say to that.

"I'm not." Agent Potts shook his head meekly.

"What gave you that idea, Agent Leon?" Agent Turner asked, laughing.

"You," she replied.

"What?" He gave her an incredulous look. "Me?"

J. Lee exhaled impatiently. "You technically did the whole debrief on your own. It made me wonder if your partner is capable of communicating at all." She glanced at Agent Potts. "You should talk more the next time I attend one of your discussions," she said bluntly, causing the agent to stare at her in wonder.

Agent Turner scoffed. "And why is that? Was I not communicating well enough with you?"

"No." She gave him a blank stare. "He communicates better with me. I prefer essence over details. That's all." A moment later, she added, "No offense."

"None taken," Agent Turner muttered, wearing a stupefied expression.

J. Lee gave them a brief nod before leaving the room. Jenn smirked. "Like this one better?"

The look on Agent Turner's face was comical. "Well ... her straightforwardness is something quite hard to get used to. I've never seen anyone like her."

Jenn simply chuckled at his reply and went out of the room to catch up with her partner. She stepped out of the building to see J. Lee already in Ben's car. She sat in the driver's seat, starting the car as Jenn climbed into the passenger seat.

"So what do you think?" Jenn asked, guessing how her friend would answer.

"A clucking hen and an owl," she muttered. "Blends well."

Jenn laughed. "The owl, I understand. But a clucking hen? Seriously?"

"Referring to him as a hippopotamus wouldn't fit."

"You've got a weird sense of humour," Jenn remarked, still laughing.

J. Lee simply stared ahead and drove on. "Where to now?"

"Since we're already outside, might as well go do some digging," Jenn mused. "Yes, that's it." She scribbled down an address on a piece of paper she found in the car and passed it over to her partner.

"This is ...?" J. Lee asked with the slightest trace of curiosity.

"The victim's house address."

"Tears and tantrums. Yay," J. Lee uttered dryly, saying nothing more. Within ten minutes, they reached their destination.

Jenn got out of the car and took a good look at the house in front of them. It was a lovely little house, only with too much red paint. Her partner paid no attention to the house and went straight for the doorbell. A few moments later, a young girl answered the door.

J. Lee flashed her badge at the girl. "We would like to have a few words with your family."

The girl looked around the age of sixteen. She stared at them in confusion. "Is this about my sister?"

"Yes. Are your parents at home at the moment?"

"It's only my mum. Dad's at work," she replied, her voice breaking. "I thought we'd already given our statements and all that." She was obviously stalling.

"Well, we have some follow-up questions, so if you don't mind, may we come in?" Jenn knew that J. Lee was trying to be as patient as possible. She didn't do well with grieving families. She and tears didn't get along.

"Please be gentle with my mum. She's still grieving," she pleaded, stepping aside for them to enter. At this, Jenn wondered what Agent Turner and his partner said when they came here yesterday.

"We all are." Jenn gave the victim's sister a consoling smile when her partner didn't make any response to that. "What's your name?" she asked the girl gently.

"Hannah," the girl replied solemnly. "Hannah Lee."

"Well, Hannah, I'm going to need your help here, okay?" Jenn said, looking into her eyes. "You said that your mum can't handle too much stress, right? So I need you to go inside and stay by her side. Help her answer some of the questions if she can't handle doing so herself, okay?"

"But the agents that came yesterday wouldn't let me speak. I was asked to go back into my room." Hannah sniffed. "They said that they would only speak with the adults."

"I know." Jenn smiled at the young girl reassuringly. So it must be that Agent Turner and Agent Potts had drilled Mrs Lee too hard. "But I trust that you're mature enough to handle this." She was sure that Hannah would know more about her sister's social life. That was why she needed Hannah to talk as well.

"Thanks," Hannah mumbled, sounding glad to be able to be with her mother. She went straight into the living room, and Jenn followed her closely. When they entered the living room, Jenn saw that J. Lee had already started without her. How typical of her.

Hannah went to sit beside her mother as J. Lee paused to give Jenn a questioning look. Jenn simply shook her head at that. She turned to Mrs Lee to give the family her condolences. She introduced herself as Agent Cole and shook hands with the grieving mother before letting J. Lee continue with the questions.

Jenn then excused herself, asking for permission to look around the house. Mrs Lee didn't give it much thought, nodding absent-mindedly at the request, obviously wanting to get this whole thing over with as soon as possible so she could get back to her grieving.

After getting permission to wander around the house, Jenn headed upstairs in search of the victim's bedroom. There were only three rooms and a bathroom upstairs, so it wasn't hard to figure out which one belonged to the victim.

It was the first room on the left of the staircase. She noticed that its door was half-open when the doors to the other rooms were closed. *Odd,* she thought. Perhaps Hannah was in here when she and J. Lee arrived and she went downstairs in a hurry and forgot to close the door. Jenn let herself into the bedroom, and the first thing that caught her eyes was the victim's perfume on the make-up table.

She picked up the bottle of perfume and held it close to her nose, taking a whiff of its fragrance. Nope, it wasn't the fragrance the killer had left behind at the crime scene. She carefully put it back where it was and continued to scan the bedroom. She saw a framed photo on a desk near the window, and she moved closer to take a good look at it.

The alder wood frame was beautifully engraved with the victim's name. It seemed to be expensive, and by the looks of the bedroom, Jenn knew that the victim wasn't a spender. Hmm, it must be a gift from someone close to her. Her boyfriend, perhaps, assuming she had one. Her guess was immediately confirmed when she saw the photo in it. The victim was smiling blissfully while being engulfed in a guy's arms. Jenn took a closer look at the guy in the photo, and her eyes widened in surprise. It was Paul Tanner, one of the suspects.

Well, this was getting interesting.

When Jenn finally finished inspecting the house, she went back into the living room. It seemed as if J. Lee was done with the victim's family too.

"Thank you for your time, Mrs Lee," Jenn said as they walked to the front door. "We're really sorry for your loss."

"Please bring the killer to justice." Mrs Lee spoke in a shaky voice.

"We will. Thank you for your time." Jenn gave the family one last glance before she went to the car. J. Lee was already in the driver's seat. The agent started the car and started driving back to the hotel.

"So did you get anything useful from the family?" Jenn asked.

"The mother was too busy sobbing. Each time I mentioned the victim's name, she just started tearing up all over again." J. Lee shuddered at the scene, which was still fresh in her memory. "As for the sister, she was pretty helpful. How did you know that she would know so much about her sister?"

"Just a gut feeling." She shrugged, not feeling like explaining her brief conversation with Hannah. It would take a long time for her to go over all the details. "What did you get from her?"

J. Lee accepted her casual answer and told her about what she had found out from the sister. Apparently, on the day of the murder, Gina Lee had made plans with her family to celebrate her birthday in the evening right after work since she was supposed to be at her birthday party later that night. However, she never made it home that evening. She'd called home to inform them that she was caught up with something at work so she couldn't get home in time for the occasion.

"Gina Lee called her family at around five thirty. But according to Agent Turner, surveillance cameras showed that she left the bank before six. That means she might be lying about staying at work," J. Lee speculated.

"Or it could be that something much more important than work happened after she made the call and she had to put her work aside for it," Jenn suggested.

J. Lee pursed her lips at the suggestion. "What could be more important than work?"

"Boyfriend, perhaps." Jenn shrugged. "You know how girls are when it comes to relationships."

"Yeah, yeah, all the 'love is blind' crap." Her friend said dryly, sighing. "Stupid," she muttered to herself, shaking her head.

Jenn gave her a light slap on the arm. "Hey, it's just a guess. No need to get all riled up over it." She chuckled.

"I'm just thinking aloud," J. Lee defended herself, unruffled.

"Wait, the sister said that she was supposed to be at her birthday party later on the day of murder?" Jenn asked, frowning to herself.

"Agent Turner said that the party was just to be a gathering," J. Lee said, plainly understanding immediately where Jenn was going with this.

"I'll ask," Jenn mumbled as she took out her cell phone to give Agent Turner a call.

The agent picked up on the first ring. "Hey, I was just about to call you."

"Oh?" Jenn uttered with slight surprise. She wanted to hear what he had to inform her about first, so she asked, "What do you have?"

"We found out that the party was actually held to celebrate the victim's birthday. Nick Jefferson and his colleagues kept it a secret because they thought that they would be the suspects if we saw it as them using the party to abduct her. Unfortunately, one of the people who was at the party let it slip accidentally just now."

Jenn's eyebrows rose at this new piece of information. Well, this certainly answered her unspoken question, but it just seemed odd of them to do so.

"So did you have anything to tell me?" Agent Turner's voice broke through her reverie.

"No. Just checking on you guys," Jenn replied smoothly. "Keep an eye on the colleagues. Good job." They exchanged goodbyes before she ended the call. Then she told J. Lee what she just heard from Agent Turner.

"Weird," J. Lee muttered after a moment.

Jenn nodded at that. "That's what I was thinking too. You only try to cover up if you have something to hide, so unless the colleagues are really that naïve, there must be something that they're hiding." Jenn turned to J. Lee. "Thoughts?"

J. Lee shook her head. "Let's ask Warner."

Thirteen

Jenn and J. Lee were back at the hotel. When the two girls returned, Ben was sitting in the living area, flipping through the case files for the hundredth time, while Ray was staring off into space yet again

"Finally," Ben said, putting the files aside as he got up and stretched his body. "What took you so long?"

"We just enjoyed talking to Turner. That's all," Jenn muttered sarcastically, walking around him to get a good look at Ray. He seemed weird.

Ben whirled around to face her. "Pardon?" There was a hint of jealousy in his tone.

"We went to speak to the victim's family," J. Lee said, watching him with mild amusement. "We've found some interesting clues." Then she walked into the office.

When he heard what J. Lee said, he looked at Jenn with a lopsided smile. "So did you really enjoy talking to Turner or were you trying to make me jealous?"

Jenn turned to him with a look of absurdity. "I was just being sarcastic. Don't flatter yourself." She rolled her eyes, turning back to Ray. "Hey, are you okay?"

Seeing this, Ben pressed his lips into a thin line, feeling annoyed. There she was again, fussing over the kid. Though he knew that Ray Darce was just a year younger than he was, he couldn't help but feel that Ray was acting like a kid. What was with all the insecurity and weird act, anyway? Perhaps the kid just loved the attention. Ben clenched his teeth and strode towards the office. When Jenn didn't move, he asked, "You coming?"

Jenn shook her head, never taking her eyes off Ray. "It's okay. Proceed without me. I've gotten what I need to know."

Ben frowned. "What are you going to do with him?"

Jenn turned to give him an impatient look. "What? You afraid that I'm going to kiss him again?"

At the mention of the kiss, Ben felt a huge ball of jealousy flare inside him. He balled his hands into fists but managed to maintain his calm expression. "No need to get all sarcastic. I was just asking," he muttered. There was a distinct edge to his voice.

Jenn bit her lips and groaned inwardly. She had not meant to say that to him. Honestly, she didn't what was she thinking to cause her to say those words. Anyway, Jenn got a hold of herself and exhaled deeply. "Well, I want to find out how Ray managed to go back into a trance under your watch," she stated in a calmer tone.

Ben widened his eyes and turned his gaze to the kid. Ray was in a trance state? But how?

"No need to look so surprised," Jenn muttered, mostly to herself, turning her attention back to Ray. "He must have done this himself, considering the fact you're not capable of inducing a trance on a person and there was no one else here when I was gone."

Ben didn't even notice that there was anything wrong with the kid until Jenn pointed it out. What a great babysitter he was. "Sorry, I didn't realise," he tried to apologise. When Jenn didn't make any response, he sighed and went into the office, shutting the door silently behind him.

Jenn waited until Ben was out of sight and then she heaved a sigh. Only he could make her feel guilty for being sarcastic. When she saw the hard expression on his face after she mentioned the kiss, her conscience kicked in. She didn't even know why she felt bad about it. Compared to what he said to her six months ago, this was nothing.

Jenn blinked and stopped that train of thought right there. Whoa, that was close. Shaking her head, she quickly dismissed those distracting thoughts. She took a deep breath to clear her mind. Then she put her focus on the person in front of her.

"Ray, can you hear me?" She made sure to lower her voice and keep it serene enough to reach into his unconscious mind. She kept her eyes on his, observing his fixated stare waver the slightest bit when she spoke to him. Then she gently held onto his wrist, feeling for his pulse.

"Ray, I want you to focus on my voice." She started inserting more force into her voice. "Okay, take a slow, deep breath … As you breathe in, you might feel a tingling or prickling sensation in your hands."

His hands twitched in her grip. Good, she was inside his head now.

"Don't worry. It's normal for you to feel that. Just focus on my voice and follow it," she said soothingly. "Now, you can see that it's getting darker and darker around you. The light is slowly fading away as you inhale … exhale … and your eyes are closing slowly …"

Ray's blank eyes started to close, his eyelids shutting slowly.

"Breathe … Relax into it, Ray. Feel your eyes close as everything gets darker around you, darker and darker, darker and darker."

Now his eyes were completely closed.

"Good. Do you still hear my voice?" She waited for his reaction. A moment later, he nodded slowly. Still smiling, she released her grip on his wrist before going on. "Okay, Ray. As I count from ten to one, remember that you feel yourself opening your eyes as you wake up."

She started counting. "Ten ... Nine ... Feel yourself opening your eyes ... Eight ... Seven ... You're breathing slowly as you wake up ... Six ... Five ... Four ... You're waking up now – and you're doing this all on your own ..."

Ray opened his eyes slowly as she spoke.

"Three ... Two ... You're awake now ... One." She gave his shoulder a light pat.

Ray blinked at Jenn as he came out of his trance. His forehead creased in confusion. "Jenn, why are you kneeling in front of me?" He tried to recall what he was doing just now. An awkward smile crossed his face. "Did I fall asleep just now?"

Jenn backed away, putting some distance between them. She continued to observe him closely. He seemed normal enough now. "What do you remember?"

He scratched the back of his head. "I was dreaming, I guess. I don't really remember much about it, but I do recall a voice speaking to me." He squeezed his eyes shut and tried to remember the voice he had heard. "This is going to sound weird." He chuckled nervously. "It sounded gentle, soft, like an angel, asking me to follow her." He slowly opened his eyes again and sighed. "I'm talking nonsense."

Seeing the look of embarrassment on his face, she had to struggle to keep her face straight. "No, you're not," she said, causing his eyes to snap back to her. "The so-called angelic voice you heard was my voice." She burst out with peals of laughter.

He snorted. "You're kidding, right?" he said in disbelief. "I mean, how would you know what I heard in my dream?"

"Ray, you weren't dreaming. You were in a trance," she explained, wearing an amused smile.

"Huh?" He stared her with wide eyes, incredulous. "But how ...?"

"Have you ever heard of self-induced trance?" she asked, cocking her head to one side. "Well, that's what you were doing to yourself just now."

"So you're saying that I hypnotised myself? Is that even possible?" He raised an eyebrow, looking dubious.

"Well, you did just put yourself in trance. Quite successfully, I might add." Then her face became serious. "But seriously, what were you thinking, Ray? Did you try to recall the hypnotist's voice again?"

Ray gave her a sheepish look. "I was just trying to see if I could match his voice with the voices of the people I know. I guess I went too far with it."

"Obviously." She stated flatly. "Ray, the killer suppressed your memories of him. It's normal for you to not remember him. That's the whole point of his suppressing your memory. This killer that we're dealing with is good with hypnosis – I give him that much. So don't you dare push yourself into doing what you did just now, okay?"

He nodded in resignation. "I was just trying to help as much as I can with the case."

Jenn sighed. "I know. It's hard to be told to sit still and do nothing when you could be doing something to help," she said comfortingly. "But if helping means you risking your mind, then I'd rather not let you do it. You'll need guidance if you want to get it right."

He grinned goofily, his mood visibly shifting all of a sudden. "Because I mean so much to you, right? You can't risk losing me," he said teasingly.

"Yeah, sure." She laughed dryly at his joke. He was testing her. "What would I do if I lost you? Your parents would surely kill me for not protecting their son from the killer's oh-so-hypnotic voice."

"You have a twisted sense of humour." He laughed, letting it slide. "Hypnotic voice? More like creepy voice." He pretended to shiver with fear.

"It's just a voice." She gave him a pointed look, her eyes twinkling with amusement. "Why are we arguing about a *voice* anyway?" she said, dismissing the topic. Then she got up. "So now that we've lifted your self-induced trance, let's see what we can do about recovering your memory of the killer."

He smiled crookedly, looking thrilled that she would let him help in some way. "Give it your best shot." He took a deep breath and asked, "What do you need me to do?"

"Just sit still and focus on your breathing," she said, her voice turning gentle again. "In and out. In ... and out. In ... Out ..." she lulled, tapping her fingers lightly on the couch in a steady slow rhythm. "Let yourself drift away as you relax into it."

Ray felt his muscles relaxing as his eyes turned blank once again. He inhaled and exhaled deeply according to the rhythm.

Tap ... tap ... tap ...tap ...

"Feels good, doesn't it?" Jenn said, watching his fixated stare. "Feel the air going in and out of your body. Now you feel your eyes closing as you breathe ... in ... and out." His eyes slowly closed. She brought her hand up to his shoulder as she continued tapping on the couch with the other one. She gave his shoulder a light pat, putting him under.

"Now, I want to bring you back to three years ago, the day of the first murder." She pressed two of her fingers against his wrist, feeling his steady pulse. Her left hand continued with the tapping.

Tap ... tap ... tap ... tap ...

"Tell me what you see, Ray," she commanded in a low voice, soothing yet assertive. "Do you see the girl at the party?" she asked suggestively, guiding his subconscious mind back to the first victim.

His eyes moved under his eyelids, but then they stilled again. "Yes, I see her," he murmured in a droning voice.

"Okay, you're doing very well, Ray. Now tell me what happens next," she prompted gently.

"I'm walking up to her." His eyes were now moving under his lids again, as if he were watching a movie. "She sees me and smiles. I smile back at her and ask for her name."

"Can you tell me her name?" Jenn asked, although she knew what the girl's name was. She was just making sure that Ray was not straying away from her.

"Anna," he mumbled. "Anna Shaw."

"Good, you're doing a great job." She decided to fast-forward the event. "You're having a great time with Anna, and the party is almost ending, but you have something you need to do, right?"

"I ... I need to get her out of there," he said, his voice turning urgent.

"Steady now." She removed her hand from his wrist. She placed it on his shoulder and squeezed it in a calming manner. "Breathe in deeply and let it out slowly. In and out."

His tensed muscles relaxed as his chest heaved in and out evenly.

"Good. Now you're bringing Anna out of the party." She led him back to the memory. "Where are you bringing her?"

"My car," he replied slowly. "She's asking where we are going."

"And what did you tell her?" she prodded.

"Somewhere where we could be alone," he quoted from his memory. "And as she strapped on her seat belt, I took out a white cloth." His brows twitched at the scene in his head. His nose crinkled. "Chloroform," he said, recognising the smell from his memory. "I used the cloth to cover her nose and mouth."

"And she struggled," Jenn continued for him. "But it didn't last long."

"No, it didn't." He shook his head.

"After a while, Anna was unconscious. And you were sitting there calm as could be," she added smoothly.

"Yes." He nodded at her suggestion, accepting it without a trace of doubt. "Then I started driving."

"Where were you headed?" she asked, still tapping with her free hand while her right hand continued to knead the muscles on his shoulder tenderly, easing him to go on.

"I was driving through a forest," he mumbled as his forehead creased with concentration.

"And the road went on and on," she said, fast-forwarding the memory again. "Until you saw a warehouse."

"Yes, and I stopped the car," he went on. "There was a person in front of the warehouse." His breathed hitched.

There it was. She moved her hand away from his shoulder and cupped his neck. "Can you describe the person? How does he look?"

"I ... I can't. I can't see his face." His heartbeat thudded against her palm, increasing as his brows twitched again.

"Hey, hey. It's okay. Just breathe. In and out." She felt his pulse slowing down. "Just take it easy, okay? Let's go back to when you stopped your car. Are you getting out of the car?"

"No," Ray said. "I just sat there watching the person."

"What was the person doing?" she asked, checking his pulse.

"He was ..." He stopped suddenly, his voice strained. Then he tried again. "He came closer and ..."

"Deep breaths, Ray," she reminded him gently. "In and out ... In ... Out ..."

Ray drew in a shaky breath. "I can't see anything," he gasped. "It hurts." He groaned, bringing his hands to his head. Beneath his eyelids, his eyes were moving rapidly.

She could see that this was as far as he could go. "Just breathe in deeply, Ray."

"Stop it." Ray shook his head, pushing her away from him. "Just stop it." His eyes snapped open as he got up from the couch, his eyes swinging around wildly. "I can't see anything," he exclaimed in desperation.

"Ray, I need you to listen to my voice." Jenn tried to hold him down, but he pushed her away again. She stumbled backwards, surprised at his strength.

"Leave me alone!" Ray shouted, clutching his head. "Stop messing with my head."

The office door flew open, and her partners came out in a rush to see what was going on. Ben frowned at Ray's condition and turned to Jenn with a questioning look. Jenn met his gaze, and something flickered in her eyes.

"Mr Darce," she called out suddenly, waving at Ben.

Ben gave her a confused look. Was she finally out of her mind?

Ray blinked, releasing his head. "Dad?" Ray let his hands drop to his sides and turned to Ben, puzzled. "I thought you were in Milan."

"Nope, he's back." Jenn said in a cheery voice. To her partners, she mouthed, "Play along." Then she said to Ray, "See, Mrs Darce is back too." She swung her gaze to J. Lee, hinting her to step in.

Immediately, J. Lee's composed face broke into a spontaneous smile. "Ray darling, come give your mummy a big hug," she said, beaming.

Jenn and Ben raised their eyebrows at her, blatantly surprised at her quick acting.

Ray grinned brightly at his "mother", not suspecting anything. "Mum, I missed you so much," he said as he engulfed J. Lee in a hug.

J. Lee visibly gulped in his embrace and mouthed to the two agents, "Some help here."

Jenn suppressed a laugh as she hurried forward and patted Ray's shoulder. "Wake," she commanded.

Ray's body tensed for a moment before he was out of his trance. "What the …?" He trailed off as he realised what he was doing to poor J. Lee. Then he quickly released her, muttering an apology.

J. Lee simply gave him a grim look. "You owe me big time." She exhaled sharply and sat down on the couch, raising an eyebrow at Jenn. "How did *he* go all haywire just now?"

"Yeah, what happened?" Ben asked.

Their questions were left hanging. Ray just stared at Jenn, still appearing dazed from the trance. He rubbed his forehead, feeling the headache after the intense session with her.

"The trance the killer induced was too deep," Jenn simply replied. "Sorry, Ray. I shouldn't have done that. How are you feeling?"

Ray plopped down on the couch. "Exhausted." He put his head in his hands. "And I feel a splitting headache coming on." He muttered, releasing a low groan.

"Can you make some tea for him, J?" Jenn said as she went and sat down beside Ray.

Ben stood there awkwardly. "Is he okay now?"

"What do you think?" Jenn frowned, studying Ray's pallid face. "He needs to get some rest."

"Got it," Ben muttered as he moved towards Ray. Carefully he placed Ray's arm around his neck and lifted Ray off the couch. "Damn. I think he's going to faint." He brought Ray into their bedroom as quickly as he could, and Jenn helped him get Ray into bed.

Ben collapsed on the bed beside Ray, who seemed to be drifting off into unconsciousness already. "What does his mother feed him?" Ben grumbled, sounding slightly out of breath.

"Don't blame him for working out too much," Jenn said with amusement. "He just wants to impress the opposite sex. Don't all guys do that?" She raised an eyebrow at him.

He smirked humourlessly. "Did he impress you?"

She sighed wearily. "Are you're implying that I'm attracted to him?"

Ben pushed himself up into a sitting position, watching her with accusing eyes. "Well, the kid's obviously interested in you," he stated flatly. "And I've seen the way you look at him."

"And what did you observe?" she asked, feigning interest.

He ignored the taunting look on her face and replied, "Well, I've never seen you treat anyone else the way you treat him."

Jenn was silent for a moment. She recalled everything that happened between her and Ray throughout the last few days and remembered the few times when she felt weird tingling feelings inside her during her time spent with Ray. She knew what those feelings meant, but she wasn't attracted to him in that way – was she?

"I care for him," she finally said, choosing her words cautiously. "I've known him since we were young. Of course I would treat him differently than how I treat others. Not everyone I know of is my childhood friend."

Ben pursed his lips. "I truly hope that you don't let your past blind you on this case," he muttered.

She laughed dryly. "Isn't that why you're here, to keep an eye on me for your dad?" she jeered. She knew that she had crossed the line, but she didn't like his tone. Ugh, why was she letting him get under her skin again?

At this, Ben clenched his teeth. "I'm just looking out for you, *Jennifer*," He said calmly with a composed face.

She smiled at him coyly. "Well, thank you, then," she replied, mirroring his tone. "I am truly touched, partner."

Just then, someone knocked on the door, interrupting their little banter. Then J. Lee walked in, holding a cup of hot tea. Jenn went over to take the tea from her and turned to Ray, who was supposedly deep asleep. Seeing this, Jenn sighed.

"Anyone else wants some tea?" she asked as she gave Ben a glance, putting their conversation behind her. When no one answered, she sighed. "I'll have it, then. Thanks, J. Lee."

With that, Jenn left the room.

Fourteen

The next day passed by in a flash. J. Lee had managed to narrow down their list of possible targets for the killer's final kill. The next target, Kayla Brown, was the only redhead in the town who had dyed her hair black over the last week right after returning home from her university studies in Ireland. It seemed that the scent at the last crime scene was the fragrance of the perfume that she used to wear. She fitted the profile perfectly. Now J. Lee was on a stake-out at the girl's house.

Jenn spent the whole day in the office with Ben, poring over the files repeatedly, but they were no closer to figuring out who the killer was. J. Lee had checked Ray's house phone and cell phone record, but there weren't any suspicious phone calls. There were just a couple of missed calls from Isabella, Tom, Nick, and his parents, all calling Ray to ask if he was okay because they hadn't seen or heard from him in days.

She had finally resolved to ask Agent Turner to conduct interviews with all people who attended the party again and with three suspects on their list. And the results were despairing. It turned out that those people were really just naïve that they thought that hiding the truth about Gina's birthday party was best for them. As for the three suspects, each of them had a solid alibi.

On the night of the party, he was having a movie night with Isabella, so it couldn't have been him crashing the party and committing the murder.

As for Paul Tanner and James Hendricks, they were back at the bank the whole time during the party. Apparently, they were trying to solve some bank account problems for their client. They had conveniently forgotten to inform Nick about that, which then led to raising all the suspicions.

So now they were basically stuck.

"There must be something that we're not seeing," Ben muttered, leaning back in his chair.

"No, I think we're seeing too much. That's the problem," Jenn mumbled tiredly as she crossed her arms on the table and rested her forehead on them. "I wish J. Lee were here instead of you – no offense."

"And why is that?" Ben asked, sounding offended despite her last two words.

"In case you hadn't noticed why I asked to have her on the team, it's because she can easily identify crucial elements in all kinds of situation. Her mind is built in such a way that she's able to sift through every grain of information we have to find the focal point of the case," Jenn explained in a bored voice. "I think that we're seeing too many possibilities here. That's why we need her to simplify things."

"Huh," Ben uttered, seeming to comprehend what Jenn had just told him. "So that's why she's always so blunt."

Jenn just grunted in response, her mind starting to run again after hearing her own words. What if the case was just how it looked? What if she was wrong about the last target? Perhaps this was just a psychopathic serial killer that they were dealing with. Then there would be no last target. It could be that the killer just had a change in his victim preference, so he started going after brunettes. Maybe this was just a thrill killer's game with them.

But then how could she explain the break in time pattern? And what about the scented note the killer left at the crime scene? The killer had made it clear that this was a scheme to get some sort of revenge.

According to his method of killing, the serial killer displayed a strong urge to break his target from the inside and to make her feel hopelessness, to let her feel the life being sucked out of her. That was the cruellest way to kill a person. The way she saw it, the killer must have suffered through some kind of psychological pain to cause him to perform such a diabolical act. It could most probably be that he lost someone dear to him and was blaming his target for being the cause of his loss. This brought her back to the relationship-gone-wrong theory.

"Hey, are you okay?" Ben's voice broke through her reverie.

She waved her index finger at Ben to silence him, not bothering to raise her head. "I'm thinking."

"Mind sharing your thoughts?" he asked again.

Jenn huffed. "Why don't you go check on Ray?" she suggested, feeling annoyed at him for breaking her train of thought. Then she heard the sound of his chair scraping noisily on the floor as he got up and left the room. He did it on purpose. She was sure of that. He knew that she didn't like it when people slammed doors and dragged chairs on the floor. She thought that it was disrespectful and unprofessional.

She rolled her eyes and went back to her perusal of the case. With Ben gone, she finally raised her head and leaned back against the back of her chair. It was rather hard to focus on her thoughts when she kept noticing his gaze on her every two minutes while they were studying the papers in front of them.

Back to the case, she remembered that she had stopped at what was the cause of the killer's revenge. Okay, so the killer wanted his target to feel his pain. But if he really wanted that, couldn't he just finish the target off straight away in the first place? She understood if he meant to use the first six murders to cover his tracks, to hide his motive, but then why did the killer decided to break pattern? What made him change his plans? Could it be that Kayla Brown had somehow provoked him again? Or was it the killer who had slipped up and raised suspicions?

More and more questions arose, but she found no answers to them. Something vital was missing. She needed to do some digging into Kayla Brown's past later.

The door opened suddenly, interrupting her thoughts again. She sighed as Ben came back into the office and closed the door behind him.

"The kid's doing fine," he said to her, sitting down opposite her. "I just don't get why he's so tired."

"Imagine the Great Wall of China inside your head and you're trying to put a hole through it to remember something. Get it now?"

"Huh," he uttered, plainly not liking the look she was giving him. "There's another thing that I don't get. Yesterday you said that you were going to lift his self-induced trance. And yet when J and I came out, he just went maniac on us instead. So what exactly were the two of you doing?"

She laughed unexpectedly. "What did it look like to you?"

He cocked an eyebrow at her, but he made a guess anyway. "He was still in a trance."

"You're just stating the obvious," she said. Her face was composed again. "Well, I did lift the self-induced trance. But then I decided to help him find the trigger, so I put him under again and brought him back to the night of the first murder."

"You did what?" He widened his eyes, leaning forward towards the table.

"I was just hoping to use his memory to get a glimpse of how the trance was induced by the killer," she explained. "If I can get him to remember his interaction with the killer, something might just jump out in the memory. You never know."

"Then how on earth did he go all haywire?" Ben asked in puzzlement.

Jenn sighed. "Well, after he got to the part where the killer steps in, I improvised a little. I asked him to try to get a look at the killer's face." She muttered with a hint of regret. "It was foolish of me to allow myself to do so. I went too far." A frown started to form on her forehead, revealing the guilt and anxiety that was building up inside of her.

"Hey, everyone makes mistakes," Ben said quietly, his eyes softening. He longed to reach out and hold her hand, but he stopped himself. Jenn rarely showed her true self to him these days. He didn't want scare her off now.

"I clearly knew that it wouldn't end well, not when he was in so deep." She turned her gaze away, feeling her emotions surfacing. "Whoever did this to him, I have to say that this hypnotist sure knows what he's doing."

His lips formed a thin line. "And I'm sure that you know what you're doing too. You're Jumping Spider, the master of human manipulation," he reminded her, sounding proud at her despite her situation right now.

Hearing his reassuring words, Jenn smiled absentmindedly. "Yeah, that's what everyone in the service calls me, but do they realise that I'm human too? That I might lose my touch someday?" Her smile became mirthless. She was so immersed in her self-doubting thoughts that she didn't notice Ben getting up and moving around the table towards her. "Do they even know that I get tired and upset like everyone else does?" She continued to speak sullenly.

"I do," Ben said as he stood behind her, placing a comforting hand on her shoulder. He felt her body stiffen at his touch. "I don't know about the others, but I do realise that your talents might just slip away someday. And when the time comes, I'll still trust you."

Jenn swallowed hard, trying to suppress the emotions that were threatening to burst out of her. She felt her will softening at his familiar warm touch. She realised that she missed him so much. But then her heart writhed as she remembered why she had banned herself from him in the first place. No, she couldn't let herself be fooled by his gentle touch and tender words anymore.

Not again.

"Thanks for your reassurance, but please know your limit, *partner*," Jenn said, her voice turning impassive. She shrugged off his hand as she stood up. She didn't turn around to reprimand him on his action just now. Instead, she just left the office and went straight into her room.

~

Catherine dug out her cell phone and dialled his number. Then she quickly pressed the phone to her ear, hoping desperately that he would pick up. It had been six months since she last saw him, back at the NSSS headquarters. Every day she would try to contact him, but he never picked up. Even so, she had never stopped calling. For six months, she had never given up on him.

She sat down on her bed and waited patiently for him to answer her call. Where was he, anyway? Jenn had briefly considered asking his father for his whereabouts, but that would only complicate things. After all, she wanted to keep their relationship a secret. Her question would surely raise suspicions in the agency.

Her heart jumped with joy when he answered the phone. *Finally.* After half a year, she had finally managed to reach him.

"Hello ..." a rough voice slurred through the phone.

A confused frown touched her forehead. That didn't sound much like him. "Ben? Is that you?"

"No, this is the president of the United States," he boomed over the phone, laughing loudly at his own silly joke.

Yes, this was definitely Ben's voice. But why was he acting like this? He sounded ... drunk.

"Ben, where are you?" Catherine asked in a worried tone. She was already guessing that he was in a nightclub or something. She could hear the loud music blaring in the background through the phone.

"Me? Well, I'm in a place where no one can find me," Ben yelled over the loud music. Then he burst into fits of laughter again. "No one can find me ..." He started singing an unfamiliar song at the top of his lungs.

"Ben!" she shouted, trying to grab his attention. "Where have you been? Do you know how worried I am? You've been gone for more than six months, you know that?"

"Wait, you're Catherine!" he exclaimed, as if he had just recognised her voice. "You've been calling me every day," he slurred happily.

"Yes, I have," she replied, sighing patiently. What was going on with him? She knew that he had always disliked drinking. He hated alcoholics – he had said so himself. But now he was wasted. "Tell me where you are, Ben. I'll come take you home."

"Don't tell me what to do, lady," he drunkenly shouted at her, sounding annoyed. "I'm perfectly happy with where I am right now, and I don't plan to leave any sooner." He started guffawing again.

Catherine was shocked at the way he had just spoken to her. Never had she ever heard him use such a tone with anyone. What had happened to him over the last six months?

She drew in a deep breath to calm herself before speaking again. "Ben, can you please just let me know where you are right now?"

Ben made an exasperated noise. "That's it!" he exploded. "I've had enough of you. Leave me alone!"

She felt as if she'd been slapped. Why was he being like this? Was it because of something she did or said? She blinked back the tears that were welling up in her eyes. "Please, Ben, come back to me. I miss you," she pleaded, hoping that he would listen to her.

Ben uttered a string of profanities. "Gosh, get the hint, will you?" he said in a mocking tone. "Leave me alone, you clingy little bitch! And stop calling me every single day! Stop bothering me!" he barked furiously.

Hot tears brimmed over as the sharp words cut through her like a thin blade. "Why?" Her voice broke, and she couldn't trust herself to speak anymore.

"You're asking me why?" He laughed coldly as the loud background music kept blaring through the phone. "I'll tell you why! I don't need you in my life! I don't need anyone in my life! You've been nothing but an obsessive little moron! You keep calling and calling every day. Every. Single. Day. Don't you have anything better to do? Well, I do, okay? So stop being an idiot and leave me alone!"

Catherine heard a girl's shrill, high-pitched laughter through the phone before Ben hung up on her. Tears poured down her face as she realised now that it was over between them. Just like that, it was over.

Over ...

She clutched her cell phone tightly, pressing it towards her chest as the tears flowed freely. He had found himself another girl, perhaps someone less clingy than she was. She laughed bitterly as his words echoed in her mind.

Sometimes life was unpredictable and things just happened unexpectedly. He'd never said anything to her before this. They were happy together with each other before he did his disappearing act. At least she thought that Ben was truly happy when he was with her. And now suddenly it all ended within a blink of an eye.

Catherine buried her face in her pillow and let out a strangled sob. Gosh, it hurt. It hurt so much. She had always thought that she was strong enough to handle this kind of emotional pain. After all, she managed to survive the pain when her parents were brutally murdered. But it turned that she was wrong. How wrong she had been about herself ...

That night, Catherine cried herself to sleep.

Jenn woke up with a start. She blinked through the pool of tears in her eyes, gasping for breath. *It was just a dream,* she thought.

Just a dream.

"Hey, you okay?" J. Lee's sleepy voice broke through the cold silence in the room. "I tried to wake you up, but you just kept crying," she uttered drowsily. "I thought I'd accidentally hit you in my sleep."

"I'm okay now," Jenn said, her voice throaty and hoarse. "Go back to sleep." She gave her friend a light pat on the upper arm, gesturing for J. Lee not to worry about her anymore.

"If you say so," J. Lee mumbled. "We'll talk in the morning, then." She yawned and drifted back into unconsciousness.

Jenn wiped the tears off her face, sniffling. She used to have this dream after she and Ben broke up that night. Since then, the bitter memory kept replaying itself every night in her sleep. But then she remembered that the dream had stopped for more than two months already.

Why was it haunting her again now?

Fifteen

The next two days were horribly tiresome for Jenn. The dream was becoming more real and vivid, and it continued to haunt her every night. During the day, she was stuck at the hotel with Ben and Ray while J. Lee went on her stake-out on Kayla Brown. The two guys, who seemed to be good terms with each other now, were constantly trying to get her to talk even though she really didn't feel like it, and when they were not, Ben would always get on her nerves. He just kept staring at her and that truly annoyed her.

Okay, maybe it was just her. But with her losing sleep at night lately – three nights, to be exact – she could hardly blame herself for being so jumpy.

Right now Jenn was in the office, trying her best to get herself back on track on the case. It had been three days since J. Lee had found the last target, and they hadn't gotten any breakthrough in the case. Jenn knew that something was missing from the big picture here.

Whenever she needed a break from the guys, she would spend most of her time staring at the timeline of the murders, the pictures of the victims, just to see if something would leap out at her. Sometimes she would just stare off into space and let her mind stray on its own to see where it would take her.

It was like searching for a needle in a haystack. She had no idea what she was looking for, to be honest. Jenn was more stressed out than ever. If she didn't find who the killer was, Kayla Brown's life would still be in grave danger. She was starting to think that she was losing her touch now.

And Ben wasn't being much of a help today. He hadn't left his room since morning after breakfast. Jenn had asked Ray what was up with Ben. Perhaps the two guys had gotten into another quarrel again and Ben had lost the fight so now he was sulking in the bedroom. Ridiculous assumption, of course, but it was possible. However, Ray had no idea why his new found friend was acting so weird either. Ray even seemed worried about him.

"Do you want to go talk to him?" Ray asked sometime in the afternoon.

Jenn let her eyes linger on him for a while, considering his question. Then she simply replied, "No."

She had already gone soft after getting stuck under the same roof with Ben for a few days. She didn't need to make it any harder for herself by showing him care and concern. He was old enough to deal with his own problems. Period.

Ray sighed. "You still care for him. Don't act like you don't know that."

She gave a short laugh of absurdity, hiding her discomfort at his statement. "I do?" she said, raising an eyebrow nonchalantly.

"Yes," Ray answered swiftly, giving her a pointed look. "I've seen the way you look at him when he's not doing the whole creepy staring thing at you. You might try to be all professional and Frosty the snowman with him, but I can see that you've never stopped caring for him."

"Oh, so now you're an expert on human behaviourism, huh?" Jenn said, feigning amusement. She tried very hard not to let his words get to her.

"Nah." Ray waved his hand dismissively. "I'm just observing. That's all." He said, obviously seeing through her façade.

"And what else did you observe?" she asked, keeping her face neutral even though she knew that he wasn't being fooled by her.

Ray smiled half-heartedly and scratched the back of his head. "Nothing else. I figured that that's enough to tell myself to back off," he muttered, sounding slightly disgruntled.

She fell silent when he said that. Why on earth was Ray admitting his feelings to her now?

"Well, this is awkward," Ray mumbled, but he never broke eye contact with her. "Don't worry – I'm not trying to put pressure on you or anything. My point is, I think you should go talk to him, just ask to see if he's okay."

Jenn scrutinised him with a certain level of intensity, frowning in mild confusion. Her scrutiny lasted for more than a minute before she finally spoke again. "I thought the two of you hated each other's guts."

A corner of his lips curled upwards into a lopsided smile. "That's just him." Ray shrugged. "But I think that we're cool now."

Jenn let out a small sigh. "Okay. I'll go check on him on behalf of you." Smiling to herself, she got up from the couch and went into the guys' bedroom. When she got to the door, she drew in a deep breath before opening it. She could feel Ray's gaze burning through the back of her head as she entered the room.

Closing the door silently behind her, she peered around the room. At first, she thought that Ben wasn't in the room. Well, he wasn't anywhere in sight. However, Jenn continued to walk slowly towards the bed, glancing around again. Then she saw him.

Ben was sitting on the floor, leaning against the dresser. He was facing away from the door so he couldn't have seen her approaching him. Jenn stopped advancing when she saw the photo he was holding in his hand. There was a girl in the photo, smiling.

Before she could get a better look at it, Ben spoke suddenly. "I'm not feeling well today, okay? Just let me be alone for a while." He didn't turn around when he spoke. Instead, he just kept staring at the photo.

"If you're not feeling well, you should stay in bed, not sit on the floor," she muttered after a moment of deliberation.

Hearing her voice, Ben got up in a dash and whirled around to face her, wearing a mask of surprise. "Catherine!" he exclaimed, sounding shocked to see her. "I mean, Jennifer," he hastily corrected himself, trying to compose his demeanour. He kept his hands behind him, obviously attempting to hide the photo from her. "I-I thought you were Ray," he said offhandedly.

Jenn merely raised an eyebrow at his reaction. "Oh, sorry to disappoint. Your dear friend Ray insisted that I should come and check on you." She said this in a detached voice, stealing a glance at his hidden hands. "Well, since you're not feeling well, I'll just let you be alone to rest." She turned away from him and headed for the door.

"Wait!" Ben said anxiously from behind her.

She halted at the door, not turning around. She just waited to hear what he had to say to her.

"Stay," he pleaded quietly. "Please?"

His soft begging tone echoed through her ears, and Jenn slowly turned to face him. What was going on with him today? She took a few steps towards him, watching his forlorn demeanour. "Are you sick?"

Ben dropped his gaze down to the floor as he sat down on the edge of the bed. "No," he mumbled in a low voice, his voice woeful. A few moments later, he looked up at her. "Come sit down. Please," he said, patting his hand on the bed beside him.

A frown appeared on her forehead as she stared at him. Something was definitely not right. Hesitantly she moved towards the bed and sat down, making sure to leave some space between them.

"Thank you," he whispered as a smile touched his lips. There was no sign of delight in his smile, just traces of solemnity and sorrow. The photo was no longer in sight. Perhaps he had put it away when she wasn't looking.

A few minutes went by in silence. Jenn just sat there watching him from a corner of her eye. She was trying to figure out what was wrong with him. It must have something to do with the girl in the photo. She would have assumed that it was his newfound girlfriend if he weren't looking so gloomy right now.

"It feels so good to be in the same room with you," he said suddenly, breaking the comfortable silence in the room. "Not bickering, not arguing, not discussing work, just sitting here …" He sighed with contentment, staring ahead. "Together."

Jenn bit her lower lip, fighting the urge to leave the room immediately. Ben wasn't himself right now. She couldn't afford to leave him alone. "Let's just embrace silence, then," she suggested, hoping that he would drop the topic already.

Unfortunately, he didn't get her hint. "I miss us," he whispered, turning to her.

She met his gaze and saw the wistfulness and yearning in his eyes. This wasn't real, she reminded herself. Heaving a deep sigh, she said slowly, "We're not talking about this right now. You promised that you wouldn't bring up anything about the past … so stick to your word."

"It's so hard, you know," Ben said in a painfully vulnerable voice. "To keep trying to hold myself down around you feels so wrong."

Jenn released an exasperated breath. Ben was crossing the line. She got up, her face contorting into a mask of disbelief as she glared down at him. "You know what feels wrong to me?" she spat, barely containing her anger. "Being in this room with you."

This was just another trick of his to play her, wasn't it? And she was foolish enough to allow herself to step into his trap again. *Gosh.*

Ben flinched at her words. His jaw clenched and unclenched as he visibly tried to hide the hurt inside him. "Why?" The word escaped his lips whilst his eyes stared into hers searchingly.

And that was it. That did the trick. That one word from him broke down every wall she had built inside her. The bitter memory of that particular night crashed into her mind as raw emotions flooded her system.

"You're asking me *why?*" Her voice came out strained, strangled. She let out an empty laugh. "What happened to 'Stop being an idiot and leave me alone'?" she asked, quoting his last words to her that night. "What happened to 'I don't need you in my life', huh?" Her voice rose along with her anger – the huge ball of anger which she had suppressed for a very long time.

Ben stared at her in confusion as he stood up. "What? What are you talking about?"

"What am I ...?" Jenn scoffed to herself, incredulous as she repeated his question in her head. She couldn't believe her ears.

He didn't remember. He *didn't* remember.

So *he* was too drunk to remember what he'd said to her that night, and *she* was the only one who had been crazily immersed in the incident that night. She let out a derisive laugh, taking a step back involuntarily and shaking her head in disbelief. "You jerk."

Ben was still puzzled by her words from earlier, but he could see that Jenn was extremely upset. *Probably not the best time to keep asking questions then,* he thought.

"Jenn, please listen to me ..." he started, but Jenn wasn't sticking around for this.

She spun around and strode towards the door. There was no point in arguing with him anymore. He couldn't even *remember*. She clenched her teeth in frustration as she reached out to grab the doorknob.

"My mum died."

Her hand froze on the doorknob. *What?*

"My mum died," he repeated bitterly, his voice shaking. "Today's the first anniversary of her death," he choked.

His mother died? Her forehead creased whilst she tried to register his sentence in her head. *Ben's mother died* ...Then a sudden realisation hit her like a ton of bricks, and she gasped softly. It was his mother in the photo.

"That was why I left last year," he continued in a weak voice. "I found out that she had bone cancer, terminal. I took off to New York immediately when

I heard that she was in the last stage. I was in such a hurry that it completely escaped my mind that I should have called you to let you know where I was going."

Ben paused to take in a shaky breath. "But still, I was too late. She was gone by the time I arrived at the hospital." He stifled a cry. "I was crushed. I became a mess. You know how I was with my dad. He was all about the agency, all about the cases and missions. Mum was the only one I could turn to when something was wrong. She was the only one who cared for me. My mum was all I had." At this point, his voice broke.

Jenn was at a loss for words. Her hand slipped off the doorknob as the anger inside her evaporated completely, replaced with a feeling of shame and grief.

He sniffled and continued. "Later I found out that my dad *knew* about mum's condition. I was so angry that I would have punched him in the face if the nurses hadn't held me back. He *lied* to me. He said that he didn't want me to be worried about her, that he thought she would be okay after going through treatments. A bunch of *lies!*" he hissed. "He took away my only chance to see her for the last time."

Jenn heard him punching the wall with so much force that it frightened her. She spun around to face Ben, only to see him letting himself fall helplessly to the floor. He leaned his head back against wall, fighting the tears that threatened to spill. This was the first time she'd seen him cry, and it broke her heart to see him so lost in his misery. She wanted to go to his side, to hug him, to let him know that he wasn't alone, but she couldn't bring herself to do it. Seeing him break down like this shocked Jenn to her very core. She was rooted to the floor, unable to move a muscle.

Ben wiped away his tears furiously, determined to get the truth out. "I lost it after that. I started drinking. I wanted to just forget everything. I was running away from the pain. Every night I visited nightclubs and bars, drowning myself in alcohol like a pathetic little coward." He forced the words out through clenched teeth. "You called me every single day, but I didn't answer any of your calls. I was ashamed to talk to you. I couldn't face you knowing the fact that I was a drunk, something I despised the most.

"After a while, it became easier. I just turned my phone off whenever I was drinking. But then the guilt still ate at me. At that point, alcohol wouldn't work for me anymore," he mumbled, reliving the pain. "So I started taking drugs."

Jenn thought that she had heard the worst part, but how wrong she was. When that last sentence came from his mouth, she literally felt as if she'd been punched in the stomach. All this time, she had thought that he was having the time of his life being away from her. And it was the exact opposite of what he was going through the whole time.

"It was like a release for me, you know. It took away all the pain ... the grief ... the guilt. I felt good again. I still refused to answer your calls, but I didn't feel guilty about it anymore. I guess I was used to it by then. It had become a habit." He smiled humourlessly. "After that, I went to parties around the city, just distracting myself from my real life. Every day and every night of my life was filled with alcohol, drugs, and parties. I didn't want to go back to the agency. The service reminded me too much of what my dad had done to me. I liked it better in New York: carefree, fun, enjoyable."

Jenn could hear the disgust in his voice. *He was disgusted with himself.* A tear rolled down her cheek as she saw how much he had put himself through. How blind she had been. He had been suffering so much – even now he was still in pain, and she saw nothing. *Nothing.*

"That was until that day – that day when I answered your call." His impassive voice had turned into a whisper at the last part of his sentence, reflecting his turmoil at this point. Then he forced himself to continue. "As usual, I was at a party when I received your call. At that time, I was so drunk and high that I forgot to turn off my phone. So I answered the call." He paused, turning to meet her gaze. His sorrowful eyes held hers for what felt like an eternity before he whispered, "I'm sorry."

Jenn just stood there, staring at him wordlessly. She felt as if her body were detached from her mind. Her body wouldn't even budge when she watched him struggling to push himself up from the floor. All she could do was stare at him and let her tears fall.

"I'm sorry that I can't remember what I'd said to you on the phone." Guilt and regret coloured his tone. "All I could remember was that I was yelling at you repeatedly." He took a small step towards her, as if being careful not to scare her off. "After the drug wore off, I remembered hearing you cry on the phone. I made you cry," he said, sounding appalled at himself. His eyes were filled with dismay as they continued to lock gazes with each other.

"That was when I realised that I was wrong. I had never been so wrong in my life." His voice broke again as he took another step forward. "I realised that I still had you. You still cared for me. I hadn't lost everything I had." He said this with such conviction that another pool of tears welled up in her eyes, blurring her vision.

Then Ben smiled through his tears as he went on. "And that was when I knew that I had to stop destroying myself. I still had something to fight for in my life. So I went for rehab to free myself from the addiction. I wanted to come back. I needed to make sure that I hadn't lost you too," he said with desperation. "I tried calling you while I was in rehab, but I couldn't reach you. It took me four months to get rid of the addiction completely, and after I got out, I took the first flight I could catch to get back to the agency."

"During the flight, I was wondering if I had gotten myself fired for leaving the agency for so long. It turned out that my dad had been keeping tabs on me the whole time. He knew about the drinking, the drugs, our relationship, everything. And he filled me in on your condition throughout the past twelve months." He took one last step towards Jenn, stopping right in front of her. "I almost lost it again when my dad told me about your change in behaviour. I thought that you were gone, that I had really lost you.

"But knowing my dad, he wouldn't have allowed that kind of thought in my mind. He said that I had to try my best to make it up to you, not to give up on you." He laughed softly. "I took his advice, despite the lies he had told me about my mum. It was really hard at first, having to watch you from afar, not being able to talk to you like we used to. I almost thought of giving up. I mean, you were so stubborn with your decision to cut me out of your life.

"But when dad decided to tell me about the nightmares you used to have before my return, I knew that I couldn't give up, not yet. I knew that my return had somehow made a change in your life once again. So here I am," Ben ended with a sad smile. Then he wiped off the last trace of tears on his face, waiting for her to speak.

Wait, how did General Warner know about her nightmares? Right, she had awaked screaming a few times back in her dorm room near the headquarters. Maybe the other agents in the dormitory reported her condition to him and that was how he found out.

His hands flew up and held her arms gently, the sudden affection surprising her. "Say something, Catherine," he pleaded, staring at her with anxious eyes.

"I …" Jenn opened her mouth to speak, but her mind wasn't really working anymore. All that she could think of right now was the look on his face when he broke down right in front of her.

"Maybe you should just sit down first," he said as he guided her towards the bed. "You look as if you're in shock."

She sat down in a daze, staring at him the whole time. *Ben knew*, she thought to herself. He *knew* about her dream, about how her life had become after that night. And yet he didn't say a thing about it. He was trying to make it up to her, even though he couldn't remember what he had said to her that night. He wanted to punish himself for it and let her have the chance to punish him too. That was why he pretended as if nothing had happened. That was typical of him.

Ben knelt down in front of her, studying her closely and worriedly. "Catherine, are you not feeling well?" he asked, wearing a concerned expression.

"No," she replied in a whisper, shaking her head. "It's okay. I'm not in shock. I'm just … thinking," she said quietly, slowly recovering herself.

Ben raised his eyebrows as a smile made its way onto his face. "Right, I almost forgot. You're always thinking."

His tender smile made her heart twist in anguish, sending pangs of sadness through her. It wasn't her who needed consolation right now, yet Ben was showering her with so much care and concern that it made her feel like a little child. Jenn stifled a sob, unable to suppress the overwhelming feeling of grief inside her. "I'm so sorry," she choked out, tears brimming again.

"Hey, hey, hey …" Ben soothed, trying to comfort her. He placed his hands on both sides of her face, using his thumbs to wipe away the tears that were streaming down her cheeks. "It's okay … It's okay …" He mumbled in a hushed voice. "You didn't know. Don't blame yourself."

Despite his reassurance, Jenn kept apologising to him as her tears continued to fall. Seeing her beating herself up like this, Ben couldn't help but feel bad for revealing the truth to her so directly. It must be hard for her to learn about his side of the story this way. But he certainly didn't regret telling her all that. At least now they could move on together.

Silently he withdrew his hands from her face, only to get up and sit beside her on the bed. Then Ben put his arms around Jenn, pulling her into a warm embrace. Jenn buried her face in the warmth of his chest and let him hold her, allowing herself this moment to fully lean on him. After that, they just sat there, forgetting time. Ben held her tightly to himself, whispering words of comfort to her as she slowly drifted off to the serene world of dreams in his loving arms.

Sixteen

In the evening, Jenn finally woke up. She brought a hand up to her face to rub her sore eyes. Her throat felt dry, and her face was sticky with dried tears. She blinked a few times and glanced around.

Wait a minute – this wasn't her room.

"You're awake." Ben's voice came from just above her head.

Jenn lifted her head and saw him watching her with an affectionate smile on his face. Then she remembered Ben holding her in his arms earlier while she was crying. She must have fallen asleep from exhaustion after crying for so long. Her head was currently lying on his upper arm, his hand wrapped around her shoulder firmly, holding her close to him.

"Are you feeling better now?" Ben asked gently in a low voice, staring at her with concern.

"Yes," she replied, her voice croaky and hoarse. As much as she wanted to stay in this bed right now, she needed to get herself some water to soothe her throat. She reluctantly pushed herself up and swung her legs over the side of the bed, feeling the floor under her feet.

"Where are you going?" Ben asked, sounding panicked. He caught her arm as he got up into a sitting position.

"Water," she said, clearing her throat.

"I'll get it," Ben offered, and he got off the bed swiftly. He strode out of the room without giving her a chance to protest.

Sighing, she stood up anyway. He really was trying to make things up to her in any way he could. Jenn figured that she might as well clean herself up while waiting for him to return. So she headed into the bathroom and widened her eyes at her reflection in the mirror. What a mess she was, Jenn thought to herself, wondering how Ben managed to stare at her for so long without laughing out loud.

She quickly started to clean herself up by washing her face first. After that, she sprayed some water onto her hair and combed her fingers through her long black hair before tying it into a loose ponytail. Then she checked her reflection in the mirror again. There, she looked much tidier now. Satisfied, she went back into the room and found Ben sitting at the edge of the bed already, waiting for her patiently.

"Hey." He stood up when she came back into the room. He handed her a glass of water which she thankfully accepted from him before gulping down the whole glass of water within seconds. "Better?" he asked as soon as she finished it.

She nodded with a grateful smile. "Is Ray doing okay on his own?"

"I would say that he's doing great." Ben chuckled. "He didn't even notice when I went out to get water just now. He's got his full attention on the TV screen."

"Glad to hear that," Jenn said with a smile of her own. "Come on. Let's go join him in the living room."

Ben's face fell when he heard that. He was hoping to have her to himself for the rest of the day, but he knew what she would say to him if he asked her to stay in the room. Even though they knew that he could be trusted to take good care of himself, Ray still needed supervision. It wasn't quite safe to let him be on his own for too long yet.

"Okay," he said, brushing off the disappointment in him. They left the bedroom together.

When they emerged from the room, Ray whipped his head around immediately. "Finally kissed and made up?" he asked curiously, cocking an eyebrow at the two agents, who went and sat on the other couch. There was no hint of jealousy in his tone.

"What gave you that idea?" Ben asked, laughing.

Ray simply smirked. "Well, you just laughed," he stated. "I thought you were all gloomy and dispirited this morning." He gave them a knowing look.

At the mention of that, Jenn froze beside Ben, worried that he would start grieving for his mother again. To her surprise, Ben simply smiled and replied, "Well, there's no kissing involved. Sorry to disappoint. But we did sort things out between us." He turned to Jenn, his smile involuntarily faltering a little. "Didn't we?" There was a slight tone of uncertainty in his question.

It seemed that Ben was still unsure of where they stood after his confession. Jenn held his gaze as she made a quick decision inside her mind. It was up to her to either turn him down or take him back right now. Then she turned to Ray, grinning. "Yes, we did." Her eyes went back to Ben, giving him a small nod as a confirmation to his uncertainty.

Ben's smile widened, and he reached out to hold her hand. He turned back to Ray and said, "And I have you to thank for this. I heard that you 'forced' her to come and check on me."

"Don't sweat it." Ray laughed, waving his hand dismissively. "I just wanted to see her happy again, not that I don't care about you. I'm just closer to her. That's all."

Ray was talking nonsense again, but this time Ben didn't mind at all. Jenn had forgiven him already, and that was all that mattered.

Ray continued to ramble. "I just hope that you two lovebirds will keep your hands to yourselves when I'm around. After all, I'm still an innocent little kid and don't want my eyes to be scarred for the rest of my life."

Jenn laughed. "Don't worry. We don't cope well with PDA anyway." When she saw Ben opening his mouth to object, she quickly added, "Well, I don't. Ben likes marking his territory."

Ben feigned an upset look. "You make me sound like a dog." Then his face morphed into an amused smile. "But I guess that it's okay for me since you just admitted that you're mine."

"Ugh, guys!" Ray complained. "Innocent kid is still here, okay? Quit flirting around." He made a face at them, and they laughed at his goofiness.

Just then, Jenn's cell phone rang. She fished out her cell phone and checked the caller ID. She got up from the couch immediately, causing Ben to release her hand rather reluctantly. "It's J. Lee," she whispered to the guys before answering the call.

"Hey. You have anything new?" Jenn asked with anticipation.

"Yes, I found something interesting," J. Lee said curtly. "You know a guy named Mason Riley?"

"Yeah, he's the mayor's son," Jenn uttered, wondering where this was heading. "What about him?"

"I just got news that he's throwing a party at his house in two days," J. Lee said. "A birthday party."

"Whose birthday party?" Jenn asked.

"Kayla Brown's," J. Lee answered in an ironic tone. "She's his girlfriend."

Jenn raised her eyebrows in mild surprise. "And you know this how?"

"I just saw him visiting her place. He was kissing her in front of her house in broad daylight," her friend explained, sounding somewhat irked. "Then some of his friends that he'd brought along with him started handing out invitations to whomever they saw. They even put up posters around town. It's an open house birthday party."

"You got one too?" Jenn asked.

"Yes."

Jenn was surprised to hear that. They didn't even know who J. Lee was. "Did you introduce yourself to them?"

"No."

"They didn't even ask for your name?"

"No. But they did ask me to spread the word," J. Lee muttered. "Rich kids. Ostentatious."

Jenn let out a laugh at her friend's tone. She could picture J. Lee shaking her head right now. "Okay, I think that you can wrap up the stake-out now that we know when the killer's going to strike again," she said, causing Ben to give her a questioning look. She simply held up a hand, gesturing for him to wait.

"Got it," J. Lee muttered before ending the call.

Jenn turned to the guys immediately. "J. Lee just found out that the mayor's son is throwing a huge birthday party for Kayla Brown in two days. She's on her way back now."

"You think that the killer's Mason Riley?" Ray interrupted, frowning.

"No. He's just an overenthusiastic kid who wants to impress his girlfriend," she stated bluntly. "Plus, you don't even know him personally, so he's already ruled out from the suspect list."

"Overenthusiastic kid," Ray snorted. "You got that right."

"So now we're assuming that the killer's attending the party?" Ben cut in, giving her a doubtful look.

"No, it's a fact," she clarified. "Our serial killer kidnaps his targets from parties. That's a pattern he didn't break in Gina Lee's murder. So I know that he's going to stick to his comfort zone this time too."

"If you say so." Ben said, obviously not convinced.

"I know so," Jenn replied with confidence.

"Okay." Ben held up both his hands in submission. "So what do you plan to do next? Crash the party?"

"If the both of you would have kindly let me finish first, you would've known that this is an open house party. The whole town is invited to attend the party," she said dryly. "That's why I'm so sure that our killer will be there. The party will most probably be filled with strangers. It's the safest place for him to take Kayla Brown."

"I see your point now. But we still can't identify the killer," Ben averred. "Our hands are still tied. We don't know who to watch out for, plus we can't stay near Kayla Brown at all times. It will set the killer off at some point."

"Yes, that will be a problem," Jenn agreed, sitting down beside Ben again. She bit the inside of her cheek as her mind started to get to work.

Ben sighed as his eyes strayed to Ray. "If only someone could break down the Great Wall of China."

"Great Wall of ...?" Ray's voice trailed off as he frowned at Ben's words, uncomprehending. "That's like *so* out of the blue." Ray shot him a weird look. "Are you stoned or something?"

"That's it!" Jenn said with a sudden burst of determination. "Ray, I'm going to help you get out of that trance soon."

Ray widened his eyes and moved away from her. "Y-you sure about that?" he stuttered, releasing a nervous laugh. "Remember how it went down last time?"

"I know. I know. Don't worry, okay? What I meant is, I'm going to get someone else to help you with it."

"Who?" Ben asked, puzzled. Then realisation dawned on him. "Wait, you don't mean Watch, do you?"

"You're going to ask a watch for help?" Ray interjected as he looked at the agents with disbelief. "How is a watch going to break my trance, with its cute little ticking hands?"

"You have a great imagination, dude," Ben said with a hint of sarcasm. "We're talking about one of the greatest hypnotists known in the agency, okay? His code name is Watch, as in observe."

"Oh, observe …" Ray laughed self-consciously. "You people have weird code names."

Jenn ignored Ray's comment. "Yes, we're going to him for help. I think that he's the only who can figure this out before the party," she mused. "It's a shame that I didn't think of this before."

"Do you even know where he is?" Ben asked, cocking an eyebrow at her.

"No," she answered with a smile, holding up her cell phone. "But I bet the general would know his location."

"Hm." Ben nodded, saying nothing else. His lips were pursed as he gestured for her to make the call.

Jenn knew that he still had bitter feelings for his father, but at least he was willing to put his personal matters aside for now. She quickly dialled General Warner's number. Just then, J. Lee arrived back at the suite. As Jenn spoke to the general, Ben started filling J. Lee in about what they had discussed.

"Sir, how are you?" Jenn greeted smoothly when the general answered the phone.

The general chuckled. "Well, someone seems to be in good mood today. I am doing very well, Catherine. Thanks for your concern."

"You're welcome." She smiled at his light-hearted tone. Then she got straight into business. "Sir, there's something we need your help with."

"Thought so. You're not one to call just to have a bit of a small talk." He laughed heartily. "So tell me. What do you need?"

"It's nothing much, actually. I just need to know Watch's current location."

"If it's not much to ask, can you tell me why you need to know Agent McKnight's location?" the general queried.

"We're predicting that we might be able to close this case in the next two days, but in order to do so, we need a confirmation of the serial killer's identity." Jenn dove into details about their plan. "So as you can see, we need to revive Ray's memory by breaking his trance for him to tell us who the hypnotist is, and Watch is the only one with enough knowledge and experience in hypnosis to pull this off before the party."

"I see," the general mumbled thoughtfully. Then the line went silent for a few moments before he spoke again. "Agent McKnight is at the Tiger's Nest in Paro Valley, Bhutan. He's guarding a national treasure at the temple. His cover is a Buddhist monk."

"Noted. Thanks for the info," Jenn said appreciatively. "There's one more request I'd like to make."

"State your request," he replied swiftly with a smiling tone.

"If it's not too much trouble, I'd like to request for a helicopter to meet us right outside Tirjuan tomorrow morning at six. Destination: Paro Valley." She stated her request clearly, waiting for his approval.

"Request approved," the general said without hesitation. Then his cheery tone dulled slightly. "How are your partners coping? Are they doing well?"

Jenn knew what his true concern was. "They're doing quite well, General," she reassured him. Then in a low voice, she added, "I'm sorry for your loss."

The general was momentarily silent after hearing her words. But he quickly recovered himself. "I'm guessing that everything has been sorted out between the both of you, then?"

"Yes," Jenn replied, keeping her voice neutral to avoid suspicions from the others behind her. "Everything's okay here."

"Well, that's good to know." There was a trace of wistfulness in his tone. "Thank you, Catherine. If it weren't for you, I would've lost Bennett forever."

She smiled. This time it felt genuine. "I could say the same to you."

He let out a chuckle. "I should be getting off the phone now. I have a meeting to attend."

Jenn could tell that it was a lie, but she pretended to believe him. The general needed some space right now. "Okay. Thank you for everything. Take care." Then she ended the call.

"We're going to the Himalayas?" J. Lee asked when she saw Jenn putting away her cell phone. Obviously, J. Lee had heard the mention of Paro Valley just now.

"Yes," Jenn said, plastering a half smile on her face as she turned around. "We're visiting the Tiger's Nest."

~

"This is awesome!" Ray shouted with a huge grin on his face.

"You should stop shouting or you'll be out of breath soon," J. Lee said. "The air at this altitude is quite thin, so try not to waste oxygen."

"But this is really incredible," Ray exclaimed, looking out the glass window.

"Fine," J. Lee replied with utter indifference. "Don't blame anyone when your face turns purple."

"Okay, you win," Ray muttered, pretending to pout as he settled down in his seat.

Jenn simply chuckled at the sight. Ray's puppy dog face was quite comical. She pitied her friend who was sitting between her and Ray. Ray could be quite hyped up when he was excited. As if to prove her point, within five minutes, he spoke again.

"Where are we headed to again?" he asked, his eyes glued to the scenery outside.

"The Tiger's Nest, also known as Paro Taktsang," J. Lee explained in a prompt manner. "It's a Himalayan Buddhist temple with more than three hundred years of history. So if you haven't finished expressing your enthusiasm, please do it here, not at the sacred site."

Ray sighed and nodded in mock annoyance. "Yes, ma'am. If it pleases you, I'll even scream my brains out."

"Better not do that," J. Lee muttered, totally unaffected by his joke. "We still need your brain to work in order to restore your memory."

In the front seat, Ben chuckled at both of them. Jenn shook her head at Ray's expression, amused. The helicopter stopped near the entrance of the temple in mid-air.

"This is our stop," Ben announced as he opened the door on his side. A gust of chilly wind blew hard into the helicopter, making them shiver. Then he jumped off the helicopter and landed on the roof lithely. His meticulous eyes scanned their surroundings for any signs of unwanted visitors before he gazed up to the others and shouted, "All clear. Next."

Ray gawked at the scene before him. "W-we're jumping?" he stuttered. "Onto a *roof*?"

"Don't worry. We're less than ten metres off the roof," Jenn said, trying to reassure him.

"Yeah," J. Lee said. "The roof won't be destroyed so easily anyway."

Ray let out a nervous chuckle. "It's not the roof that I'm worried about."

"Just jump already," J. Lee said from behind him, sounding rather impatient.

"Here goes nothing." Ray drew in a deep breath before jumping off the helicopter, trying to refrain from yelling his lungs out and failing miserably.

Ray's landing was clumsier than Ben's, but at least he didn't slip off the roof. Ben steadied Ray before gesturing for the girls to jump. Jenn let her friend jump first, and she turned to the pilot to give him directions about when to fetch them back to Tirjuan. Then she too jumped off the helicopter and landed lightly on her feet.

After making sure that everyone was okay after the jump, Ben led the others down the roof with a long rope he'd brought along. He climbed down the rope first, and J. Lee went next. When it came to Ray's turn, he froze once again. Jenn had to threaten to leave him alone on the roof in order to get him to start climbing the rope. With his stamina, Ray had no problem with the rope climbing part. But when his feet finally touched the ground, his legs suddenly became wobbly and he almost stumbled into J. Lee. After Jenn had gotten down from the roof, a monk came out to greet them warmly with his thick Asian accent.

"Greetings, young ones. I've been expecting you. Come."

Jenn trailed behind the monk, and the others followed suit. They were led into a small room which seemed to be a little prayer room. The monk quickly closed the door after they had all entered the room.

"Have a sit, young ones," the monk said politely as he moved towards a small table in a corner of the room and started pouring tea for them. "I've made some tea for you to warm yourselves. The weather is getting cold these days."

"Thank you very much for your hospitality," Ben said in a polite tone, stepping forward, "but we're here to see someone."

"You can drop the act now, Watch," Jenn interjected, smirking.

Ben blinked at Jenn. "He's Watch?" he asked in disbelief, pointing at the monk.

"Bennett Warner, don't you know that it's rude to point at a senior agent." Watch scolded, dropping his fake accent. "I'm almost the same age as your father, young man."

Ben apologised immediately, dropping his hand to his side.

"You are forgiven," Watch said with a pleased smile, hitting Ben lightly on the shoulder. Then he turned to Jenn with a huge grin. "My favourite girl," he announced with his arms wide open.

Jenn laughed gaily and gave him a huge hug. "It's been a while, Watch."

"Indeed, it has," he said as he released her. "Look at you. You've changed so much."

"I'm assuming that you two know each other?" Ben interrupted, looking rather stupefied at the situation before him.

"Yes, we do. I was the one who discovered her talent and talked her into joining the NSSS, Warner," Watch stated proudly. "Vibrant young lady, isn't she?"

"Now, now." Jenn put a hand on his shoulder. "Let's not get all fatherly right now, okay? We have pressing matters at hand."

"Ah, yes. Major General Warner did say that you needed my help with something," Watch said, looking around. "So how can I help you, Spidey? Don't be shy with me."

"Trust me, I won't." Jenn smiled wryly. "But let me introduce to you my friends first." She gestured for J. Lee to come forward. "This is Agent Leon."

"I'm Agent Justine Leon, detective from the Criminal Investigation Department." J. Lee introduced herself with a tone of respect in her voice. "Pleasure to meet you, sir."

Watch shook her hand, smiling at her. "Likewise."

Then Jenn gestured for Ray to come forward too. "And this is Ray Darce."

"Nice to meet you, sir." Ray stared at him nervously.

Watch gave him a short glance, cocking his head to one side. "He's the 'pressing matter at hand'," he stated with a small frown.

"Yes, he is," Jenn said, her tone turning serious.

Ben and J. Lee exchanged impressed looks. "That was fast," Ben murmured under his breath.

"Did you do this?" Watch asked Jenn, wearing a disapproving frown. "How many times have I told you? Hypnosis is—"

"Unethical and immoral unless it's for hypnotherapy," Jenn said dryly. "Yes, I do remember that. And no, this" – she gestured towards Ray – "wasn't me."

Watch turned back to Ray, scrutinising him. "Well then, the hypnotist is really skilled. He's in deep."

"Yes. I tried to lift the trance, but I can't figure out the trigger." Jenn sighed. "That's why I've come to you."

"Huh," Watch merely uttered, continuing to study Ray. "Sit down, Ray," he commanded, locking his gaze with his subject.

Watch was getting to work already. Seeing this, Jenn turned to the other two agents and gestured for them to sit down too. J. Lee shook her head, refusing to sit. She felt more comfortable standing anyway. Ben sat in one of the chairs at the side of the room and Jenn took the seat beside him.

"Did he just call you Spidey, like Spiderman?" Ben whispered to her, keeping his eyes on Watch and Ray.

"Yes. He's been calling me that ever since the day he discovered my so-called talent back in Tirjuan," she whispered back, her eyes glued to Watch. "At first, it didn't make sense to me, but after I joined the agency and got my code name, I figured it out."

Watch had already put Ray into a trance now. He stopped to think for a moment. Then he turned around. "Where is he from?" he asked Jenn in a low voice as a strange look came across his face.

"My hometown, Tirjuan," she replied swiftly. "Why?"

His thick eyebrows rose when he heard her reply. "What a coincidence," he muttered in an ironic tone before turning back to Ray. He snapped his fingers once in front of Ray as he said, "Wake."

Ray blinked a few times and glanced around. A mixture of bewilderment and surprise filled his face. "What on earth is this place?" he mumbled in a disoriented manner. Then his eyes went to the person standing in front of him. "And who are you, monk?"

"Your saviour," Watch said flatly before bringing his hands up to both sides of Ray's head and pressing his thumbs against Ray's temples. He applied just enough force at the intended spots, rendering Ray unconscious within seconds.

"Hey!" J. Lee called out, stepping forward to stop him.

"It's okay, J. Lee," Jenn said reassuringly as she stood up and walked towards Watch. "How did you do that?"

"I was just confirming a hunch," Watch said in a low voice, his expression grave. "I've taught my nephew about hypnosis before, but it was just for fun, so I taught him only one of my tricks, one of the oldest tricks in the book."

"Snapping fingers. Indeed, it never occurred to me when I tried to lift the trance," Jenn mused.

"You were never a big fan of the classics."

Jenn let out a dry laugh in response. "But why are you mentioning your nephew?" she asked, her tone becoming serious.

Watch closed his eyes and released a sigh. "He lives in Tirjuan."

"What?" Jenn stared at him in disbelief. "Are you serious about this?"

"Yes. You've never wondered why I visited Tirjuan when I met you for the first time, have you?" Watch asked, raising an eyebrow at her.

Jenn shook her head no. "I assumed that you had a case there."

"I was visiting my nephew," he simply replied.

Jenn lowered her gaze to the floor as she felt her heart drop. "I see." It seemed as if they might have found their serial killer.

Watch went forward and put his hand on her upper arm. "Do what you have to do," he said, giving her a rueful smile. "I don't care what kind of case you're investigating here. If you need to take him in, just do it."

"Okay. Thank you." She returned the smile. Then she inhaled deeply. "I'll keep you posted."

"No need for that," Watch muttered. "I'll find out for myself the next time I visit Tirjuan."

She nodded. Then she glanced at her watch to check the time. "Well, we should get going now. The helicopter will be back soon."

"So soon?" Watch asked, looking mildly disappointed. "You really trust my skills that much, huh?"

"You're my mentor. Of course I trust you," she said in a lighter tone. "Come on, guys." She turned to Ben and J. Lee. "Finish up your tea before we leave." Then she turned to Watch again and hugged him. "Take care," she whispered softly.

"Remember to send me an invitation to your wedding." Watch said teasingly as he let go of her, keeping his arm around her shoulder. "That Warner kid is like an open book when he's around you. Totally smitten," he whispered into her ear, chuckling.

"No, he's not," she objected. Jenn's eyes went to Ben and caught him glowering at Watch. Yep, he really was an open book. Watch was her mentor, for goodness' sake. What was there to be jealous about? When Ben saw her staring at him with a knowing look, he quickly averted his gaze and turned to Ray, pretending to study his unconscious friend. She felt her mouth twitched as she tried to suppress a smile. Such an open book, she thought.

"Smitten," Watch teased, laughing.

She shot him a witty smile and said to the others, "We're leaving now."

Watch pulled her in for another hug. "Go make me proud, Spidey. Stay sharp." Then he released her and went to open the door for them.

Ben and J. Lee went forward to help Ray up. Ben put Ray's left hand over his shoulder while J. Lee did the same on the other side of Ray. They thanked Watch as they dragged Ray's limp body out of the room. Jenn and Watch followed behind them until they had reached the front door of the temple. The helicopter was already there in mid-air waiting for them, and hanging from the helicopter were four long white ropes.

"How are we supposed to get him up there?" Ben shouted over the deafening whirring noise of the helicopter.

"Tie him with one of the ropes and pull him in after we've gotten into the chopper!" J. Lee shouted back, and they got to work immediately. Jenn went forward to help them hold Ray's body upright while they did all the tying.

"Why did we have to jump off the chopper when there are ropes available for us to use?" J. Lee asked as she strapped the rope around Ray's waist.

Ben tied a tight knot with the rope. "Who cares? It was fun."

When they were done with Ray, each of the agents tied the remaining ropes around their waists too.

"I call shotgun," J. Lee shouted before giving the pilot a hand signal to pull them up.

The ropes started lifting them off the ground, pulling them up. J. Lee got into the helicopter first, and she climbed into the front seat, settling down beside the pilot. Ben got in next and he helped Jenn into the helicopter. Then they quickly pulled Ray in too before closing the door with low grunts.

Ben placed Ray on the back seat, pulling his limp body into a sitting position. Ray's head knocked against the window, but the impact didn't wake him. Jenn sat near the other window as Ben positioned himself between her and Ray. The helicopter started moving, and she kept her eyes on Watch until he was out of sight.

Seventeen

"Why didn't you ask who the nephew is?" Ben asked at some point during their trip back to Tirjuan.

"We have Ray for that, remember?" Jenn replied in a low voice.

"Right," Ben responded. After a while, he spoke again, seeming rather embarrassed. "What did Watch say to you back at the temple before we left?" Ben asked her in a low whisper.

Jenn shot him a glance. He seemed to be so curious about it. "Watch said that you're like an open book to him," she whispered back in indifference, keeping her face straight.

Ben blinked. "I am not," he protested. Then his eyes became unsure. "Am I?"

Jenn let out a low chuckle. "Well, Watch thinks so."

"Why would he say that?" Ben muttered with a small frown, looking genuinely troubled. "Did he mean it in a bad way or in a good way?"

"I don't know." She shrugged, wearing an innocent smile. "But he did seem quite amused when he told me his impression of you."

Ben narrowed his eyes at her sceptically. "You're hiding something from me," he said in a low voice, just loud enough for her to hear him. "What else did he say?"

"About you?" she asked, stalling. She was enjoying this.

"There's more?" He raised his eyebrows at her. "Tell me everything."

She looked at him in amusement. "What makes you think that I'll do as you tell me to?"

Suddenly, Ben realised the game she was playing with him. His gaze turned playful as he rearranged his face into a serious look. "Don't tell me, then. Let me assume the worst."

Playing games now, were they? Jenn smirked inwardly. He wanted to play? Too bad. She was just thinking about ending the game. She leaned closer to his ear, exhaling a long breath. She felt his back stiffen, and she suppressed a laugh. "Watch said that you're totally smitten. He also told me to send him an invitation to our wedding," she whispered into his ear, sending a shiver down his spine. Then she backed away slowly to see his reaction.

The look on Ben's face was priceless. "W-wedding?" he stuttered, his face turning red. He visibly gulped as he stared ahead, clearly not sure how to respond to that.

Game over, Jenn thought. Then she finally grinned. "He was just joking, Ben."

Ben turned to look at her. His expression was a mixture of embarrassment and disbelief. "How can you take it so calmly?"

"I just told you. It's a joke." She gave him a weird look. "Why are you getting so worked up?"

"Nothing," Ben mumbled. Then he went silent, his expression unreadable as he stared ahead.

However, one look at Ben's withdrawn face and Jenn knew that he was actually considering the wedding thing. Jenn silently wished that she hadn't said anything to him at all. It was just a joke. She didn't want to put any weird ideas in his head, especially when they had a series of murder cases to solve right now.

Jenn released a silent sigh. She would have to leave it to Ben to sort out his own thoughts. Hopefully, he wouldn't get ahead of himself at a crucial moment like this. She still needed his mind for their game plan during tomorrow's party.

Moments later, the helicopter started to lower itself to the ground. They landed in a piece of rural land which was the exact same spot where they had taken off earlier that morning. As soon as the helicopter touched the ground, J. Lee opened the door and got out. Their car was still parked where they'd left it that morning, and J. Lee quickly unlocked the car for the others. Meanwhile, Jenn helped Ben bring Ray down from the helicopter; then they brought him over to the car.

"I'll drive," J. Lee offered as she swiftly got into the driver's seat.

Ben gestured for Jenn to take the passenger seat as he helped Ray into the back seat. When they were all in the car, J. Lee revved up the engine and drove back to the hotel. Ben kept Ray's face out of sight to avoid his being recognised by his friends on the streets. It was around noon, and the town was packed with the residents and some visitors. Within ten minutes, they reached the hotel and hurried to bring Ray back to the suite without attracting too much attention.

Once they were in the living area, Ray was placed on the couch while the others waited for him to regain consciousness.

It was almost five in the afternoon now, and Ben was getting tired of the long wait.

"How much longer will he be out?" Ben asked in exasperation, crossing his arms across his chest. He was sitting on the other couch with Jenn beside him.

"I'm not sure," Jenn murmured, keeping her eyes intently on Ray's unconscious figure. She was starting to get worried about him. What if Watch had put too much force on Ray's pressure points? Then she saw a twitch on his forehead.

J. Lee noticed that too. "Guys, he's back," she said, coming closer to the couch.

Ray stirred and let out a low moan. He brought both his hands up to his head and pressed his fingers against his temples, massaging them as he slowly opened his eyes. Seeing this, Ben leaned forward to get a better look at Ray while Jenn got up from her seat and went to help Ray up into a sitting position.

"How are you feeling, Ray?" Jenn asked gently as she sat down on the coffee table so that she was directly in front of him.

J. Lee automatically went into the kitchen and came back with a glass of water. "Here. Drink some water first before you start talking," she muttered, holding out the glass of water to him.

Ray stared at her, blinking. Then his blank eyes swung to Jenn and then to Ben. "Who are you people?" he asked, his expression wary yet befuddled. His gaze returned to Jenn, and recognition sparked in his eyes. "Wait, I know you." After a moment of hesitation, he added, "At least I think that I've seen you before."

"Jennifer Cole." Jenn said with a friendly smile. So her guess was right. Three years under the influence of hypnosis really did quite some damage on his mind.

Ray's wary expression dissolved into a puzzled look. "Jenn?" He cocked his head to one side, studying her carefully. "You look different … Aren't you supposed to be overseas right now?"

"I came back for my holidays," Jenn lied, keeping the smile on her face.

"Huh," Ray uttered, nodding whilst frowning. Then he brought his hand up to rub his forehead. "Ugh. My head feels fuzzy right now."

Jenn took this as an opportunity to slip in her partners' introductions. "Ray, these are my friends from school, Bennett Warner and Justine Leon." She introduced them briefly, giving her partners a pointed look.

Ben and J. Lee quickly caught up with her act and played along. They exchanged hellos with Ray and faded into the background, letting Jenn do the talking. They were currently all back to being strangers, except for Jenn, so it was only wise for her to do the digging.

"Where am I, anyway?" Ray mumbled as he glanced around the room, scratching his head.

"My place," Jenn replied, starting to make up a cover story for now. There was no time for her to explain about the real situation here, so a lie would just have to do the trick. "I invited you over, remember?"

Ray's forehead creased in confusion. "Did you?"

"Yes." She chuckled. "You fell asleep while watching the morning news. I didn't wake you up because you seemed tired after the morning run, so I just let you sleep through the afternoon. I think you've slept too long, Ray." She gave him a pat on the head to make her lie look real.

Ray blinked, trying to recall his memory of their event this morning, and shook his head slightly to rearrange his thoughts. "But I don't recall anything about a morning run. In fact, I remember myself in a helicopter with her," he mumbled, pointing at J. Lee. "Wait, all of you were there with me."

"You remember?" Jenn asked.

"Fragments," he muttered, frowning in concentration to recall the rest of his memory. "What's going on here?"

Jenn exhaled a long sigh. Lying to him wasn't going to work now. But she certainly couldn't afford to lose any more time on filling him in about what had happened to him over the years. His mind was practically stuck in the period of three years ago. "Okay, Ray. I need your full attention right now," she said in a serious tone, dropping her act.

"I'm listening," Ray said, looking at her nervously. He took in a deep breath to calm his inner turmoil.

"The truth is, I'm not back here for a holiday or anything. I am now a special agent from the National Security Secret Service. I'm here to investigate a series of murders in Tirjuan," she explained in a rush. "These two friends" – she gestured at Ben and J. Lee – "are my partners in this investigation. Now, I have a few questions for you regarding the case, so the rest of the story will have to wait. Bear with me, can you?"

Ray stared at her as if she had grown an extra head. He opened his mouth, only to shut it again when he couldn't think of something to say.

Jenn sighed and took out her badge. "Here's proof," she said, showing him the badge. "Now, just try to answer my questions without leaving out any details, okay?"

Ray gulped audibly and nodded.

"Good," Jenn said with a smile. "I want you to first tell me the last thing that you can remember most clearly before you woke up just now. Just close your eyes and let it flow."

Hesitantly, Ray shut his eyes and did as she told him to. He searched through the jumble of images in his head, looking for a memory that made sense to him.

"Don't push yourself too hard," Jenn said in a calm voice, watching his face closely.

Ray continued to sift through his memory – and voila! His eyes snapped open and met Jenn's immediately as the words started to spill out of his mouth.

"The last thing I remember was that I was with Nick in his car," Ray said in a hurry, stumbling over his words.

Hearing Nick's name, a slight frown appeared on Jenn's forehead, but she quickly smoothed it out. She nodded, encouraging Ray to go on.

"Nick was giving me a ride home from his house. Tom, Isabella, Paul, James, and I were at his house for dinner. It was sort of a gathering to remember Jules, you know."

"Why were you guys having a gathering to remember Jules?" Jenn asked, puzzled. Something didn't add up here.

"Um, if I'm not mistaken, it was because the next day was the first anniversary of Jules's death," Ray said, struggling to put his memory into words.

"Wait … Jules's *death*?" Jenn repeated, not believing her ears. She'd thought Jules had run away with her prince charming. How on earth did she end up dead?

"Oh, you didn't know?" Ray asked, blatantly surprised. "Jules committed suicide," he told her sadly, his expression solemn.

What? She committed suicide? Once again, Jenn was dumbfounded. "When did that happen?" she prodded, determined to learn what had happened.

"The day after you left, actually," Ray replied straight away, his head getting clearer now. "She hung herself in her room. Nick found her body the night she killed herself. Poor Nick. He was crushed. He locked himself in his house for more than a week after Jules's suicide."

"Did the police find out why she committed suicide?" Jenn pressed on.

"She left a letter on her bed before she killed herself," Ray answered. "In her letter, Jules confessed that she was cheating on Nick. She felt sorry for betraying his trust, so she hoped that her death would bring him peace. Shocking, isn't it?"

Jenn was silent as she listened to Ray's answer, her mind processing his words. So Jules didn't run away with the other guy that she liked. Instead, she killed herself out of guilt. When Nick knew that he had lost Jules, he went crazy and turned into a psychotic serial killer, seeking revenge by killing innocent girls. Jenn tried to summarise everything she could think of right now. Then she proceeded with her questions.

"Okay, now back to the car," Jenn said, recollecting her thoughts. "You said that you remember yourself with Nick in his car on the night of the gathering. Did you notice anything strange about him when he brought you back home?"

Ray thought about it for a while before answering the question. "I thought that he was managing himself quite well at the time. Of course, he tried to keep his mind off Jules by rambling about our friends and families, but I thought that it was normal for someone who was still grieving for the death of his girlfriend."

Something was definitely fishy about Nick now. Ray said that Nick was rambling, but knowing Nick, he wasn't quite the talker. In fact, he was an introvert to the extreme, so the fact that he rambled felt really off.

"Can you recall what he talked about in particular in the car?" Jenn asked, hoping to know how he had managed to put Ray under.

Ray gave her a bewildered look. "You want me to remember a random conversation I've had with him from …" He trailed off all of a sudden. "How long has it been since that night?"

Jenn hesitated. "Three and a half years, give or take," she replied warily, gauging his reaction.

Ray's eyes nearly bulged out of his sockets. "Three y-years …" he stuttered, trailing off again.

Jenn placed a hand on his elbow, comforting him. "It's okay. Take your time," she said soothingly. "Do you think that you can go on now?"

Ray took in a few deep breaths, forcing himself to accept the truth. Then he smiled at her grimly. "I can manage a few more questions."

"When was the last time you saw Jules before the suicide?" Jenn continued.

"Uh …" Ray touched a hand to his forehead, trying to remember. "The day before she died, during the last VCS meeting, I think. You were there too."

Jenn paused for a moment to think. Yes, she did attend a VCS meeting the day before she left Tirjuan. She also remembered that Jules had pulled her aside after the meeting and confessed about her falling for another guy, saying that she did not have feelings for Nick anymore. Then her train of thought came to a sudden halt.

"Uh, I'm sorry," she muttered to Ray before turning to J. Lee. "Hey, do you mind taking over for me here?" Jenn said distractedly, getting up from the coffee table.

"Sure," J. Lee said, stepping in to continue with the interview.

Heaving a deep breath, Jenn turned to Ben and gave him a look, hinting for him to follow her. Ben saw the look on her face, and his face turned alarmed. He followed her silently into the office, where she then spun around with a puzzled frown.

"Something's not right here," Jenn muttered in a low voice.

Ben let out a dry laugh. "Tell me about it," he said with a sigh. "I mean, if this really is about getting revenge or whatsoever, Nick Jefferson should be hunting down his girlfriend's secret lover, not a bunch of innocent young girls. And what's the girlfriend's name again?"

"Juliana Owens. Jules was just a nickname. But no, Nick's target is not what I'm talking about here," Jenn said. "I'm referring to the part where Jules committed suicide out of guilt." She spoke in a calm manner, concealing the fact that she was still shaken up after finding out that Jules was dead.

"Okay," Ben nodded, prompting Jenn to go on. "What about her?"

"So you heard what Ray said just now, right? That Jules hung herself because she felt guilty for cheating on Nick."

"Uh-huh." Ben nodded again, still not getting where this was going. "The girl was found dead in her bedroom, and there was a note left behind to explain why she had killed herself. I don't see what's weird about that. This kind of melodramatic scenes can be found all over the news lately."

Jenn had to stop herself from lashing out at him for talking about Jules in that kind of tone. "The girl used to be my friend, okay? Watch your tone."

"I'm just saying," Ben said to her in an innocent tone.

Jenn rolled her eyes at him. "My point is, I don't think that she committed suicide," she said, sounding quite confident about herself.

"Uh, mind explaining why?" Ben asked, giving her a confused look.

"Jules wasn't cheating on Nick," Jenn stated, crossing her arms in front of her chest as she leaned back against the conference table.

"And how do you know that?" Ben frowned, cocking his head to one side.

Jenn sighed. "Look, Jules and I used to be quite close. The day before she died, which was also the day before I left Tirjuan to join the NSSS, Jules confessed to me that she had no feelings for Nick anymore and that she liked another guy. Then she asked for my opinion about her situation, whether she should dump Nick and be with the guy that she liked or stay with Nick until the feeling faded away. She didn't mention anything about seeing the other guy while she was dating Nick, okay? So technically she didn't cheat on Nick."

Ben stared at her, trying his best to comprehend her words. "Maybe she conveniently left out that part?" he suggested.

"I'm sure that she didn't leave out anything," she said in disagreement. "Jules was saying that she wanted to be with the guy that she liked. I think that statement had made it quite clear that she wasn't seeing the guy yet."

"So you're saying that someone else killed her and made it look like she committed suicide?" Ben asked to confirm his hunch.

"Yes, and I think Nick did it," Jenn said grimly. "Nick killed her when she decided to break up with him."

"When you put it that way, it kind of made sense," Ben said thoughtfully, nodding. "Did you tell her to dump Nick?"

"No, I told her that she should follow her heart," she said glumly, sighing.

Ben made a face. "Seemed like her heart didn't guess that her boyfriend was a cold-blooded bastard," he muttered in an ironic tone.

"Nick isn't a cold-blooded bastard," Jenn argued, giving him a disapproving look.

Ben gave her a half smile. "Seven victims plus Juliana Owens's death says otherwise."

She exhaled sharply. "Okay, maybe Nick changed. But he wasn't like that before I left. He was a good guy."

Ben looked at her with a frown and sighed deeply. "Catherine, you have to let go of the past," he said calmly, bringing his hand up to hold her shoulder gently. "Maybe you're still subconsciously thinking that your friends are the same as they were before you left. You haven't been as sharp as you used to be, no offense. I think that the personal feelings you have for your friends are clouding your judgement."

Jenn bit on her lower lip, looking away from Ben's intense gaze. She could feel her mind refusing to accept what he had just said, regardless of how true she knew it was.

Ben called her name, pulling her gaze back to him. "Catherine, it's okay to make mistakes. I mean, who doesn't? No matter what talents or gifts you possess, you're still human. You said so yourself, remember?"

She stared at him for a moment before nodding. "Yeah, I guess you're right." She slowly dropped her eyes to the floor. "Can I have a moment to myself? I need to rearrange my thoughts."

"Sure." He smiled tightly. "Just don't stress yourself out, okay?" He gave her shoulder a gentle squeeze before heading out of the office.

Releasing a tired sigh, Jenn got off the table and took a seat in one of the chairs. Ben was right. She hadn't really let go of anything from her past. That was why she didn't manage to see through Nick at Eiry's Garden when she first arrived in town. It was time to have her mind reprogrammed now.

Feeling determined, she took out all the files of the murders and went through them again. This time she made sure that her judgement wasn't affected by her personal feelings.

When she was done, Jenn paid a visit to the local PD to get the case files on Jules's death. She went through every detail of the report and found several loose ends on Jules's case, which indicated that it was a homicide case. From what she saw, it was obvious that the case was wrapped up without thorough investigation. The agents in charge of Jules's case didn't put much effort into it before closing the case. So Jenn decided that her hunch about Jules's death was confirmed.

After she finished filling Agent Turner and his partner in on the progress so far, she headed back to the hotel. On her way back, she bumped into Nick and Tom in front of the hotel, which she considered quite strange. Tom seemed to be glad to see her, and he asked her if she knew about the party the following night. Meanwhile, Nick was wearing a friendly smile the whole time. Jenn kept her cool and saw through Nick's happy façade almost immediately.

Nick was pretending to be indifferent about the party, and she noticed the way his ears pricked when Tom brought up the topic. Since she was attending the party – for a different reason, of course – Jenn nodded at Tom and exchanged a few comments on the town and the weather while she kept her eyes on Nick. He seemed to be eager to leave when he noticed the way she was studying him, so Nick excused himself and Tom as smoothly as he could. Jenn found herself suppressing a smug look as she made her way back to her suite. Yep, she was definitely seeing things clearer now.

Later she had a small discussion with her partners while Ray sat in a corner in the office. They planned the operation for the birthday party, going over details about guarding Nick and keeping an eye on Kayla Brown. They still couldn't find a connection between Nick and Kayla Brown, but she remained the most possible target, so they would still be shadowing her at the party.

That night, as Jenn lay in her bed beside J. Lee, the thought of Jules's death kept swimming around in her mind. That was obviously the missing piece of the puzzle from the big picture of her investigation. But somehow she still felt that there was something that she didn't see. The connection between Kayla Brown and Nick was still unknown, and that was the vital part of the case right now. She was almost drifting into sleep when something finally clicked in her mind about the case.

That was it – the final piece to the puzzle.

She had figured it all out, the entire case. And now all she could think about was how blinded she had been all this while.

Eighteen

The next morning, Ben woke up with a start and saw Ray sitting at the corner of the bed, already awake. Ray was staring out the window, hugging his knees tightly to his chest. He seemed to be in deep thought, as his eyes were unmoving, as if fixated on a distant object, and his expression was blank.

Last night, when he filled Ray in about the case, the hypnosis, Ray seemed more than stunned to hear that he was under the influence of hypnosis for over three years. Perhaps his mind was still on the whole hypnosis thing, Ben guessed.

"Why are you up so early today?" Ben mumbled groggily, sitting up too.

Ray didn't seem to hear Ben; he just remained silent and stared ahead. Ben blinked sleepily and moved closer to Ray. He gave Ray a nudge on his shoulder, calling his name. Ray jumped, startled by the sudden contact. He quickly snapped his head around, looking alarmed.

When he saw Ben behind him, his tensed expression relaxed into a friendly smile. "Oh, you're awake," he said, changing his position so that his body was facing Ben.

"What were you thinking about?" Ben asked, stretching his body lazily as he let out a yawn.

Ray raised his eyebrows. "Oh, it's nothing," he muttered, waving a hand in dismissal. "Just some random musings. That's all."

"You worried about tonight?" Ben asked, seeing straight through Ray's lie.

Ray gave him a surprised look. "Yeah," he admitted, smiling sheepishly.

"Don't worry about it," Ben muttered, getting off the bed. "You'll be staying here during the party. No harm will come to you."

"That's not what I'm worried about," Ray mumbled, frowning to himself. "It's Jenn that I'm worried about."

Ben's eyebrows rose at the mention of her name. "Mind explaining that?" he said over his shoulder, walking into the bathroom to wash up.

"Well," Ray said, raising his voice slightly so that Ben could hear him from inside the bathroom, "I don't know about now, but Jenn used to trust Nick very much. She sees him differently than how the others see him." He paused for a moment before going on. "Tom, Isabella, Paul, James, and I think that Nick is someone who is extremely sensitive in his personal relationships – and he was totally obsessed with Jules."

Ben's ears pricked at the mention of Jules. Nick was obsessed with his ex? Huh, Catherine had never said anything about that to him. He kept his expression curious, hiding a look of surprise from Ray.

"As for Jenn, she sees him as someone who is socially challenged and an introvert. She's kind of a natural when it comes to socialising and communicating her thoughts, so she pities him for his lack of ability to express himself effectively. She also made it quite clear that she thought that he was a softie with everyone. With Jules being her best friend and everything, she thought that they were the perfect couple and that Jules brought out the best in him." Ray smiled wryly at his own words. "I suppose that's why she never put her guard up with Nick, why she trusted him so much."

So she used to have a misconception about Nick. That actually explained a lot, Ben thought. That was why she didn't suspect Nick at all about the murders. She thought that he wasn't capable of doing such a thing. But things had changed now. Last night he observed the way she handled the discussion, and he was extremely sure that Catherine was back on track.

"You know what?" Ben said as he leisurely walked out of the bathroom. "I think that Jenn can handle him now. She's no longer stuck on her previous impressions of her past associates in Tirjuan."

"You think so?" Ray asked, meeting his eyes.

"Of course." Ben replied. He stood by the bed, smirking. "She's one of the top agents in the NSSS."

Ray nodded. "What about you?"

"It's sort of different in my case." Ben hesitated. "I've been trained to be an agent since I was young. Catherine is a natural, plus she has a rare talent of her own."

"You make it sound like she's the best," Ray said, watching him curiously.

"She is," Ben stated proudly. "That's what everyone in the agency thinks anyway. I'm not ashamed to admit that I think so too."

Ray suddenly burst out laughing. "Dude, you're so whipped!"

Ben quickly hushed him, trying not to laugh at himself too for being so obvious. "Keep your voice down, man." Then he walked out of the bedroom and into the kitchen to get some water.

Jenn was already in the dining room sipping her coffee when Ben came out of his room. He got a glass of water from the kitchen and went to the dining table to join her.

"You're up early," Ben said as he sat down next to her.

Jenn kept her eyes on her coffee. "I didn't really get much sleep last night," she muttered, leaning her elbows against the table.

"Nervous?" Ben asked half-jokingly, putting a hand on her lap.

She stiffened at his touch, but then her body relaxed again. "I guess so." She sighed.

Ben studied her closely, his hand caressing her lightly through the tight denim jeans. She seemed to be acting kind of weird today, Ben observed. Maybe she was still trying to cope with the fact that one of her most trusted friends was now a serial killer. It must be hard for her, no matter how professional she was.

"What's on your mind?" Ben asked as he downed his glass of water. He saw her hesitating for a moment before answering him.

"We don't have anything to pin him down," Jenn said with an edge to her voice.

So that was what she was worrying about, that they had nothing to prove that Nick Jefferson was responsible for the murders of the seven girls plus Juliana Owens's death. Ben looked at her, sighing deeply. "Well, that's why we're counting on catching Nick Jefferson red-handed tonight. That way we can make him confess for all the other murders he committed."

Jenn finally turned to meet his gaze. "Have it ever occurred to you that Kayla Brown might not be Nick's target?" she asked in a quiet voice.

"Look, I know that we still haven't found any connection between Nick Jefferson and Kayla Brown. But she's the best shot we've got," Ben said calmly. He could see that Jenn was worrying too much. "You know, maybe there's still more to this case. Maybe there's another secret inside this big secret – something we haven't yet managed to discover. That's why we can't find a connection between them."

Jenn let out a quiet sigh and turned her gaze back to her drink. "You're right. Maybe something happened between Nick and Kayla Brown while I was gone. That's why I can't find the connection between the both of them."

But her voice sounded detached, and Ben was starting to get unsettled by the way Jenn was acting right now. He could feel that her mind was still reeling but she was shutting him out – something she would do when she thought that it was pointless to argue over a matter anymore.

"Catherine, some things are better left unexplained for now. When we take Nick Jefferson down, he will reveal the truth about Kayla Brown himself," Ben advised, bringing his hand up to her shoulder to give it a gentle squeeze. "The main thing is that we will take him down before he can hurt her. So stop thinking too much, okay?"

"Okay," Jenn mumbled, getting up from her seat. She plastered a lazy smile on her face, turning back to face him. "Let's just focus on the party, then," she added in a lighter tone, walking into her bedroom.

Ben stared after her retreating figure, pursing his lips into a thin line. He couldn't help but feel troubled about tonight. She would need her full attention on the operation later. If she couldn't take her mind off these details, she might accidentally arouse the killer suspicions, especially when she was assigned to stick by the killer throughout the party to monitor his movements. Even if Nick Jefferson didn't know her true identity, it would still raise suspicions if she slipped up on her cover.

~

After having breakfast, Jenn and J. Lee went to the mall at approximately ten in the morning. They went out to get their dresses and shoes for the party that night since none of them had brought along anything appropriate for an occasion like this. Meanwhile, Ben stayed behind to watch over Ray because he did bring along semiformal attire for the case.

The girls came back to the hotel at around three in the afternoon. Then the agents started checking each of their weapons, making sure their guns were loaded and ready to be used during the operation. After that, they started getting ready for the party.

Ben was done within half an hour since all he needed to do was throw on a white dress shirt and a pair of slacks. He decided not to wear a tie, considering that it would be too much for a small-town party. After all, he needed to fit in the crowd, not to stand out and attract the killer's attention.

As for the girls, they took a longer time to get ready because they still needed to do their hair and make-up after getting into their dresses. Jenn got herself a light blue chiffon dress. She applied her make-up lightly so that it matched the simple dress she was wearing. Then she put on a silver teardrop necklace to accentuate the dress. To finish her look, she tied her hair up into a tight ponytail, giving herself a neat appearance. On the other hand, J. Lee was wearing a black long-sleeved minidress. Her make-up was heavier, and she wore her light brown hair loose, going for a sharper look.

At five, they gathered in the office for their final walk-through of the operation. The overall plan was that Ben would be watching the target from afar, the suspect would be shadowed by Jenn and J. Lee would be observing the entire party for any suspicious movements from the crowd.

Ben and J. Lee would be posing as a couple so it would be easier for them to communicate during the party. As for Jenn, she would have to keep her distance to avoid suspicions. They wouldn't be using any gadgets on this operation so they would be solely using non-verbal communication with Jenn, which of course wouldn't be a problem for her.

During the walk-through, Ben watched Jenn from a corner of his eye. It seemed that Jenn was doing just fine now. He couldn't be sure if she was just acting or not. After all, she could be a damn good actress when she wanted to be.

When they were finally all prepped up and ready to leave for the party, Jenn gave Ray strict instructions that he was not to answer any phone call unless it was from her or the other two agents. Also, for his own safety, he should not leave the suite at any cost. Then Jenn went off first in a taxi, followed by Ben and J. Lee, who left a few minutes after her in the rented black sedan.

On their way to the mayor's house, J. Lee suddenly spoke. "I think that something's going on inside her head."

Ben knew immediately that she was referring to Jenn. "Well, you're not the only one who thinks so," he replied.

"She's hiding something from us," J. Lee stated flatly.

Ben laughed wryly, but he was secretly amazed at his blunt partner for being so observant about Jenn. "Do you any idea what she's hiding?"

"No," she simply replied, expressionless.

At this point, Ben was already used to her lack of emotion and bluntness. He just sighed. "Me neither."

The party had already started when Ben and J. Lee arrived. The first thing that they did when they stepped foot onto the huge lawn in front of the house was locate their partner, the suspect, and the target. Ben scanned the crowd and found Jenn having a conversation with her friends near a massive potted plant in one corner of the lawn. One of them was Tom Gallner. He recognised Tom from the photo of the list of suspects. He also saw Nick Jefferson among her group of friends.

Meanwhile, J. Lee saw Kayla Brown near the front door of the house, welcoming her guests with a friendly smile. She quickly gave Ben a nudge in the ribs and pointed in the target's direction. Ben got her message and gave her a slight nod. The fake couple started moving towards the target, stopping a few feet away from the birthday girl.

Jenn caught sight of her partners, and she exchanged glances with them to acknowledge their presence before going back to watching Nick discreetly. He was standing beside Tom with a stiff smile, his trademark expression for the night. More and more people were joining their little group, but Nick made no move to socialise other than exchanging a few hellos with them.

It was almost eight now, and the mayor's son clinked on his wine glass with a teaspoon to get everyone's attention. He led his girlfriend towards a table with a huge birthday cake on it, and the guests started singing "Happy Birthday" to Kayla Brown. The birthday girl actually shed a few tears as she made a wish before blowing out the candles.

Seeing this, J. Lee rolled her eyes and muttered under her breath, "Drama queen." This earned her an amused chuckle from Ben, who was also shaking his head at the birthday girl.

By midnight, the party was in full swing. There were kids and youngsters dancing wildly inside the house, while the older town folks remained outside on the lawn, chatting and sipping their champagne. Fortunately, Nick Jefferson and Kayla Brown didn't enter the house at all during the party so the team didn't have to split up.

While he shadowed the target, Ben threw a few occasional glances in the suspect's direction and noticed something weird – Nick Jefferson had never looked at Kayla Brown since the party had started, not even once. This struck Ben as odd. He was about to point this out, but J. Lee beat him to it.

"Did you notice that the suspect hasn't given his target a single glance throughout the whole evening?" she muttered in a low voice.

"Yes." Ben nodded. "It could be that either Nick Jefferson was a killer actor or his target wasn't Kayla Brown at all." Just then, Jenn's question from this morning flashed through his mind. She had asked him whether or not it had occurred to him that Kayla Brown might not be Nick Jefferson's target. At that time, he had fully disagreed that it was possible, but now he wasn't so sure.

J. Lee continued with her observation. "Nick Jefferson seemed to be staring at Spider a lot. I'm starting to wonder if he had a thing against her dress or …" She trailed off, her expression turning dark the slightest bit as something clicked inside her head.

"Or she was his person of interest." As Ben finished off her sentence, he felt his heart sink, realising the truth. "Catherine is the target," he blurted out as his eyes widened in panic and his face grew pale.

Seeing the look on his face, J. Lee pulled Ben to the farthest corner of the lawn and away from the crowd, where no one would notice them. She took hold of his shoulders and shook him, trying to get him out of his shock.

"What do we do now? What do we *do*?" Ben muttered, his eyes running wild.

"You're the planner. You tell me," she said with a frown. "But how is this possible? How could it be that she became his target in the first place?"

Ben swallowed hard, trying get hold of his unruly thoughts. He breathed in deeply, reanalysing everything as fast as he could. Then suddenly things started to make sense to him. "Catherine said that Nick Jefferson's ex, Juliana Owens, didn't cheat on Jefferson. Owens confessed that she fell for another guy, so she was thinking about dumping Jefferson so that she could be with the other guy," Ben said in a rush, explaining his theory as quickly as he could manage. "The day before Owens died, she asked for Catherine's opinion about dumping Jefferson.

"Catherine told her to follow her heart, so she did," Ben continued. "Owens decided to break up with Jefferson the next day. She must have let Catherine's name slip during their breakup. Jefferson was obsessed with Owens, so he couldn't accept the breakup. He ended up killing Owens in a jealous rage, and he then covered up his tracks by staging her suicide act."

J. Lee listened intently to his explanation as her expression became grave.

Ben paused to take a quick breath. "So now Jefferson misunderstood that Catherine pushed Owens to break up with him, and he blames Catherine for Owens's death. All those girls he had murdered before this were merely substitutes for the real target. When Catherine came back, Gina Lee was killed shortly after her return as a warning. He was expecting the murder to be reported on the news and to frighten her a little before he came for her. The hair colours matched Catherine's perfectly." He ended with a look of horror, feeling the air being sucked out of him.

So when he and Jenn went to the crime scene where Gina Lee was murdered, he had thoughtlessly said that Catherine could be the target because of the change in the choice of victim, and Ben had actually been right about it.

J. Lee snapped her head back in the direction of the crowd. "Where's Spider?"

Oh no! They had totally forgotten about her shadowing the killer at the moment. Dread filled his chest as he hurried back to the crowd, searching for Jenn. She wasn't anywhere within sight. Not giving up hope, he said to J. Lee, "You look inside the house. I'll search the backyard."

J. Lee gave him a curt nod and disappeared into the crowd, moving towards the house. Ben went to the backyard and scanned his surroundings. There was still no sign of her. A few seconds later, J. Lee appeared in the backyard to meet up with him, her expression grave.

"She's gone," J. Lee muttered. Her usual emotionless voice shook slightly, betraying her worry for her friend. "He's taken her."

Nineteen

"Car," Ben managed to utter before they started darting out of the backyard and back to the black sedan that was parked right behind to the mayor's house. Ben got to the car first, and he slid into the driver's seat, starting the engine as J. Lee got into the passenger seat before slamming the door shut.

"Search for an abandoned building around this area," he commanded, his hands clenching tightly to the steering wheel as he started driving. "A warehouse, an old factory, a cabin – anything that would work for the killer."

J. Lee typed furiously into a specialised GPS she had brought along. A moment later, she frowned when the results were shown. "There are only two abandoned sites in this area, but the nearest would also take about fifteen minutes to reach by car."

"Just let me see the damn thing," Ben snapped.

"Here." J. Lee placed the GPS on the dashboard. Ben immediately stepped harder on the gas, and the car picked up speed.

"Sorry," Ben apologised after a few moments of silence, staring ahead. His expression was still bleak, but his voice was composed now. "I didn't mean to snap at you."

"I know," J. Lee muttered.

Ben drove on, revving the engine. He was driving way past the speed limit, but he didn't care, and from the looks of it, neither did J. Lee. Both of them were consumed in each their own thoughts, leaving an atmosphere of tense stillness hanging in the car as they watched the scenery outside zooming past the car windows in blurred movements.

Then J. Lee spoke again. "Knowing her, Spider would have seen through Nick Jefferson's game and sent us a signal. It's hard to believe that he managed to abduct her just like that. I can't even imagine how Jefferson could have lured her out of the party without raising suspicions."

A cold, scornful laugh escaped Ben's lips. "My guess is that she had gotten everything figured out already before the party," Ben said through clenched teeth. "She *let* herself get abducted. She must think that she could deal with him on her own and make him turn himself in."

"Stupid," J. Lee uttered in an irritated tone.

Ben gave her a sideways glance, momentarily distracted by her typical reaction. If things weren't so urgent now, Ben would have laughed at that.

"There's the warehouse," J. Lee said suddenly, pointing at the building ahead of them.

Ben parked the car randomly and turned off the engine. Then they got out of the car and took out their guns, taking slow careful steps towards the old-looking warehouse. Ben peeked inside through one of the broken windows and saw that it was empty.

"Why do you even bother?" J. Lee asked from behind him. "We don't even see his car here. Of course they're not in there."

"Just being thorough," Ben muttered as they ran back to the car and headed towards the next destination.

Unfortunately, when they reached the second location, Nick Jefferson and Jenn were still nowhere to be found. Ben was getting more and more anxious as they drove around town in circles, trying to figure where Nick Jefferson would bring Jenn.

"Go to his house," J. Lee suggested suddenly, turning to give her partner a confident nod. "He's not planning to get away with this. He would have known that his friends must have noticed that he and Spider are missing from the party now. If Jefferson didn't care about covering his tracks, he certainly doesn't care about being caught." As she explained this in a swift manner, she was searching for Nick Jefferson's house address on her GPS.

When she found it, she placed the device back onto the dashboard. Ben started driving to the destination straight away, glancing at his watch. It had been almost an hour since they'd left the party to search for Jenn. Apprehensively, he increased his speed, praying silently that he would get to her before it was too late.

Jenn stirred, feeling her heavy, foggy mind drifting in and out of awareness. She knew that she must have been unconscious for quite some time now. She noticed that there was a weird noise echoing in her surroundings. Judging by the intensity of the sound and its faint echo, she guessed that she was in an enclosed little room.

She tried to open her eyes, only to realise that she had been blindfolded when she saw nothing but pitch-black darkness everywhere. Then she squirmed slightly, causing her delicate skin to flinch in pain as her wrists rubbed against the ropes around them. The ropes were so tied so tightly that she felt her blood circulation had been mostly cut off. Her hands felt numb, her fingers cold and stiff due to the diminished blood supply.

Jenn focused her attention back to the weird noise that was moving nearer to her. It sounded quite familiar actually, almost like a ... It was the sound of someone sharpening a knife, she realised, finally recognising the noise.

So this was the eerie atmosphere Nick created during his previous murders. He certainly knew what to do, she gave him that much. A low chuckle echoed through her ears, and Jenn had to stop herself from laughing aloud. Now that was way too much.

"Jennifer." Nick's gentle voice spoke suddenly as he continued sharpening the knife.

She kept her expression blank, suppressing a sneer that was making its way up to her face. "Nick," she replied, mirroring his tone.

"Yes, it's me," he replied in a smiling voice.

"Why am I here?" Jenn asked, feigning curiosity. She could have added some fear into her voice but she didn't want him to have the satisfaction of even thinking that he had managed to get to her. Well, she did have quite an ego after all, so she wouldn't show weakness in front of her enemy, not even the slightest bit.

Nick chuckled lightly. "Wrong question, dear." He said smoothly, obviously trying to intimidate her.

Jenn felt like gagging when she heard the gentle tone he was using. "Look, I already know what you have planned for me," she said with a sigh, showing him that his feeble attempt of intimidating her wasn't working at all. "So why don't you tell me why I'm here already?"

He scoffed in disbelief. "You're not afraid of anything at all, are you? You still think that you have the upper hand here, huh?" he said tauntingly. "Well, I'll show you who the boss is here."

She felt something grazing against her wrist despite the ever-increasing numbness in her hands. It must be the knife sharpener, she thought, making a smart guess. Then she heard the sound of liquid dripping on the floor. It was meant to make her think that her wrist had been cut and that her blood was dripping onto the cement floor. But unfortunately for him, she already knew all the secrets to his trick; it wasn't going to do much harm to her.

Jenn laughed. "I know what you're playing here, Nick." She couldn't resist the urge to smirk. "Why don't you save yourself from looking like a fool and take off my blindfold?" She heard him grinding his teeth together in frustration, and she knew that he was speechless by now. So she continued to speak. "You didn't really cut my wrist. You just made me feel like you did, and then you let me hear some dripping sound to trick me into thinking that my life was over, that my life was slipping away through my fingers ..." She heaved a sigh, shaking her head. "Not going to work on me."

The blindfold was pulled off her head, quite roughly she might add. Her eyes scanned her surroundings swiftly, and she realised that Nick had brought her to his house. She had been to his house before, so she knew clearly that they were in his basement right now. However, the pictures of Jules that filled the walls showed that Nick had done some redecorating for his act tonight.

Nick's face came into view, and he didn't look very thrilled after hearing her unravel his secret just now. "You always think that you know it all," he spat, sneering. "Too bad. This time you don't even know what you did wrong."

"This is about Jules," she stated, proving him wrong. She gave him a humourless smile. "Ray told me."

Nick barked a laugh. "That idiot," he muttered in irritation under his breath.

"Yeah, he was an idiot," she agreed, causing him to give her a look of absurdity. "He was a fool for letting himself be hypnotised by you."

Nick laughed dryly. "So you know about that too. What else do you know?" he asked, challenging her as he leaned his back against the wall with a scowl on his face.

"Everything," she said in a relaxed tone. "I know that you are responsible for the seven girls' deaths. I can even list their names if you don't believe me. The first was Anna Shaw, followed by Rachel Clark, and then it was Leigh Burnham, Vanessa Reece, Jane Lowry, Sharon Dylan, and lastly, Gina Lee. The fragrance on the card, vanilla peppermint, was the scent of the Jules' favourite fragrance mist. The dates you chose for those murders were the beginning and the end of your relationship with Jules. August first: the day you started dating her. May fifth: her death."

"Impressive." He smiled darkly. "You did some homework."

"I certainly did," she said, smiling. "I also know that Jules was murdered by you too."

His cold smile morphed into a condescending sneer. "It was your fault!" he hissed through clenched teeth, narrowing his eyes into slits. "If you didn't convince her to break up with me, she wouldn't even have to die."

Jenn laughed coldly. "She never had to. You could've just let her go."

"And let the bastard have her to himself? No, no, no, I don't think so." He chuckled cruelly, shaking his head. "Jules was *mine*. If I couldn't have her, no one else could." Nick wore a most gruesome smile, as if he really believed his own words. "She loved me. If it weren't for the bastard who seduced her away from me, we would be having a happy family by now."

"You're delusional," Jenn mocked, unable to hide the horror and disbelief in her tone. "You hypnotised her into falling for you ... and you call that love?" she said in a disgusted voice. When she saw the look on his face, she added, "Don't look so surprised. It wasn't really hard to figure that out after learning about Ray being hypnotised by you. A simple art of deduction would have done the trick.

"Jules had a certain look on her face when she started being with you. At that time, I didn't think much of it. I thought that it was the look of a girl in *love*." Jenn's voice turned derisive at the last word. "But when I learned that Ray was under hypnosis and remembered that same peculiar look on his face, it all became clear to me."

"H-how could you ...?" Nick stared at her, uncomprehending and hardly believing his ears. "Who are you?"

"Do you remember an uncle of yours who taught you about hypnosis?" Jenn asked suggestively with a ghost of a smile. "He's my mentor."

"What?" he blurted out, breathless and shocked. "You know Uncle Steve?" Then a wary expression appeared on his face. "You ... You're an agent too?"

Jenn was surprised to know that Watch had told his nephew about his identity as an NSSS agent, but she kept her face composed and calm. "Yes," she said smoothly, revealing the truth. "I'm Special Agent Catherine Nelson."

Nick's face paled. "Jumping Spider?"

Again, he surprised Jenn. Watch told Nick about her, she realised. Wow, he must be really proud of her, she thought as she mentally shook her head. She wondered what Nick knew about Jumping Spider. "Yes, I am," she said, keeping her voice as cool as possible.

Nick got over his shock quite fast after that. His face twisted into a sneer again. "Well, well, well." He put on an evil grin. "What a pleasant surprise. I never thought that killing you would be so interesting and exciting."

Nick masked his emotions well, but Jenn caught the tiniest bit of wavering in his eyes and smiled mirthlessly. "Really? Because I'm starting to get bored here," she drawled, wearing an indifferent look. Nick bared his teeth as his eyes sparked with determination. But before he could counter her words with a snide remark, Jenn continued smoothly, saying, "So you're thinking that you can still end me psychologically and physically. Enlighten me, please. How are you planning to do that?"

"Don't think that I don't know where you're going with this," Nick retorted, chuckling lowly. "You're trying to make me doubt myself about what I'm planning to do with you."

"Am I succeeding?" Jenn asked, her voice unruffled.

"No," Nick growled, clearly getting upset at her calm exterior.

"Really?" she said, looking at him with an amused expression. "Because I doubt that you have anything planned for me at all. You know, after I revealed your huge secret about that little trick of yours."

"Well, you're wrong." He laughed mockingly, but there a hint of nervousness in his tone.

She merely shrugged, giving him a knowing look. "If you've known my true identity now as Jumping Spider, you would've guessed how much better I am at playing mind games with people. And you're really willing to risk your sanity to play with me?" She pretended to laugh at the thought. "Well, I don't mind sitting here watching you go round and round about how you're going to end me and all that crap, but can you really handle that?" She forced her gaze on his, her face turning expressionless.

Nick's eyes hardened at her taunting words. "I can see what you're doing, you know. I can see it very clearly."

"Huh." She gave him an unimpressed look. "Well then, I wonder if you can see yourself clearly." She kept her tone relaxed, maintaining eye contact. "I wonder if you can see how out of control your brilliant plan has gone, how desperate you've become, how disappointed Jules would be to see you right now."

"Oh, you're psychic now?" Nick's calm voice had started to tremble slightly. He took a long breath, making an effort to calm himself. "You won't do yourself any good by bringing up Jules right now. Your pathetic attempt to rile me up isn't going to make me end you any sooner. I'm going to make sure that you suffer a slow, painful death."

Jenn let out a jeering chuckle. "You think I'm mentioning Jules to infuriate you?" She sighed. "No, I was just trying to test you to see if you really do love her. Turns out I'm wrong. You don't love her at all. Because when you love someone, you would show traces of grief or guilt in your eyes at the mention of your loved one. You showed none."

"You can't be more wrong," he stated, narrowing his eyes. He clutched his knife tighter in his hands, trying to keep his emotion in check. "I loved her, and I still do right now. If you're Jumping Spider, you would have known that right from the beginning."

"You call this love?" she asked in a flat voice. "Killing her when she didn't love you back anymore and then sacrificing innocent young girls in the name of vengeance, putting the blame on me because you lost your grip on her mind. That's love?"

He scoffed. "Don't you see? I was willing to sacrifice everything I have for her – my time, my job, my future, everything. You don't call that love?"

"No." She shook her head with a serious look on her face. It seemed as if her friend was in this deeper than she had thought. "I call that madness. You're so consumed with the idea of her being your possession. You're obsessed, and she was starting to think that too. That was why she broke through the trance. She couldn't take it anymore, and her subconscious wouldn't allow her to be tied up against her will. That was why it was becoming harder for you to plant suggestions in her mind. She had subconsciously shut you out."

"No, no, no," Nick repeated to himself, shaking his head with a frown. "No, that's not right."

However, Jenn took this as a sign of weakness from him and pushed on. "So actually, your obsession with Jules was the cause of her pushing you away. To tell you the truth, I didn't encourage her to break up with you when she asked for my opinion."

Nick's eyes snapped to her, and he gave her a look of confusion. "What? Then what did you say to her?" he asked, putting on a look of wariness.

A corner of her lips rose slightly as she saw that he had taken the bait. "I simply told her to follow her heart, and she made her own decision after that. She might have mentioned my name during the breakup, but she didn't really say that I encouraged her to end the relationship. Try to remember. You'll remember that she didn't say that. Go on. Recall what happened that night."

"Shut up!" He was definitely worked up now. "Shut up, okay? Stop trying to put those awful memories inside my head." His grip on the knife became even tighter as his fist turned white. "If you don't shut your mouth right now—"

"Those awful memories were all caused by *you!*" Jenn continued, ignoring his comeback. "*You* killed the girl whom *you* claimed to have loved, because *you* were pushing her way too hard. So now *you* have no one to blame for her death but *yourself!*" She spat. "You want vengeance? No problem. Just stick that knife through your heart and all is solved! Go ahead! Kill yourself if you want to. I don't care."

Nick found no words to refute her. Suddenly, he seemed lost and helpless. His eyes fell to the knife in his hands. They were filled with guilt and grief which Jenn had never dreamt of seeing in him. Well, at least he still had a teensy bit of conscience in him.

Jenn feigned a sneer before she continued. "You want to proclaim about your undying love for Jules? Go ahead then, if you dare. Just don't pull any other innocent young girls into this mess you caused." She pretended to pause for a moment to take a deep breath, rearranging her expression into a calm mask. She waited for her words to sink in his head before continuing. "You know, you might have gotten her to like you – and I do mean genuinely like you – if you haven't been too wrapped up with the idea of having her to yourself."

His face rose as he stared at her with a desperate look. She could see in his eyes that he really wanted what she had said to be true. "You believe that?" he asked, barely a whisper.

"Yes, I do," she lied, smiling gently. "You were loyal, gentle, loving to her. That was exactly what Jules was looking for in a guy. If only you had been patient with her and given her some space ..." She trailed off with a sigh.

"If only," Nick mumbled, staring down at the knife in his hand once again.

"Yes, if only," Jenn whispered, luring him into her voice. "But it's too late for that now. All you can do to make it up to her is show remorse for what you've done, prove that you're worth her forgiveness ... and love."

"Yes," he murmured, glancing at the knife with new hope. "I'm worth her love. I will prove to her that I'm worth it." Holding the knife tightly, he touched its sharp blade with his other hand, caressing his wrist lightly. "She will take me back."

"She will take you back," Jenn repeated in a low voice, serene and smooth. "All you have to do is show remorse for what you did. Apologise for all the lives that you've taken so that the seven girls you killed may rest in peace. Then you do whatever you need to do to get Jules to take you back."

"Jules ..." Nick said with a slight tremor of wistfulness in his voice, staring down at the knife. "Wait for me ..."

Twenty

Nick brought the knife to his wrist, and Jenn widened her eyes. He was really going to do it. But before he could touch the blade to his skin, the door burst open.

"Police! Put your hands where I can see them!"

Nick's head snapped up, his face morphing into a furious mask. "Lying bitch!" he sneered, moving swiftly behind the chair that Jenn was tied in. He lowered his body behind her, using her as a shield. He grabbed her shoulder roughly, his nails digging into her bare skin. She flinched, biting back a gasp. Jenn moved her gaze to the door and saw her partners. Ben and J. Lee were both pointing their pistols at her, trying to get a clear aim at Nick, who was hiding behind her.

J. Lee spoke in a firm and calm voice. "Nick Jefferson, this place is surrounded by our men. You have nowhere to escape. Do yourself a favour. Put down your weapon and release the hostage."

Nick laughed derisively. He brought his lips near Jenn's ear and whispered, "You've got everything planned out so well, Jumping Spider, except for the part where you're still trapped to this chair and I have the weapon. I win." Then he plunged the knife into her stomach.

Jenn's breath seemed to be knocked out of her as a strangled scream escaped her mouth. Behind her, Nick was chortling insanely. Then he pushed the knife deeper into her, twisting it violently and cruelly. Jenn's face contorted in agony, gasping. She couldn't manage a scream this time.

In front of her, Ben was shouting at J. Lee to arrest Nick while rushing towards her. Then she felt Nick's hands releasing both the knife and her shoulder as she heard him being tackled to the ground with a grunt.

Black spots started clouding her vision. Sirens of police cars outside the house echoed in her ears, but the sound slowly started fading as she felt her body going limp in the chair. The last thing she could remember was Ben anxiously untying her hands and calling her name before she was pulled into the darkest depth of nothingness.

~

As soon as he finished untying her, Ben quickly laid Jenn on the floor. She was already unconscious as he gingerly pulled out the knife from her stomach. "Man down! I need paramedics!" Ben yelled, pressing his hands onto Jenn's stomach to stop the bleeding. "Paramedics! Please!"

Agent Turner appeared in the doorway of the room, looking out of breath. "Jumping Spider!" he blurted out in shock as his eyes fell on Jenn. Before he could move in closer, J. Lee pushed a cuffed Nick into his hands.

"Bring him back to the department now," J. Lee ordered. Agent Turner nodded in a daze and dragged the guy out of the house.

J. Lee rushed to Jenn's side, throwing the bloody knife aside as she knelt down beside Ben. Her eyes went to the necklace which Jenn was wearing and noticed something odd about it. She brought her hand to the teardrop pendant and turned it around. She frowned when a small black object came into view. It was then she had realised that Jenn had planted a bug on herself. Jenn was recording her conversation with Nick to get his confession.

Just then, the paramedics arrived in the room. J. Lee quickly took the necklace off Jenn before stepping aside. The paramedics took over the situation and moved Jenn's unconscious body onto a stretcher, bringing Jenn out of the house and into an ambulance as quickly as possible. Jenn's body was transferred onto a hospital bed in back of the ambulance. Ben was about to enter the ambulance when J. Lee put a hand on his upper arm to hold him back.

"What?" he asked distractedly, giving J. Lee a fleeting glance before turning his worried gaze back to the ambulance.

J. Lee held up the bug in her hand. "I think she did this to get Nick Jefferson's confession for all the other murders he's committed."

Ben snapped his head around and saw what his partner was holding. His forehead creased as he let out an angry groan, cursing under his breath. Then he sighed deeply and spoke in a rush. "Take this back and see if Catherine got us the confession. Then bring it to the local PD and make sure that the bastard pays for what he did."

J. Lee nodded grimly. "Ray Darce?"

"He's free to leave."

As soon as everything was sorted out, he hopped into the back of the ambulance. His hands were full of Jenn's blood, but he didn't seem to notice. He held Jenn's hand tightly in his as the ambulance sped to the nearest hospital. Her hand felt so cold. He rested his eyes on her pale face as he silently prayed for her to survive this. On the side of the bed, two paramedics were still working on stopping the bleeding from her stomach.

A few minutes later, they arrived at the hospital. Nurses and doctors hurried out and took over, rushing Jenn into the emergency room. A nurse stopped Ben from entering the ER, asking him to wait outside the room so that the doctors could do their job. Ben didn't argue further. He sat back on the bench which was on the opposite side of the room, waiting in silence. Suddenly, he became aware of how violently his hands were shaking on his lap. In fact, his whole body was shaking. He decided to ignore it, knowing that the adrenaline would eventually wear off.

Fifteen minutes later, J. Lee arrived. She had managed to get rid of her dress and change into a plain white T-shirt and a pair of cargo pants. She sat down beside Ben and waited with him for the doctors to come out of the ER. It was almost three in the morning now, yet neither of them felt exhausted, even after all they had been through just now. Ben's eyes were glued to the door, hoping that the doctors would come out any moment now. His body was still shaking, but it wasn't as bad as before.

Half an hour went by, and Ben was getting more and more anxious. He got off the bench and started pacing around, no longer able to force himself to sit down and do nothing. He tried to convince himself that Jenn would be okay soon, that the doctors would be out any moment now to give them good news, but the longer the wait, he felt hope slipping away. He didn't even realise that his cheeks were wet with tears until J. Lee spoke up.

"I think you should go clean yourself up first," J. Lee said quietly. "Give yourself something to do while you wait."

Ben glanced down and saw that his hands were still covered in blood, though it had probably dried up by now. Splotches of blood stained the white cloth of his dress shirt too. He could picture himself looking like a complete psycho right now, but he couldn't care less. His eyes returned to the door as he continued to wait for the doctors, ignoring J. Lee's words.

J. Lee sighed and turned her eyes back to the door too. Just then, there were footsteps approaching them. She turned her head and saw Ray walking down the hallway towards them. Ray's eyes nearly bulged out of their sockets when he took in Ben's bloody appearance. Gulping, he went and sat down beside J. Lee.

"How's Jenn?" Ray asked in a whisper, trying not to stare at Ben.

J. Lee simply sighed and shook her head in response. Ben was still pacing around in front of the ER, paying no attention to whoever who had just arrived. Another ten minutes passed by. Suddenly, the door opened. Ben spun around with hopeful eyes, only to see a nurse rushing out of the room. He quickly stepped forward and caught hold of her.

"How is she?" he demanded, controlling his emotions.

"The patient's condition is still in critical state, and she's losing a lot of blood right now," the nurse explained in a hurry. "Now can you please let go of me? I need to get to the blood bank."

Ben released the nurse immediately, stumbling backwards involuntarily as the words sank inside his head. Jenn's life was still in danger. His back hit the wall, and he let himself fall onto the cold hard surface of the hospital floor. He buried his head in his hands as silent tears started to flow. No, he couldn't lose her, not after everything he had done to get her back.

"God, don't take her away from me. Please … I'm begging you," he mumbled in a trembling voice while his tears wet his blood-covered hands. His muffled voice came out as desperate sobs as he repeated the words like a mantra, again and again.

J. Lee watched Ben's vulnerable state wordlessly, sadness colouring her usual poker face. The nurse had returned from the blood bank, and she was pushing a trolley into the ER. Staring as the nurse rushed back into the room, J. Lee inhaled deeply, intertwining her fingers on her laps as she leaned back against the wall. She really hoped that her friend would make it through this. Jumping Spider was one of those rare people who accepted her truly for who she was, and she appreciated that. So she certainly did hope that she would not lose this special friendship between them.

Ben kept on mumbling inaudibly, pressing his forehead against his wet palms. He rocked his body back and forth, completely consumed in his fear of losing the girl he loved. She was all he had to fight for now, yet he was about to lose her too.

"Son?"

Ben's body suddenly went stiff when he heard the familiar voice. He kept his eyes closed, refusing to believe that he had heard his father calling him. Perhaps his mind had gone haywire after everything that had happened and now it was making him hear things – strange, insane things.

There was no way his father would have been informed so soon. And even if he had been informed about the situation here, his father would've never personally make such a long trip over here over such a trivial matter. After all, he knew his father well enough to know that the general was never one to mix his private life with work, not when he had so many oh-so-important meetings and cases he needed to attend to.

"Bennett?" His father's voice sounded nearer this time, and it was filled with concern.

Ben frowned and lifted his head from his palms to check if his ears were really playing tricks on him. It wasn't possible, he thought.

Yet it was.

The general stood a few feet away from Ben, staring down at him. He did a double take, silently gasping when he took in his son's current state. "Son ..."

Ben pushed himself off the floor, wiping the tears off his face. His face was smudged with Jenn's blood, but his appearance was the last thing on his mind right now.

"Sir," he said in a stiff tone, directly meeting his father's gaze.

The general frowned at his son's defiant expression. "Enough with the formalities." Concern filled his eyes again as he moved forward to engulf Ben in a warm hug.

His sudden act of affection left Ben totally flabbergasted. Ben blinked, unable to react. His whole body was immobile in his father's arm, stoic and awkward.

General Warner, however, tightened his arms around Ben, sighing. "I'm sorry I haven't been around for you. What happened after your mother's death has proved me wrong about my ways of treating you all this years. I hope that you'll forgive me for my ignorance towards you and your mother." The general spoke calmly, careful not to push his son over the edge.

"I want to make a change, if it's not too late." The general released Ben hesitantly, but he kept his hands on Ben's arms. "Agent Leon told me what happened to Catherine. I just want you to know that no matter what happens, I'm here for you."

Ben nodded stiffly, not meeting his father's gaze. He didn't know what to say to his father. He very much wanted to believe what the general had just said to him, but Ben thought that it was quite impossible for a leopard to change its spots. A simple apology and a promise wouldn't mean anything if his father was going to turn around and go back to being the almighty Major General Warner after this.

However, Ben remembered how his father had been monitoring him when he had run away. His father had also kept an eye on Catherine for him while he was gone. That ought to count as something, right?

Ben's thought started to jumble up. He wasn't sure what to think of his father now. He couldn't even think straight right now.

"Can we talk about this later?" Ben said quietly, his eyes falling onto the white tiles of the hospital floor.

"Sure." The general nodded, sighing again. He patted his son's shoulder lightly, taking a step back. "Why don't you go clean yourself up?"

Ben started to shake his head, but the look on the general's face told him that it was best to do as he was told. Shoulders slumped, he moved to the nearest washroom he could find and washed himself up as quickly as he could. After he managed to get most of the bloodstains off his hands and face, he strode back to the ER.

The doctors had finally come out of the emergency room, and Ben's heart nearly leapt out of him as he made a dash down the hallway to hear what the doctors had to say. But his steps faltered, slowing down when he saw the doctors' faces. Ben was still out of earshot, but the furrowed brows and grim expressions that the doctors wore made his heart drop. The doctors were saying something inaudible to him, and they kept shaking their heads.

Why were they shaking their heads? Why were they looking so downcast? Then, with sudden comprehension, his feet stopped moving and he just stood there for a few moments, staring at the doctors, Ray, J. Lee, his father … None of them seemed to notice his presence.

After that, Ben turned around and started running, not bothering to hear what the doctors had to say anymore. He just kept running and running. He was out of the hospital before he knew it, but he didn't stop. Angry tears blurred his vision, but he never stopped. Ben wasn't sure where he was headed, but he just kept continued running. He was aware that he was being irrational, but he didn't care and commanded his legs to keep moving forward, as if he could outrun the truth, the harsh reality that was bound to haunt him for the rest of his life.

Finally, he felt his lungs begin to burn, begging for oxygen. Ben saw a few benches in front of him and he slowed down to a stop, catching his breath. He plopped down on one of the benches, glancing around and seeing flowers everywhere.

He knew this place. This was the park named ... Eiry's Garden, he recalled. Jenn was the one who told him about the name of this park on the second day he arrived in town. He remembered the look she had on her face when he brought up the topic to start a conversation with her, the way her dark brown eyes studied him warily as she responded to his comment about this park.

He shut his eyes, letting his head fall into his hands. What was he thinking, running away from the hospital, only to come to this place to let memories of her flood his system?

Behind the lids of his eyes, he could see her smiling softly at him – the twinkle in her warm brown eyes, the faint blush on her cheeks, her full lips curving into a gentle smile – and the harder he tried to push her out of his mind, the clearer he saw her. He swallowed hard, trying to suppress the bittersweet feeling that was welling up inside of him.

A doleful smile pulled at the corner of his lips as her face continued to burn in the back of his mind. She was so special, so perfect, so beautiful, yet it seemed that she was always out of reach – just like incense. Just when he thought that she was coming back into his arms, death pulled her away, dissolving into thin air. Just like incense, so gentle and beautiful yet untouchable.

Why must she leave him too? *Why?*

Twenty-One

What seemed like an eternity passed, and Ben was still sitting alone in Eiry's Garden, wallowing in self-pity. He felt that he was losing himself all over again, just how it was after his mother passed away. Gripping his head in his hands, he let himself dwell in grieve and sorrow, replaying memories of Catherine. From a distance, the sound of footsteps approached, but he chose to ignore whoever had followed him here.

"Warner." It was J. Lee.

"Go away," he groaned, covering his ears. "I don't want to hear it. Leave me alone."

Instead of walking away, J. Lee moved closer and sat down beside him. "Spider's not dead, if that's what you're thinking," she said flatly.

Ben froze for a moment as her words registered in his head before lifting his face, his eyes filled with new hope. He stared at J. Lee with a confused look. "But the doctors ..."

She sighed, her expression back to her usual emotionless mask. "I know. Their faces really made my heart stop for a moment too. It was a good thing that I stuck around to hear what they had to say about Spider's actual condition," she said pointedly.

Joy filled his chest as he began to smile, finally letting himself believe that Catherine wasn't dead, but then he remembered the grave expressions the doctors wore outside the emergency room and his face fell. "How is she?" he whispered, bracing himself for the worst.

"She managed to survive through the worst, but the doctors said that her condition is still unstable. She suffered severe internal bleeding. The doctors managed to stop the bleeding before it became fatal, but she lost quite a lot of blood, so there's still a possibility that hypovolemic shock might occur if her heart can't cope with the blood transfusion. The doctors are keeping her in the ICU for further observation. Do you want to go see her?"

The bridge between his brows creased. "No," Ben said after thinking for a moment. "She went through all of this to make sure that Jefferson pays for every murder he committed. So I'm going to make sure that he's brought to justice. I want to make that bastard feel sorry for what he did to her," Ben snarled, standing up with clenched fists. "I'll be back ASAP. Stay here and watch her for me, will you?" He didn't wait for J. Lee's response as he strode away.

J. Lee stared after his retreating figure, releasing a long breath. "Good luck cracking the nutcase," she muttered under her breath before heading back to the hospital.

~

Catherine lay still in the darkness, unmoving. Her chest rose and fell ever so slightly with each breath, inhaling and exhaling the stale, cold air around her. Even breathing felt so strained right now. Her eyes moved back and forth under her closed eyelids. She tried to open her eyes, to break the darkness, but the effort required was too great. Somewhere in the foggy mist in her mind, she remembered what had happened before she woke up in this rotten state.

Nick had stuck a knife in her stomach.

She mentally groaned at the memory. She couldn't believe that she had actually managed to pull through that whole incident. Catherine thought that she was going to die right there and then. She remembered how much it had hurt when the sharp blade cut through her skin. Damn, it was the most traumatic physical experience in her life – ever.

Thinking about the injury magnified the pain in her stomach even more. She felt her stomach muscles cringing in response as her sedated mind started becoming clearer. She could hear a beeping sound near her, getting faster and faster as the pain increased in her, pulling her back into consciousness. She also heard people shuffling around her, muttering to each other in low voices. It was hardly possible for her to make out what they were saying, but one thing was for sure: they sounded alarmed and a bit panicked.

She ignored the agonising sensation in her stomach, trying to recognise the voices around her. None of them sounded familiar. Where was Ben? Why wasn't he here with her? Her breathing became shorter, faster as the pain started clouding her mind. Where was J. Lee? Had they found the bug in her necklace?

Her train of thought started drifting away as a sudden wave of heaviness washed through her. She felt her tensed muscles loosen as the pain faded into the background, along with her consciousness.

"Doctor, how's the patient?" J. Lee asked when the doctor came out of the ICU.

The doctor sighed. "Well, her heart rate's back to normal. She seems to be coping well with the blood transfusion so far. The patient's body went into minor shock just now due to the physical pain that she was feeling from the injury. We had to increase the dosage of sedation we're giving her to keep her in an unconscious state. Her condition is now under control but she's still under observation." With that, the doctor gave her a quick nod and left.

J. Lee turned back to the window, staring at her unconscious friend in the room. She wore a small frown as she silently studied Catherine's pale figure.

"How is she?"

J. Lee turned her head to the left to see a worried Ben hurrying down the hallway. She raised an eyebrow at him, contemplating what to tell him. However, Ben must have caught something in her expression that made him rearrange his face into an alarmed mask.

"I can handle the truth," he assured her, but it sounded more like he was trying to convince himself.

She stared at him, giving him a blank look. "If you say so." She turned back to the window. "Sedation was wearing off just now, and she was waking up."

Ben wore a confused look. "That's good news, right?"

J. Lee gave him a sideways glance before continuing, "Her body couldn't handle the physical pain just yet. She went into minor shock. The doctor had to increase the drug dosage to keep her under until they're sure that her body can manage the stress."

Ben released a frustrated breath. "So her condition's still unstable?"

J. Lee responded by shaking her head. "Her condition is as stable as can be. If it makes you feel any better, the doctor said that her body is coping well with the blood transfusion."

Hearing her reply, Ben gave a faint smile. "Considering that's the best news I've heard today, that will have to do for now."

"Huh," she uttered under her breath and dropped the topic. "How did things go down with Nick Jefferson? Everything sorted out?"

"Mostly. Turner and Potts are finishing up with the paperwork," Ben answered monotonously. Then his expression turned dark. "I hope that the bastard rots in hell."

J. Lee didn't make any comment on that. "Did you listen to the recording?"

Ben clenched his teeth. He had heard every single detail of the conversation from the recording, and he had to fight the urge to strangle the bastard while listening to it, knowing how the conversation was going to end. "Yes, I went through the whole thing."

J. Lee didn't say anything more after that. Ben had a feeling that she was itching to ask him something but felt that it might cause unnecessary trouble. He could easily guess what her question would be, because he was wondering about the same thing too.

Was Catherine trying to manipulate Nick Jefferson into killing himself back there in the house?

~

Catherine had felt herself drifting in and out of consciousness over the past few hours – or was it days? Well, time did pass differently in the realm of unconsciousness. It felt as if it had been months since light had hit her eyes. She missed the colourful world outside this boring, empty realm. Cold darkness was all she could see and feel right now, and it wasn't pleasant, though sometimes she could feel a pair of warm hands holding on to her hand and caressing her face gently, giving her the only reassurance that she was still alive.

It must be Ben, she guessed, considering that she heard him talking to her once or twice. She didn't know what he had said to her, but she could recognise that silvery smooth voice anywhere. Worry tainted his usual calm and collective tone, and Catherine didn't like it one bit. She felt bad for making him go through this on his own, but no matter how much she tried to open her eyes, she just couldn't manage to do so just yet. The drugs were still running through her system, so it would be impossible for her wake up and give him the comfort he needed.

So right now, all she could do was to endure the helplessness until the drug wore off. Patience would have to be her only companion – for now.

~

Ben gripped Catherine's hand tightly in his hand, his eyes never leaving her face. Some colour had returned to her cheeks, but she was still looking pale and fragile. And it hurt him so much to know that it was because of his ignorance to the hints she had left him that Catherine had ended up like this. If only he had decided to hear her out, she might not be in this condition right now. Maybe they would be back in the headquarters already, safe and unharmed.

It had been five days now, and she still had not awakened. After spending three days in the ICU under close observation, the doctors finally announced that her condition was stable enough to have her released from the unit. According to her doctor, her recovery was slow but steady. But if she was doing well, why wasn't she opening her eyes? Why hadn't she woken up? Indeed, the doctors had kept her under during surgery, but the drugs should be wearing off by now.

Ben brought his head down to the bed and rested his forehead on her lap, not releasing her hand. "Please come back to me," he whispered, pressing his lips to her fingers. "Open your eyes, Catherine, please."

Exhaustion washed through him as he stifled a yawn. A small part of him tried to recall when he'd slept the last time, but he couldn't remember. He had dozed off a couple of times, but that was all the rest he had. All he knew was that he wanted to be awake when Catherine woke up – if she ever woke up. That possibility seemed to become smaller and smaller as days passed by with her lying unconscious in the bed. However, exhaustion was overpowering his will right now, and he soon drifted off into a soundless sleep.

In his sleep, he found himself standing in an empty room with Catherine right in front of him. She was staring at him with a smile, but her smile seemed off. There was an edge to it. This was a dream, he told himself. It must be.

Catherine opened her mouth and closed it again when no words came. Her eerie smile was still on her face, but her dark brown eyes lacked their usual touch of sharpness. Instead, they were empty, depthless, unfathomable.

Suddenly, a shrill of evil laughter pierced his ears, and Ben saw Nick Jefferson entering his sight from behind Catherine. Even in a dream, Ben felt the fear start pulsing through his veins when he saw the knife in the murderer's hand. Ben's eyes flashed back to Catherine, trying to warn her, but before their eyes met, the knife was already stuck in her stomach.

Ben felt his breath being knocked out of him as he widened his eyes at the scene before him. He knew exactly what would happen after this. His instinct told him to step forward and take the cold bastard down, but his body refused to obey his commands. His feet were rooted to the ground as he just stood there helpless, watching the girl he loved so dearly bleed to death.

The difference between reality and nightmare was that everything was beyond your control. This time no one was there to help him stop Jefferson. So being stuck where he stood, Ben could only let out strangled cries as the murderer drew the knife out of Catherine and plunged it back into her frail body repeatedly. He kept yelling and begging for that sick lunatic to stop torturing her, but it seemed as if an invisible wall between them was draining out his desperate pleas.

Then, just when he thought that this would go on forever, he heard his father's voice. "Bennett, it's just a dream," his father's voice soothed in a hushed tone. Ben glanced around, searching for the source of the voice. "Wake up, son, and it'll all be over."

His father's gentle voice continued to lull him back to the present, and the dreadful bloody scene slowly melted away before him. Then his eyes snapped open, searching for Catherine's hand and realising that he was still holding on to it. Breathing hard from the horrible dream just now, he allowed himself to close his eyes and draw in a deep breath.

The general's voice came from beside him. "Have some water."

Ben jumped a bit in his seat, realising that his father really was the one who had brought him out of his nightmare just now. His father handed him a glass of water, and he mumbled a thanks as he accepted it. Holding the glass with one hand, the other still clinging to Catherine's, he gulped down the whole glass of water and felt better immediately. Whether it was because of the water or his father's presence, he didn't take the time to ponder. But a huge part of him knew that it was the latter.

The general took the empty glass out of his hand, sighing. "She's going to be fine, son. I promise." He gave his son an encouraging pat on the back and left the room.

Ben knew that his father was just trying to console him. However, it surprised him that he really believed his father's comforting words. He could already feel the reassurance building up inside him. At this point, he knew that he had already forgiven his father. Deep down, he knew he already had when his father came to him with news about Catherine's condition when he had finally returned to the agency two months ago. However, he was too stubborn and arrogant to admit it back then.

But right now, being able to finally admit that to himself felt good. He felt as if a huge weight had been lifted off his shoulders. It turned out that his mother was right. The only way to free himself from the bitterness inside him was to learn to forgive others and accept changes in people.

A sudden twitch in his hands pulled him back to reality. He almost thought that he had imagined the whole thing, but then he saw Catherine's hand twitch again in his hands. His green eyes widened, and his jaw dropped. Could it be? His gaze flew up to her face, and he could hear himself laughing with relief and disbelief as he saw Catherine's eyes fluttering open.

She was back.

Twenty-Two

"Catherine?" Ben asked warily, not believing his eyes. He brought a hand up to her face and touched the side of her cheek gently. "Catherine, can you hear me?"

"I was stabbed in the stomach, you know, not the ears," she replied in a hoarse voice, blinking her eyes a few times to adjust to the bright fluorescent light that hit her eyes. "Water?"

Ben laughed quietly at her witty remark and reluctantly withdrew his hands from her to get the bottle of water on the coffee table near the couch in the room. He returned to her side quickly, fumbling to open the bottle and put in a straw for her to drink from. "Here, let me help you." He supported her head so she could drink from the straw. When she was done, she gave him a nod and he laid her head gently back onto the pillow. He set the bottle on the floor beside the bed, not willing to step away from her this time. "How are you feeling? Does your body hurt anywhere?"

She smiled half-heartedly. "I'm a big girl, Ben. I can survive a little knife wound."

Obviously, that was the wrong thing to say, for Ben's face suddenly twisted into a mask of anger as he balled his hands into fists. "That little knife wound nearly killed you, Catherine," he spat through clenched teeth, his tone mirroring his emotions. "Did you ever consider how big of a danger you put yourself in that night? You could've gotten yourself killed."

"But I didn't." She shrugged. "And I've gotten what I wanted. Have you guys closed the case yet?"

"Yeah, you got the confessions from him all right. And the case is officially closed," he muttered darkly. "But was it worth it? Risking your life and getting stabbed – was it worth it?"

"That," she said with a pointed look, "was not part of my plan at all. I would've gotten myself out of there alive in the end if you didn't come looking for me."

"You're pinning this on me?" He scoffed. "You know what? Never mind that. What I want to know is how exactly you had planned to get yourself out of the situation." He said this with a deep frown, staring at her intently.

Catherine studied him for a while and remembered the recording she had made for them. Well, he must have heard the last part, then. "You think that I was going to manipulate him into killing himself. Commit suicide out of guilt," she stated, quirking an eyebrow.

Hearing her say that only made him feel a whole lot more frustrated. "Honestly, I don't know what to think of you right now."

She expected that from him, but hearing it said in reality hurt more than she thought it would. She sighed and looked away from his intense gaze. "Oh, I truly doubt that, judging from the anger and accusation that is written all over your face right now."

He released a breath that he was holding. "You won't even deny it?" he said in a defeated tone, sounding disappointed.

"Sometimes I really wonder if you know me at all," she mumbled to herself tiredly. Then in a louder voice, she explained, "Okay, I guess I'll have to spell it out for you. I was planning to turn the tables around, make him the puppet so that I could convince him to untie me, go to Turner, and turn himself in. Guilt is the best way to placate someone in such a hostile situation. I was never going to let him as much as draw blood on himself.

"I would never stoop so low for revenge," Catherine said. "Rotting away in jail sounds better than a free ticket away from the worldly miseries, plus I did go through great lengths to get his confession to all the murders he had committed. So I would really be contradicting myself if I just went and convinced Nick to end his life right there and then, right?"

Ben stared at her with pursed lips, though he seemed satisfied with her explanation. "I'm still not letting you off the hook. Even if you weren't seeking revenge, that doesn't mean that you were doing the right thing by improvising on your own. A team means no secrets, remember?"

"I was going to tell you." She simply replied, not even attempting to defend herself.

"But it would have been after the operation, assuming that you were still alive if we didn't figure it out in time," he retorted, feeling his anger boiling again. "Did you know how selfish it was of you to do that, to go on your own operation without backup? What if something did go wrong with your plan? What if you really did end up ... dead?" He struggled with the last word. "Have you ever thought what it would have done to everyone else? To me?" The last part came out in a low whisper. Ben looked away, swallowing the emotions that were swimming inside him.

Catherine watched him with a thin smile. "You don't really mean that."

He turned his gaze back to her and scoffed, incredulous. "I don't?"

"No." She shook her head, sounding sure of herself. "In fact, selfish is the furthest thing you have in mind about me," Catherine stated, still wearing the same watchful expression. "Because deep down, you know that I went solo on the operation because you would've stopped me if I told you beforehand. You wouldn't even let me go anywhere near Nick if you knew that I was the target. But it had to be me if we wanted to talk the truth out of him, to get him to confess willingly about all the other girls that he'd killed without his guard up. That was why I made it easier for you by improvising on my own." She was quoting his words.

Catherine let out a long breath before she continued, "You were too aware that it was because of the huge part of you which wanted to keep me safe that I said nothing to you, and it's eating you up from the inside." She paused and stared at him with gentle eyes. "Don't let it pull you down, Ben, because it's understandable for you to want to keep me safe. After all, you just got me back – or at least that's what you think." The truth was, he had never lost her – not her heart – but she didn't say it aloud.

Ben was speechless. Catherine's words had hit the bullseye. She was right. He was covering up his guilt. It was stupid for him to think in such a way, but he couldn't really help it, considering that he and J. Lee barging in was the exact reason Catherine was stabbed. In a way, it was them who had compromised her operation and put her in this situation.

"Ben," Catherine called out, pulling him out of his messed-up thoughts. "Why don't you just say it outright?" she suggested softly. "Just try apologising to me."

He blinked at her, obviously taken off guard. But then his stoic expression softened a little as he went forward and took her hand in his. "I'm sorry," he began slowly, staring right into her dark brown eyes. His voice was thick with emotions. "I'm sorry for compromising your operation and putting you in so much danger. I'm sorry for misunderstanding your words and actions. I'm sorry that I broke my word, that I didn't truly trust you ..." He opened his mouth to continue, but Catherine cut in before he could say anything else.

"That's quite a long list you have there." She inclined her head to one side, her eyes twinkling. "How about you sum it all up in one go?"

Amusement flickered in his eyes, and the solemn atmosphere in the room lifted. "Okay, I'm sorry for everything – except for the part where I wanted to keep you safe. It's selfish of me, but I won't apologise for wanting to protect you."

"Okay, I forgive you." A smile tugged at the corner of her lips. "Feels better, doesn't it?"

His lips twitched. "Looks like you haven't lost your touch," he mused, smiling now.

Catherine sighed dramatically. "My preconceptions of my associates here might have clouded my judgements for a moment, but yeah, I'm still stuck with my oh-so-sharp senses, so you're not climbing above my rank any sooner."

Ben chuckled lightly. "I might not be able to outsmart you, but I still know how to get you to shut up about showing off your skills." He sneered mischievously.

Her eyebrows rose at his words, accepting the challenge. "And how do you—"

She was cut off mid-sentence when Ben suddenly leaned in and softly pressed his lips to hers. Catherine reacted almost immediately. She moaned and tilted her face up to meet his, closing her eyes to savour the sweetness of the moment. She felt him smirking against her lips, and all too soon, he pulled away.

"Works like a charm," he said in a smug tone, grinning happily at her. "Every time."

She was unable to resist smiling at his self-satisfactory look. "It works both ways, you know," she shot back wittily. Then she grabbed his shirt, pulled him in and kissed him fiercely.

Ben responded just as eagerly, holding her face dearly in his huge warm hands. He ran his fingers through her long dark hair, his right hand gripping the back of her head as the other slid down to cup the side of her neck. Her rapid pulse thudded against his palm, and he continued to bring his hand down lower, brushing his thumb along her collarbone. Catherine gasped and laced her fingers through his thick soft hair, pulling herself up to deepen the kiss. She ignored the stinging sensation from her injury and continued to kiss him passionately, wanting more.

Without breaking the kiss, Ben brought his hands to her shoulder and pushed her down gently, forcing her to lie down on the bed. Then, he slowly pulled back, panting. "Easy there, Spider," he mumbled, his voice husky, smiling down at her, and leaned in again to plant a soft kiss on her forehead.

Her heart fluttered at his thoughtfulness as she held his tender gaze with a content smile. Then she noticed a hint of uncertainty in his eyes, just a ghost of it beneath the euphoria inside him, and she raised her brows at him questioningly.

Ben straightened up, pressing his lips into a thin line. He seemed to be having some conflicts inside his head. Then his torn expression was suddenly replaced with a determined look. Catherine didn't know what was going on inside his head but she knew that whatever decision he had just made, she was most probably not going to like it very much. Ben put his hand into his pocket, and Catherine sucked in a sharp breath. Then he pulled out a little black velvet box and opened it.

And voilà! Catherine could heard her mind exclaim in dry humour. How she wished that she could shut that annoying little voice in her head right now.

"Marry me," Ben said, his emerald-green eyes filling with so much conviction and love that it made her momentarily speechless. Her eyes flew back and forth between his face and the ring. It was a simple yet elegant ring made up of a gold band with an engraving on it that read *Le seul.* In French, it meant "One and only".

It was beautiful.

Biting his lower lip, Ben took the ring from the box, and his hand was visibly trembling. He took a deep breath. "This might seem a bit sudden to you, but I have been waiting for this moment to come for quite some time. So here it comes." He let out a puff of air and got down on one knee.

Catherine widened her eyes at the sight before her, and the first thought that entered her mind was, *Oh. My. God.*

"I, Bennett Lucas Warner, would like to ask for your hand in marriage. I promise to love you unconditionally, in sickness and in health, until the end of time. It doesn't matter who you want to be; whether Jennifer or Catherine or just Jumping Spider, I would still love you with all my heart and soul."

Catherine blinked. "It's okay. I prefer Catherine," she interjected with a tiny smile.

Ben's eyes twinkled with hope at her reaction, and he nodded once at her input. Then he continued. "So, Catherine Jane Nelson, will you do me the honour of marrying me?"

Her breath hitched. Then without thinking, she blurted out, "Is this a proposal, or did you fast-forward to the marriage part already?"

His lips twitched as he tried to suppress his amusement. "This is me proposing to you," he reassured in a smiling tone.

She nodded. "Okay." She bit her tongue, embarrassed by her stupid question. Damn, she never knew that a proposal could make her so nervous – or maybe it was just Ben. He tended to have that kind of effect on her.

"Catherine?" Ben called her name softly, his tone turning hesitant.

Her throat went dry. She opened her mouth to speak, but when no answer came out, she closed it again. Suddenly, his sharp words from that particular night flashed through her head, and she cringed involuntarily, causing her to look away from him. Man, she had totally forgotten to deal with that part of her – the part of her that was still hurting like hell even though Ben had explained everything to her. The truth was, the memory of that night and the feeling of betrayal from his words had been rooted too deeply in her heart, and she had no idea how to get it out of her right now.

"You're thinking about that night, aren't you?" Ben asked, breaking through her reverie. His voice was dull and impassive.

Her eyes flew up to meet his, genuinely surprised that he knew her so well, despite the earlier confrontation they've had about the operation.

"What exactly did I say to you, Catherine?" Ben asked with a concerned frown. "Because I really can't imagine what I could have said to you to have such a huge impact on you. So please tell me."

She couldn't speak, so she just shook her head. No, she wasn't going to tell him. He would be appalled to hear the truth, maybe even feel disgusted at himself. She didn't want to see him get hurt over some silly words he had said in the past. It wasn't worth it. He had suffered too much.

Then remembrance shone in Ben's eyes, and his face fell. "That day in my room, before I told you about my mum, you said something about 'leaving me alone' and 'stop being an idiot'." He grabbed her hand with sudden desperation. "Was that what I said to you that night? That I don't need—"

"No." She cut him off firmly, making a quick decision in her head. "This is not about what happened that night. I forgave you for that long ago, when you told me the truth about your mum. I've put it past me already." With every word she said, Catherine felt herself getting lighter and lighter. This was her way of letting go. Saying it aloud made her decision feel more real and concrete, and there would be no going back on her words. "I promise you, Ben. What you said to me that night doesn't bother me anymore, so don't let it get to you." With that, she knew what her answer was already.

Ben didn't look completely convinced, but at least he was starting to let go of the topic. "If that's the case, then what's holding you back? Don't bother denying it. I saw it in your eyes. You were scared to say yes."

"You seem pretty confident that I will be saying yes," she pointed out, evading his question completely. And her diversion seemed to be working.

Ben blinked. "You ..." He trailed off, his forehead creasing. "Is this your way of saying no?" he asked warily, clearly not knowing what her point was.

"You're assuming things again, Ben." She sighed, relieved that he had dropped the previous topic.

"And you're stalling," he muttered. He wore a dissatisfied frown and a tiny pout as he stared at her accusingly.

Catherine had to fight the urge to pat his head when she saw that adorable expression on his face. Only Ben could manage such a cute look in a tense moment like this without even realising what he was doing. For someone normally so collected and thoughtful like him, it was really hard to believe that he could portray such a childish look.

She smiled at him dearly, deciding to free him from his misery. "Yes."

"Yes, you're stalling?" he mumbled, confused. Then it clicked in his mind and realisation dawned upon his face. "Mrs Warner," he mumbled dreamily with a look of pure bliss.

She stuck her hand out and gave him a meaningful smile. Ben understood immediately and put the ring on her finger, grinning happily the whole time as he got up from the floor. They stared into each other's eyes, and Ben started to lean in towards her slowly. Catherine felt her eyes fluttering closed, anticipating his next move. When their lips were about to meet once again, the door swung open, startling them both. Ben pulled away reluctantly, turning his head to see who in the world would have such impeccable timing.

"Congratulations!" Ray exclaimed as he literally jumped into the room. A nurse passing by outside the room shushed him, sending him a disapproving frown. Ray clapped his hands to his mouth, giving the nurse a sheepish look. Then he turned back to the couple, the excited glint back in his eyes. "When's the wedding?" he asked, rubbing his hands together with apparent glee.

Behind Ray, J. Lee stepped into the room wearing her trademark poker face. When her eyes found Catherine and Ben, she offered them an apologetic smile. "Welcome back, Spider. And congratulations on the engagement," she said in a light manner before turning her gaze to the back of Ray's head. "Leave them, Ray. I'm sure they have some catching up to do after not being able to talk to each other for five days." She dragged Ray out of the room, ignoring his protests, and shut the door again to give the couple some privacy.

Ben shook his head as he turned back to Catherine with an amused smile. Catherine's expression mirrored his. Raising an eyebrow, she asked, "Five days?"

He nodded. "You can only imagine what it did to me."

She wanted to tell him that she understood exactly how he'd felt – that maybe she understood the feeling even better, that he had once kept her waiting for six months without making any contact – but she thought better of it. She didn't need to spoil the moment by bringing up the past now. So instead, she smiled and said, "Good thing it's over now."

"Indeed," he agreed. "It was totally worth it." The blissful grin was back on his face. "Mrs Warner." He took her hand, running his thumb over the ring on her finger. "So worth it," he whispered to himself, staring at the ring in contentment.

Catherine felt her heart swelling with emotions as she watched his tender expression. Yes, it really was worth it. Then a sudden thought occurred to her. "Ben," she began, pulling him out of his euphoric thoughts. "When did you get the ring?" she asked with a curious expression.

"Uh …" Ben chuckled nervously. "I …" He swallowed, looking quite embarrassed. "I got the ring made right after I was released from rehab. I've had it with me all the time ever since."

"Oh." She didn't know what else to say. She hadn't expected that at all. She'd thought that he got it while she was unconscious. Wow, he really meant what he said about waiting for a long time to propose.

"That phone call from you … was my wake-up call, I guess," he continued to explain. "Knowing that I might have really lost you …" He inhaled deeply, trying to put his thoughts into words. "I think that was when I hit rock bottom. It made me realise that it was time to rise again, and this time I decided that you will be the essential part of my life – my new life." He smiled, looking down at the ring again. "And now I've made it happen. You're mine to love and cherish now."

As much as she hated to admit it, Catherine felt her heart melt at his last sentence. She stared into his warm green eyes, memorising every detail of his glorious face. Silence filled the room, but instead of feeling uncomfortable, it made the moment feel even more intimate to them.

The scene of the first time they met flashed through her mind, and Catherine realised how much they had gone through together over the years – and how much their differences complemented each other. While she was more withdrawn about her feelings and emotions, Ben was open and more ready to express himself. He also had the potential of being a great leader. Catherine was more of a soloist and could work well with only a number of people without driving them mad.

Sure, they have some differences in their personalities and modes of operation. So it might not have been love at first sight between them at the agency, but they certainly had grown to understand each other well. Catherine knew that there would still be arguments and disagreements between them in the future, but what would life be without its ups and downs?

Life was filled with crazy twists and turns, and they couldn't possibly control things that were beyond them, so they might as well live it to the fullest, despite all odds. Because even if Catherine were to lose her gift at some point in life, at least she knew that there was someone she could lean on – her very own Cougar.

About the Author

Christine J. W. Chu lives in Malacca, Malaysia. She started her writing journey on Wattpad, an online writing community. With the publication of *Codename: Jumping Spider*, she has achieved a long-held ambition of becoming a published author.